The Wicked Rebel

Blackhaven Brides
Book Three

MARY LANCASTER

Copyright © 2017 by Mary Lancaster
Print Edition

Published by Dragonblade Publishing, an imprint of Kathryn Le Veque Novels, Inc

All rights reserved. No part of this book may be used or reproduced in any manner whatsoever without written permission, except in the case of brief quotations embodied in critical articles or reviews.

Books from Dragonblade Publishing

Knights of Honor Series by Alexa Aston
Word of Honor
Marked By Honor
Code of Honor
Journey to Honor
Heart of Honor

Legends of Love Series by Avril Borthiry
The Wishing Well
Isolated Hearts
Sentinel

The Lost Lords Series by Chasity Bowlin
The Lost Lord of Castle Black

By Elizabeth Ellen Carter
Captive of the Corsairs, *Heart of the Corsairs Series*
Dark Heart

Knight Everlasting Series by Cassidy Cayman
Endearing

Midnight Meetings Series by Gina Conkle
Meet a Rogue at Midnight, book 4

Second Chance Series by Jessica Jefferson
Second Chance Marquess

Imperial Season Series by Mary Lancaster
Vienna Waltz
Vienna Woods
Vienna Dawn

Blackhaven Brides Series by Mary Lancaster
The Wicked Baron

The Wicked Lady
The Wicked Rebel

Highland Loves Series by Melissa Limoges
My Reckless Love

Clash of the Tartans Series by Anna Markland
Kilty Secrets

Queen of Thieves Series by Andy Peloquin
Child of the Night Guild
Thief of the Night Guild

Dark Gardens Series by Meara Platt
Garden of Shadows
Garden of Light
Garden of Dragons
Garden of Destiny

Rulers of the Sky Series by Paula Quinn
Scorched
Ember

Viking's Fury Series by Violetta Rand
Love's Fury
Desire's Fury
Passion's Fury

Also from Violetta Rand
Viking Hearts

The Sons of Scotland Series by Victoria Vane
Virtue

Dry Bayou Brides Series by Lynn Winchester
The Shepherd's Daughter
The Seamstress
The Widow

Table of Contents

Chapter One 1
Chapter Two.. 14
Chapter Three.. 26
Chapter Four.. 38
Chapter Five 49
Chapter Six.. 63
Chapter Seven.. 80
Chapter Eight..101
Chapter Nine 113
Chapter Ten..124
Chapter Eleven 134
Chapter Twelve 146
Chapter Thirteen 157
Chapter Fourteen..170
Chapter Fifteen 182
Chapter Sixteen..194
Chapter Seventeen..209
Chapter Eighteen 219
Mary Lancaster's Newsletter 221
Other Books by Mary Lancaster 222
About Mary Lancaster 223

At eight-and-twenty, Lady Arabella Niven is gentle, sickly, and firmly on the shelf. Having disobliged her father by refusing her last chance of marriage, she has been sent in disgrace to Blackhaven with two domineering aunts. Her one wish is to be left alone in a quiet cottage to write books on history.

However, everything changes when she tries to rescue a naked man apparently drowning at sea. Thus begins an odd, fun friendship that quickly becomes passionate. For Captain Alban, the hero with a shady past, is rebellious and unconventional by nature.

Marriage between such a man and a duke's daughter is inconceivable, and yet Alban's feelings for her drive him to face his past in order to create a new future that would be unendurable without her.

Oppressive family, neglected children, fortune hunters, past loves, and old crimes all contrive to keep the pair apart. But when danger threatens Alban, it is the duke's gentle daughter who rides to his rescue.

Chapter One

LADY ARABELLA NIVEN backed toward the bedchamber door. Her breath came in short, shallow gasps and her throat seemed to be closing up. Her aunts' furious argument had just about reached the stage where they wouldn't notice her departure, even though it was Arabella they were quarrelling over.

Surreptitiously, she lifted her old travelling cloak and bonnet from the chair by the door and stepped out of the room. Her next gasped breath brought a rising cough with it, but somehow, she swallowed it down, whirled around, and sped across the sitting room. Jenson, her maid, entered the room from the passage, carrying a glass of warm milk which was supposed to help Bella sleep.

The woman paused, her eyes widening. Clearly, she meant to demand where her ladyship was going alone, but Bella pressed her finger to her lips in warning. Jenson closed her mouth, though worry was still etched into her stern face. Bella smiled at her to lessen the blow, and then fled past her into the hotel passage.

She fought the cough until she reached the empty stairs, from where no one was likely to hear her. But even when it erupted, harsh and wracking, she refused to let it slow her. She didn't think Jenson would tell her aunts for a little, at least, but she couldn't be sure.

She clapped the bonnet over her smooth brown locks, and flung the cloak around her shoulders as she ran. Good sense then forced her to walk calmly across the foyer, past the hotel reception desk to the front door, which had taken on the importance of the promised land to her. Her cough had quieted by then, so she could smile pleasantly at the doorman and even murmur a word of thanks as she passed into the street and blessed fresh air.

She inhaled the scent of sea which pervaded everything in Blackhaven. She was outside and alone. And she no longer wheezed.

As she hurried along the street, her shoulders relaxed a little in relief. She didn't really care where she walked, but her whole body and mind seemed to scream for the release of exercise and the space to be alone.

Of course, Blackhaven was a busy, thriving little town, but since she'd only arrived here with her aunts yesterday, and been nowhere but the pump room to take the waters, she hadn't yet been introduced to anyone. She doubted she would be recognized, or even stand out. Country customs pertained here, and she was not the only respectable young woman walking unaccompanied about her daily business.

She supposed she would feel guilty later for causing her aunts anxiety, but at this moment, her selfish priority was to extend her time alone as much as possible before they found her. Without solitude, she feared exploding into a million tiny pieces.

Following the lesser-used roads, she came at last to the harbor. It was quiet at this hour and picturesque, even to Arabella's myopic gaze, with its colorful fishing boats bobbing on the water and bumping against the harbor wall.

A gnarled and weather-bronzed individual sat on a crate mending ropes. A couple of young fishermen were in earnest conversation about something important—the weather perhaps, or where the best fishing was to be had this season. Simple, uncomplicated concerns of vital consequence to their lives.

Since no one paid her any attention, she walked to the wall that ran part of the way around the harbor, and gazed out to sea. The Irish Sea, and beyond it, the vast Atlantic Ocean. A ship seemed to have anchored beyond the confines of the harbor, only half visible because of the jutting headland to the south of Blackhaven. It must have been a large vessel, since even her short-sighted eyes could pick it out.

Arabella allowed herself a moment's fantasy of being alone on that ship for weeks, with just her books for company. But, of course, she could not sail a ship alone, and in any case, she would probably only worry about her family. To say nothing of her complete inability to manage the basic tasks necessary to survival—such as cooking.

She sighed.

"Beauty, isn't she?" the old rope-mending fisherman observed, nodding toward the anchored ship.

"Yes," Arabella agreed. Although she knew nothing about sailing vessels of that size, and it was in fact more than a little hazy to her, she could imagine its sleek lines, the fluttering of its sails, the notion of all the exotic places it might have been and would sail to next.

"That's *The Albatross*, that is," the old man informed her.

Arabella glanced at him. *"The Albatross?"* she repeated.

"Captain Alban's ship."

"Ah." Captain Alban's name was known to her as that of a somewhat shady character probably involved in illegal trade and even piracy. In recent months, he'd become something of a national hero due to running French blockades and even helping out in the odd naval skirmish. "What would bring such a ship to Blackhaven?" she wondered.

Smuggling, no doubt.

"Brings in prisoners sometimes," the man said, surprisingly. "Well, he did once a few weeks ago. Maybe he's got some more. Prisoners-of-war, I mean. But I did hear he's headed round to Whalen for repairs."

Reluctantly, Arabella let go of her impossible fantasy of sailing alone in the large ship. Instead, her gaze drifted over the fishing vessels and rowing boats tied up in the harbor.

She turned her head, regarding the old man with speculation. "Do you have a boat, sir?"

He grinned at her and let the rope fall at his tattered boots. "Not like that, I don't."

"A rowing boat, perhaps?"

"I got one of *them*," he said, clearly disparaging of the idea of someone who didn't.

"Which one?" she asked with interest.

He pointed out the boat bobbing directly in front of him. It was well used, with space only for two people, maybe three at a pinch. But it was neatly painted and solid looking, and the idea wouldn't go away. Even if her aunts saw her, it would take a while to row back. If she was quick enough now.

"Would you rent it to me for an hour or two?"

His gaze was steady. "I would, ma'am, but I haven't got time to take you today. Tomorrow, I could, if I make the right arrangements."

"I wouldn't need you to take me. I can row myself, and the sea is beautifully calm."

His gaze skimmed over her. "Begging your pardon, ma'am, but you don't look fit to even *lift* the oars."

She smiled. "That's where you're wrong. I am quite used to rowing on the loch at home."

"Lakes are not the sea," he said severely.

"I won't lose your boat, I promise. Um, I'm afraid I have no money with me just now, but I will pay you. Or you may come to me at the hotel for it later on. My name is Arabella Niven."

"I know who you are," he said unexpectedly, and grinned when she blinked at him in consternation. "The arrival of a duke's daughter is an important event in Blackhaven, even nowadays." He stood up. "Very well, in you go."

Arabella suspected he only gave in to watch her flounder and give up before the boat was even untied. But she hadn't lied. Alone at Kelburn for so much of the year, she'd rowed quite frequently.

"Don't go too far out," he warned as she descended the steps and clambered into the rocking boat in her clumsy way. "It'll be harder when the tide turns."

All the same, as he cast off the rope, he was clearly dubious about her chances of getting anywhere at all, let alone far enough out to be in difficulty. She took a modest pleasure in proving him wrong, in setting the oars and pulling in slow, rhythmic strokes.

"Thank you," she called. Pulling away from him, she prepared to enjoy her adventure. She even had hopes that no one would think to look for her at the harbor. And when she went back, she would be good. Or at least submissive. Up to a point.

Banishing all the nastiness of recent weeks from her mind, she listened only to the cries of the gulls, the creaking of the boat, and the light splash of the oars. Peace…

The sky was a fine, bright blue, with fluffy clouds drifting past the sun. It was a beautiful summer's day, and she was delighted to enjoy it at last. In the town it had been a little too warm for comfort, but here she had all the benefits of the light sea breezes.

Drawing out of the harbor, she rowed away from the headland and *The Albatross*, not allowing herself to drift too far from the coast, but far enough that no one could see her. Only then did she rest the oars and rub her aching shoulders. Lying back, she sighed contentedly and allowed the boat to drift. It might have been pleasant to read out here—perhaps she'd bring a book the next time she escaped—but for now, she was happy just to enjoy the sea, the sky, and much desired peace.

Until something moving in the water caught her eye and she sat up, peering shortsightedly toward it. She wished she'd brought her spectacles—Aunt Sarah had confiscated them—for it looked like someone struggling and splashing. In sudden fear for whoever it was, she picked up the oars and rowed toward it as fast as she could. The breeze gave her a little help, as did the tide, which seemed to be turning. She should go back, just as soon as she'd made sure this person was not in trouble.

However, even as she drew nearer, the figure suddenly vanished beneath the water and she rowed all the harder, searching desperately.

Dear God, someone is drowning before my eyes, and there is no one to help! I can't see him!

Even as the thought entered her head, the boat rocked mightily, causing her to drop one of the oars and hang on, as a figure rose out of the water right next to the boat, gasping for air and shaking its head like a dog.

Arabella lunged to the side of the boat and leaned out to grasp his wrists. "Hold on!" she cried, pulling as hard as she could. "Get into the boat."

The man, emerging from a spray of seawater, gazed at her in astonishment. It struck her that there was no pull against her supporting hands. He didn't appear to be going under again. On the contrary, everything about him seemed suddenly still and steady, including his eyes which locked on hers.

He didn't look like a drowning man. Or even a frightened man. On the contrary, there was a hint of arrogance in the fearless tilt of his head and the firm lines of his mouth and chin. He hadn't been drowning at all. Like a dolphin, he'd merely dived under the water. Her stupid, useless eyes…

Since he grasped the side of the boat, she hastily released his wrists. His gaze dropped to the region of her mouth and lower.

"Well, I will," he said. "But you might want to pass me that blanket."

She couldn't at first think what he meant, and turned stupidly to look at the blanket on the bench. Of course, she'd told him to get in the boat.

The vessel rocked wildly as the man hauled himself aboard in a fresh spray of water. She turned back to him in alarm and realized her mistake—and why he'd suggested the blanket.

He was stark naked.

Anyone else would have landed in an embarrassed and undignified heap inside the boat. This man simply pulled himself up out of the sea, threw one powerful leg over the side and stepped in.

Heat rushed up from her toes to the roots of her hair, mostly from embarrassment, but also because she had never realized before how beautiful men's bodies could be. Lean and muscled, tapering from broad shoulders to narrow hips, his was bronzed by the sun, though less so on his lower half. Coarse, black hair was scattered down his big forearms and chest, running in a thin line down his stomach to…to the place she should not be looking.

Apparently quite unabashed, he reached over and lifted the blanket, and at last she could look away, her face burning.

"Sorry," he said mildly. "I suppose you weren't expecting that. Are you in trouble?"

"Of course not," she said indignantly. "I thought you were!"

She risked glancing back at him. He sat on the boat's other seat, the blanket wrapped loosely about his hips and legs. His eyes—a strangely turbulent blue-grey, like the sea on a stormy day—remained on her face. He didn't laugh at her or even smile, and yet she had the impression she did amuse him.

"Thank you for rescuing me," he said gravely.

"I'd take your gratitude more to heart if I thought you'd actually been in need of rescue."

"It's the thought that counts."

"But... where are your clothes?" she demanded.

He pointed in the vague direction of the headland, where *The Albatross* stood at anchor. "In the boat."

When she screwed up her eyes she could just make out a rowing boat about half way to the ship. She thought it was empty, though she couldn't be sure.

"You wanted peace, too," she guessed.

His eyebrows twitched, as though she'd surprised him. "Perhaps. Is that what brings you out here alone?"

"Yes."

She waited for him to ask if she didn't have family or servants to row for her, but he didn't. Instead, he said, "I thought you were a mermaid, come to tempt a desperate sailor."

"No, you didn't," she said dryly.

"Well, maybe I wished it. You're certainly beautiful enough to knock a man's senses out of him."

She blinked. "Are *you* short-sighted, too?"

His breath hissed out. It might have been laughter but it was hard to tell from his expression. "Not in the least. It wouldn't be good in my profession."

"Ah. Are you one of the sailors from *The Albatross*?"

"I am. Which explains my need for solitude. What is yours?"

He was a disreputable sailor from a disreputable ship. He had no idea who she was, and she would never meet him again, socially or otherwise. "I'm in disgrace," she blurted. "Scolded, defended, and smothered with disappointment, anger, expectation and even kindness. I thought my head would explode, so I escaped."

She gave a quick, apologetic shrug. Such reasons would be laughable to a man like him.

He didn't laugh, merely regarded her with a thoughtful expression. "I didn't realize young ladies of quality led such exciting lives these days."

"Well, I'm hardly young, being turned eight and twenty—which is part of my family's disappointment, since I am not yet married."

"I was more interested in the disgrace."

"Ah. Well, I refused an offer of marriage from a man my father *particularly* wanted me to accept."

"Because you are on the shelf?" the sailor asked brutally.

"Yes. And because he's a political ally. But I don't want to get into that," she added hastily.

"Why would you?" the sailor agreed cordially. "They would be stupid reasons to marry anyone."

"Well, I didn't like him either," Arabella admitted. "He is nearly sixty years old and portly. Which I wouldn't mind except he has eyes like a fish. But, I fully understand I am no catch. I am quite old and inclined to ill health, and I've had several London seasons where I did not *take*, and watched my younger sisters snatch up very eligible husbands before me. It is quite humiliating for my father."

The sailor blinked. "Why?"

"Having an old maid on his hands," Bella explained without heat. "And I expect he promised me to S…his friend and then I made him look bad. But truly, I have no desire to marry. I have a small independence inherited from my mother and I would be much happier in a cottage on my own, somewhere quiet, with my books." She glanced at

The Albatross. "Or perhaps on a yacht, only I would need servants for that, wouldn't I? I couldn't sail it with just myself and a maid and a manservant, could I?"

He shrugged. "It's my belief you can do whatever you like if you find the right way."

"Really?" she said, brightening.

His gaze remained on her face, unsmiling but steady. "Of course. What is wrong with your health?"

"I am just sickly," she said dismissively. She didn't want to think about it. The knowledge that however many years were left to her, she would never grow old was constant, but she preferred it in the background. On the other hand, she had brought the subject up. She kept her voice light. "I have a cough. My aunt Maria is convinced I have consumption and has brought me to Blackhaven to drink the waters."

The sailor blinked. "Water does not cure consumption."

"Apparently Blackhaven water does," Arabella said humorously. "Also, barrenness, tumors, headaches, indigestion, gout, joint-pain, and bad temper."

"In that case, drink on. And when you are better, you will buy your cottage or your yacht and tell everyone else to go to the devil."

She sighed. "No, I don't suppose I will. They mean it for the best. What of you, sir? Do you not lead a carefree life at sea? Although I have heard it is a difficult one."

"I shall keep living it, if I can avoid the other responsibilities people keep trying to thrust upon my shoulders."

"You don't like responsibility?" she asked curiously.

"Only what I choose."

"Have you sailed all over the world?" she asked enviously.

"Yes."

"I would love to do that, visit around the Mediterranean, Africa, the Ottoman lands, the east, China, the Americas…have you visited these places?"

"Yes, at one time or another, some more than others." His gaze seemed to have rivetted on her face. Surreptitiously, she brushed her hand over it to remove whatever blemish attracted his attention. Again, came the faint hiss that might have betokened amusement. He leaned forward, and she tried not to look at the thick muscle in his shoulders or the tempting hair on his chest. She wanted to touch them suddenly, and flushed at the unmaidenly urge.

He stirred. "Then I have a different proposition for you. Join me on *The Albatross* and I'll show you all those places and more."

She laughed. "I couldn't possibly do that. For one thing, your captain might well object."

"Oh, trust me, he'll make no objections at all. Don't you want to come?"

"Only if I don't consider reality. And I know you are not serious."

"Nonsense. I'll row you across now, fetch your things from wherever you're staying, and we'll sail with the next tide. No more scolding or smothering or fish-eyed suitors."

She knew he was joking and that she would never do it anyway, but just for a moment, something leapt in her, an urge to escape the humdrum and see the wonders of the world with this peculiar stranger. Even to know *him*, for he intrigued her. And it was nothing to do with the way his naked body had made her feel. Well, not *much* to do with that.

She smiled, letting her hand trail over the side of the boat and into the water. And when she refocused on his face, it was curiously intense, his stormy eyes heated and predatory and more than a little dangerous, though in what way she couldn't quite work out. It just made her heart race uncomfortably fast. Which was silly. Despite his unashamed nakedness, he'd made no threat of any kind, only a jesting offer to take her away with him on his ship.

But she was being foolish.

She drew in a breath. "The tide is turning. I need to go back and I can't possibly take you with me without your clothes." He wouldn't try and keep her here, would he?

His eyelashes—incongruously long and dark—lowered, veiling his eyes. "Give me the oars," he said. "We'll catch my boat and my clothes and I'll row you into the harbor."

"There is no need," she said quickly, but he was already moving to her bench, his half-naked form far too close for comfort. His hip, his blanket-covered thigh, brushed against her.

"Unless you throw caution to the wind and come with me to China," he said flippantly, "there is every need."

Hastily, she threw herself across the boat onto the other bench, blushing at the warmth he'd left behind.

"I am a strong rower," she said indignantly.

"The currents are treacherous. You should really have rowed back instead of rescuing me."

She regarded him. "I can't tell when you're jesting," she observed. "You never smile."

"I never jest."

"I don't think I believe that."

Now that she was thinking properly once more, she was very aware of her danger, alone with a mostly-naked man, being rowed in a different direction to the one she needed to go in. Especially when that mostly-naked man was one of Captain Alban's, and his ship was closer than the shore. She was the Duke of Kelburn's daughter and could probably command a considerable ransom. Her father would pay, of course, but she would never hear the end of it.

However, the man showed no inclination to abduct her, despite his previous, not entirely serious suggestion about running away with him. In fact, as they drew closer to his rowing boat, he simply stood up, threw down the blanket, and dived into the sea, giving her a glorious glimpse of his naked back as he jumped. Her stomach tightened with sensations much more pleasant than fear.

Perhaps I am a voluptuary at heart, she thought. More probably she was simply astonished by his open behavior, the like of which she had never encountered before.

She tried not to watch as he hauled himself into his own boat and hurriedly donned a shirt and pantaloons. That done, he threw a rope over to her and invited her to tie it to her own boat. When she had done so, he pulled on the rope, drawing her boat closer to his until he could step from one vessel into the other. Then he picked up the oars and rowed once more, quickly and efficiently in the direction of the harbor, while his own boat bobbed along behind them.

"Thank you," she said ruefully, watching his muscles tense against the pull of the currents. "I *would* have struggled."

"Then I'm doubly glad you rescued me."

She smiled. "Now I know you're joking. I hope Captain Alban does not object to your sortie ashore."

"He would insist upon it."

"Then he is a gentleman at heart?" she asked, curious but happy to believe the best of anyone.

"God, no. He's an unscrupulous bas—swine," he corrected himself at the last moment.

"You don't like him?" For some reason she didn't like to think of him at the mercy of such a person.

"No, I don't."

"Oh dear. No wonder you never smile."

His gaze brushed hers before returning to the harbor and the quay she'd directed him to. "For whatever it's worth to you, I've rarely come closer. Don't waste your sympathy on me, my mermaid, I am quite content." He rose, his balance perfect, and threw the rope to the old man who was reaching for it. Then, steadying the boat with one hand on the wall, he held out his hand to help her over to the steps.

Inevitably, she stumbled, but his grip tightened, steadying her, and for a moment, their eyes met. His were unreadable, but something in them, or in his touch, sent butterflies soaring in her stomach. Her throat felt suddenly dry.

He said, "I hope you find your escape. But I'll still take you to China whenever you like."

She laughed breathlessly, but suddenly she felt sorry, almost panicked, that she'd never see him again. The strength of it took her by surprise. She dragged her gaze free and stepped out onto the narrow stone stairs.

"Thank you," she said again. "Goodbye, sir."

But unexpectedly, he followed her, his large person all but crushing her into the wall in that cramped space. His head bent, blotted out the sun. "Goodbye," he said huskily, and kissed her lips.

His mouth was warm, firm, parting her shocked lips. No one had ever kissed her like that before, which might have been why her stomach seemed to dive and tingle. But there was no time to debate the matter, because it was over almost at once. She gazed up at him, bemused.

"You're too sweet for a mermaid," he murmured, his breath caressing her stunned lips, "but just as tempting. Run."

He stepped down on to the stair below, despite the lapping water. Confused, she opened her mouth to say something, only she'd no idea what it was. She had a vague idea she should be offended or frightened, though in fact she felt neither. She wanted to stand close to him again.

Instead, she turned almost blindly and walked up the steps. She thought he followed, as if making sure her clumsiness didn't cause her to fall off into the water. But she didn't look back. Her whole body trembled, and yet for some reason, she didn't dislike the sensation at all.

Chapter Two

WILL CONWAY HAD never before entered the dingy portals of the Blackhaven Tavern. It took only one step inside the taproom to remind him why.

The place stank of stale rum, ale, tobacco smoke, and unwashed humanity. He could barely see through the thick fog of smoke, and those few people he could make out were not comforting. Even the whores, who appeared to ply their trade openly, looked as if they'd slit your throat for your necktie.

His chances of finding his quarry in this stew were minimal. Why couldn't the wretched man have picked somewhere more salubrious? Somewhere they weren't actually guaranteed to have their throats cut. Although, as he made his way slowly through the room, trying to peer at the patrons without actually catching their eyes, he didn't like to think of his old friend as being reduced to this company. He didn't want him to be used to it.

From nowhere, a stool appeared in front of Will's feet, brushing his shin as it arrived, as if pushed there by someone at the nearest grubby table. Will halted and raised his eyes from the stool to the man watching him from the shadows.

Surely it wasn't...

The man leaned forward, pushing a mug of ale across the table toward him. It wasn't a comforting face. It was saturnine and hard. Even in the gloom, Will could tell it was weather-beaten and bronzed by warmer suns than Britain's. An alien face, and yet that determinedly pointed chin and those turbulent eyes fixed so steadily on his, were quite familiar.

"Alban," he said in relief, dropping onto the stool. "You can't be so afraid of arrest that we had to meet here."

Alban raised one brow and leaned back into the shadows. "No, I just like it here. Good place to pick up fresh crew."

"I'll take your word for it." Will dragged his gaze away from two sailors squaring up to each other and back to his old friend. His eyes must have been growing used to the poor light, because he could see his companion better now. "How are you?"

"Busy."

"I wasn't sure you'd come."

"I wasn't sure either. I bear you no ill will, my friend, but I don't really care to be reminded of auld lang syne, as the Scots put it."

"I don't blame you," Will said ruefully. "But I think there are some things you should know." Taking a deep breath, he looked his old friend in the eye. "Your father is dead."

Alban's face didn't change. He'd known already. "Rest in peace, old man," he said flippantly. "You never did when you were alive." He lifted his mug of ale and drank. It might have been a toast. "Did you really go through all this fuss to get me here, just to tell me that? It was years ago."

"Do you know Nicholas is dead, too?"

That one got his attention. For an instant, the hard eyes stared into his with disbelief, and then a flash of pain so intense that Will felt it like a blow. Almost at once, Alban's eyelids came down, hiding, protecting with those ridiculously long lashes. But it was too late. With relief, Will had already seen Alban still cared for his family. He hadn't known about his brother.

"How?" he barked.

"Fever. Spread round the neighborhood like wildfire, the winter before last. Nicholas's youngest died, too, as did my mother."

Alban's eyelids lifted. "I'm sorry," he said.

Will nodded once. It was genuine, and it was enough for both of them.

Alban stirred. "Nicholas's youngest, you said. How many children does he have living?"

"Two still living. Leo is his heir. He's a good boy, full of life and fun. You'd like him."

Alban said nothing. As if he knew he'd never get the opportunity. It was impossible to tell if he cared, but Will had hope.

"He's the new Lord Roseley, of course, inheriting all the entailed property along with the title," Will said. "But…you should know that Nicholas willed you the lands in Scotland, including your mother's."

Alban's in-drawn breath was almost a gasp. At the same time as his eyelashes swept down once more, he pushed himself to his feet, clearly meaning to leave. "Tell them to give it to the younger son. Or daughter."

"Daughter. Florence. I'm not sure how that can be done."

"Well I can't inherit it. I'm a criminal in my own name, and I've certainly added to those charges in another. Is that how you found me?"

"Alban isn't such a common name. A smuggler and a pirate with hints of honor sounded just like you."

Alban snorted, but at least he sat down again. "Honor? I'm a mercenary. Whatever I do, I make sure I get paid."

"Did the Royal Navy pay?" Will asked with interest.

Alban's lips twisted. "They will. Don't confuse our childhood games with real life."

Will sipped his ale.

Alban looked around him restlessly. "What the devil are you doing in Blackhaven anyway? They've turned a dreary little town into a fashionable spa for the sick and the gullible."

"I suppose I must be sick. Or gullible."

Alban threw him a piercing glance. It struck Will that his old friend had been too on edge to look properly before.

"You're too thin," Alban said at last. "And pale as a convict."

Will shrugged. "I'm on the mend. I had a fever, too, this winter past. Couldn't quite shake it off, and my doctor recommended I come here a few weeks. I was about to go home again when I saw your ship from the harbor yesterday."

Alban finished his ale and pushed the empty mug away. "Who looks after Nicholas's children?" he asked abruptly.

"His wife." Will shifted on the stool. "Of course." He took a deep breath. "Marianne," he admitted.

Alban pushed out his breath. Once, it would have been a laugh, though perhaps not a very good one. "So, she married Nick in the end? Good for him. I hope she made him happy."

"Happy enough," Will said uncomfortably. "It was two years after you left."

"You don't need to defend them. We were children, and Nick always wanted her, too. So did you."

"She was engaged to you," Will retorted.

"I think running away without so much as a farewell constitutes a breach of contract. Why are you looking so glum? What more is there, for God's sake?"

"Marianne remarried at Christmas. Her husband is Julian Radnor."

"Never heard of him," Alban said without much interest. Will guessed he really didn't carry a torch for Marianne any longer.

"He's ensconced his own servants at Roseley, and swanned off to London with Marianne and her money."

"It's not my concern," Alban said impatiently.

"Isn't it? When I left, there were only servants—*his* servants, not any of your people—in the house with the children."

Alban's frown deepened. "You mean they're not with Marianne in London? Don't they have governesses or tutors or something?"

"No. There was a governess, I believe, but she left. I can't interfere, Alban, but you can. Nicholas named you their guardian."

Alban stared at him. "What sort of idiot names a dead man as his children's guardian?"

"A brother who trusts him to be neither dead nor neglectful."

Alban stared at him. "Low blow, Will."

"Think about it."

Alban stood up, and this time, clearly, he meant it. "I have to go."

"Perhaps I can return the hospitality. Tomorrow morning at the coffee house in High Street?"

"Don't hold your breath," Alban said rudely. "Goodbye, Will."

ARABELLA WAS SO absorbed in her adventure with Captain Alban's sailor—and his most improper farewell which she could still feel imprinted on her lips—that she didn't pay any attention to the direction of her steps.

She didn't even notice she was out of breath until she found herself back in the hotel, dragging her feet upstairs to the suite of rooms she shared with her aunts. By the time she stood outside the door, she couldn't even hear the shouting over her own breathless coughing. Trying to disguise it only made it worse. But as she waited for the paroxysm to pass, the door flew open and Aunt Sarah hauled her inside.

"Where on earth have you been?" she demanded.

"Just out to take the air," Arabella said as the coughing subsided. She was grateful that only Aunt Sarah was in the sitting room. Aunt Maria would have her in bed or at least wrapped in stuffy blankets. "It's not necessary to take a maid here," she added excusingly, "and at my age, I hardly need a chaperone."

Unexpectedly, Lady Sarah brushed that aside. "I expect you're right, dear. But I have had the most wonderful idea. We shall go to the Assembly Room ball tomorrow evening."

"Oh no," Arabella said instinctively.

"Now I know Maria will try to coddle you and bore you to death, but trust me, there is nothing like a dance to raise the spirits! And I know she will say we have no escort, but I've taken care of that, too."

"You have?" Arabella said, sinking wearily onto the sofa. Only now did she feel the exhaustion of her adventures.

Aunt Sarah smiled, an alarming mixture of conspiratorial mischief and triumph. "I wrote to Smedley."

Arabella blinked. "You invited Aunt Maria's husband here to escort us to a ball?"

"Well, he's staying with friends in the north. He might as well be useful."

"Aunt Maria won't see it that way," Arabella murmured. Neither did she. James Smedley inclined toward bullying to get his own way, and Arabella rarely did what he thought she should.

"Well, it might stop her from smothering you and let you have some fun."

"Truly, I'd have much more fun left alone with my books," Arabella said faintly.

"Nonsense, you are still a young woman, and your father and brother are quite wrong that Sir George was your last chance. Dash it, the man's so dull I wouldn't marry him myself. He's nearer my age than yours. Here in Blackhaven, I am convinced you will encounter a most superior gentleman. One who is kind to his sick old mother, perhaps. Or a grieving widower. A scholarly gentleman, who needs help with his great history of…something or other."

"Aunt, who *are* these people?" Arabella asked in bewilderment. "I don't believe they exist."

"They do," Aunt Sarah said firmly. "That is, they might. They are *possibilities* and quite likely to be encountered at the Assembly Room ball."

"Ball?" Aunt Maria repeated, emerging from her own bedchamber in a mist of scarves and shawls. "What ball?"

Sarah cast her eyes to heaven before turning to face her sister. "The Assembly Room ball, of course. I know you are going to say she doesn't deserve it and that she is too ill, but honestly, Maria, you must see that it would be good for her."

Aunt Maria gazed somewhat doubtfully from her sister to Arabella. Arabella was tempted to look as ill as she could just so that Maria would forbid the ball. Only then, she would be coddled mercilessly and forced to stay in bed for days without any books. And it would only cause more arguments with Aunt Sarah, who'd clearly set her heart on the event.

"Why don't you two go," Arabella suggested brightly. "I can have an early night and you may tell me all about it in the morning."

"Don't be ridiculous," they snapped in almost perfect harmony, and Arabella realized too late that she'd played her hand badly. All she'd succeeded in doing was uniting her warring aunts.

"I'm here as a punishment," Arabella reminded them with a hint of desperation. "Not to go to balls. Besides, no one wants a dancing partner who will cough all over them."

"Then you'd better not cough," Aunt Sarah said tartly.

"Sarah! As if she can help it."

"Of course, she can. She only does it when something she doesn't like is required of her! Like going to a ball. Honestly, Bella, do you imagine you'll get a husband just by sitting at home with your books?"

"I don't want a husband." She stood up in agitation, as the cough seized at her breath. "Look, why don't I just go and stay with Frances? She will want help with the new baby—"

"You'll do no such thing!" Aunt Sarah said, scowling. "Your sister has an army of paid servants to help her. As does your brother. Your father sent you here, and here you shall stay! Now, what do you have to wear to a ball…?" She barged off into Bella's bedchamber without a by-your-leave.

Bella sighed.

Aunt Maria sat down beside her. "She means it for the best, you know. She can't bear the thought of you ending up an old maid like her, at the beck-and-call of all your siblings' families, with no life of your own."

Arabella smiled faintly. "I don't believe Aunt Sarah's at anyone's beck and call."

"Don't you?" Maria said at once. "She makes a fuss, but she always goes. And here I am too, because our brother sent us. In fact, it makes no difference whether you're married or not. A Niven lady always does her duty."

"Except me. It was my duty to marry Sir George Beaton."

"Well, it was a mistake to refuse him," Aunt Maria allowed. "You'd have had a fine home and an interesting life as a political hostess, and enjoyed much more freedom than an unmarried lady is permitted."

Arabella gazed at her lap. It seemed to her she'd just have been swapping a set of chains she could manage for one she couldn't. Her family—some of them at least—bullied her from kindness. Sir George, she was sure, was not a kind man. She didn't care for the look in his fishy eyes.

Aunt Maria drew in her breath and metaphorically waved Sir George aside. "However, perhaps Sarah is right. We can use this time to find a different husband. He might not provide the kind of alliance my brother hoped for, but at this stage, I imagine Kelburn will no doubt be glad just to have you off his hands. He did *say* he'd washed his hands of you."

Arabella raised her eyes thoughtfully. "He did, didn't he?" Her thoughts began to race around the long-standing fantasy of her own quiet cottage full of books. And dogs, perhaps… It was possible. It could be done.

"So, we are doing nothing wrong in attending this ball and enjoying a little company along with your Blackhaven waters. I wonder if we know any gentlemen here who might escort us…"

Arabella smiled unhappily. "I'm sure someone will turn up."

ALBAN, DRAWN BY old and unwanted bonds, did row ashore the following morning and venture further into Blackhaven than he had in years. The old high street was barely recognizable in the impressive buildings that had since sprung up on either side of the road and extended it at either end. Smart shops selling gowns, hats, and fripperies flanked impressive Assembly Rooms, a hotel and even a theatre at the far end. Alban walked the whole length of the street, trying to bore himself into returning to *The Albatross*, but in the end, he turned and walked into the coffee house opposite the hotel.

This time, Will was waiting for him. Well, it was certainly a more salubrious place to wait. Making him come to the tavern had been unkind. Especially if he'd been ill.

Will grinned and stood up, thrusting out his hand. "I didn't think you'd come."

"Neither did I," Alban confessed, gazing at the hand for an instant before he took it briefly.

Will called for more coffee and breakfast, and they sat opposite each other. Alban didn't want to ask, didn't want to know. But he'd come ashore, he'd entered the coffee house, and he'd shaken hands. It was inevitable now.

"What have you been doing with your life?" he asked, reluctantly, and Will began to talk.

Alban had discovered this talent many years ago and it had often proved very useful. He asked a mild question, spoke a few words, and information flowed without him having to say or do much more. This was the first time he could recall doing it when the information wasn't to his advantage. In fact, it churned him up, reminding him of the life he'd left behind. He'd learned very early on not to regret it, to accept the consequences of the actions he had chosen. Yet, hearing about the old neighborhood, old friends, and family *did* hurt. He didn't know why, just let Will talk. He didn't even want to shut him up.

Even more unusually, it took him a while to become aware of the curious glances of the other patrons. Not that the place was crowded. But when he glanced around the house, a few old soldiers at the back and a scattering of gentlemen with newspapers all looked away too hastily.

"I gather they don't see many strangers here," Alban said sardonically.

"Oh, people come and go all the time." Will cocked an eyebrow at him. "Are you being modest? Or do you really not know you are the popular hero of the hour?"

Alban frowned. "I'm what?"

"A hero. People are delighted to see the great Captain Alban with their own eyes."

Alban cast him a look of derision. "The great who?"

"Captain Alban who entered the late battle in Biscay, scuttled one French ship and captured another, thus preserving the reputation, to say nothing of the survival, of the British naval vessels being attacked. It's been in all the newspapers."

Alban swore, dragging one irritable hand through his hair. "You knew who I was and where to find me. Surely they don't all know?"

"Of course not. I guessed. I doubt anyone else has cause to. In any case, yours is an old scandal."

Alban grunted and finished his coffee.

"I gather you've prospered in the years since you left," Will said, just a little diffidently, as if he were eager to know but loathe to offend by unseemly intrusion. He kept it light and humorous. "Rumors of great wealth, secret treasure—and even piracy!—abound."

"As I said yesterday, I'm a mercenary. I make sure I get paid well and I don't ask too many questions. How much longer do you intend to stay in this wretched town?"

"Just a few more days." Will smiled faintly. "You could come back with me. If you like. Stay. Visit Roseley, perhaps."

"No," Alban said. "But thank you. *The Albatross* put into Whalen today for repairs. I'll be gone in a couple of days."

"Then stay in Blackhaven and keep me company until you're ready to leave."

"I need to be with my ship," Alban said shortly.

Will blinked. "Truly? Don't you have underlings to take care of things like repairs? Or can't you trust them?"

Alban, twisting the handle of his empty cup, regarded him without favor. "You're still a manipulative bastard, aren't you?"

"We have beautiful women in Blackhaven," Will coaxed. "Guaranteed to gladden every sailor's eye."

"Then you have a whorehouse?" Alban said crudely.

"Actually, yes," Will replied. "I was thinking of the Assembly Room ball, but the brothel is good, too."

Alban stood, throwing a handful of coins onto the table. "You haven't changed at all, have you?"

"Devil a bit. This was meant to be my treat."

"I couldn't bear to be beholden," Alban said sardonically, striding toward the door.

As he stepped outside, a figure across the road caught his eye and he paused.

If she hadn't been wearing the same bonnet, he probably wouldn't have noticed her, for her posture was completely different. She looked…frailer. Not cowed exactly, but vague. Without any of the vitality that had so charmed him yesterday when she tried to save a naked man from drowning and held her own quite impressively with that same naked man in her small boat. Today, she was neat and conventional. No soft, brown hair escaped the bonnet to fall so appealing over her cheek. No laughter lit her face and there was no sign of the humor that had lurked constantly in her bright, intelligent eyes.

The woman whose soft, gasping lips had opened to his with such instant passion—however shocked—should not look like…*that*. As if all the stuffing had been knocked out of her. Her shoulders seemed almost hunched, her head drooping. She didn't look to the right or left as she walked between two smartly dressed, older women.

As Alban watched, she stumbled over some obstacle in the road. Both the other women grasped her arms and turned her into the hotel doorway. *Like a prisoner*, he thought irritably. The only sign of life in her was when she turned her head toward the doorman to thank him, a courtesy few would have bothered with. Her companions certainly didn't. But the smile that went with her words was singularly sweet. He'd noticed that yesterday.

As the hotel door closed behind her, he became aware that Will stood beside him. "Who are these people?" he asked abruptly. He didn't even know her name.

"No idea," Will said. "They must be new here. I haven't seen them at the pump room, or at the Assembly Rooms."

"Don't you stay at the hotel?" Alban demanded.

"No. I've borrowed a house on Harbor View, closer to the sea front. Which means I don't always hear the latest gossip first. On the other hand, there *is* a spare room. Easy enough to squash you in."

Alban regarded him in silence.

Will grinned. "Whoever she is, she's bound to be at the ball tonight."

Chapter Three

"IF I COULD just have my spectacles back," Arabella said reasonably, "I would be much more comfortable."

"Don't be ridiculous," her aunts snapped, in unison once more.

"You can't wear a ballgown with spectacles," Aunt Maria added dismissively. "You would be a figure of fun."

"I shall be funnier when I fall flat on my face," Arabella murmured.

If they heard, they pretended not to, so she sighed and followed them out of the hotel rooms. It had been a faint hope. Watching people would have passed the time. She knew from experience that sitting against a wall for several hours was incredibly dull with nothing to occupy one's mind. Her nerves were usually too jangled to concentrate on books she had read, or the one she had begun to write. But tonight, she thought optimistically, she would be invisible, close herself into her imaginary bubble and make plans.

She didn't expect to dance. She was rarely asked, except by gentlemen who wished to oblige her father or brother. Even gazetted fortune hunters avoided her for fear of her powerful family. There were always easier pickings than the Duke of Kelburn's plainest daughter. In any case, she never looked her best in the overelaborate costumes foisted on her by her worldly sisters and aunts. She looked like a coat stand someone had thrown a gown and too many jewels over. And they *would* curl her hair, which always made her feel like a stranger with a tight scalp.

Not that it mattered. If tonight was not a success, and she could imagine no reason why it would be, her aunts would simply give up on what they saw as her last gasp.

Uncle Smedley, Maria's husband, awaited them in the foyer. He made a ponderous compliment about the bevy of beauty it was his pleasure to escort, and offered the older ladies his arms. Which at least gave Bella, trailing behind, a brief moment of amusement as the three of them tried to get out of the front door in a row.

Although the summer daylight was only just beginning to fade, the Assembly Rooms were lit up by a thousand candles. Carriages were dropping people off at the door and driving off to make way for the next one. Presumably, these passengers were local gentry coming into town for the event, or those too frail to walk the distances from the further edges of town. Arabella gritted her teeth and prepared to endure.

If she'd hoped to pass the evening in dull anonymity, she was doomed to disappointment. A man in a black coat took their cards from them at the ballroom door and announced loudly: "Mr. and Mrs. Smedley. Lady Sarah Niven and Lady Arabella Niven."

Even Arabella could see the immediate turning of heads. As the old fisherman had told her, the presence of the Duke of Kelburn's family could not but cause a stir.

Bella peered at her feet to make sure there were no stairs to stumble down.

"Look up!" Uncle Smedley hissed. "And smile, for God's sake."

She wasn't sure baring her teeth at this point would have quite the effect Uncle Smedley hoped for. The thought of her snarling at the inoffensive revelers at least made her want to laugh, though for everyone's sake, she swallowed that back, too.

"Don't skulk behind your aunts," Smedley commanded. He had, apparently, taken his wife's scheme to heart. "Allow yourself to be seen. Promenade with grace. Look as if you're graciously pleased to be among them."

I'm not, she thought miserably. *I want to leave.*

Since she couldn't, without making an almighty fuss that would be unbearable, she walked blindly behind her aunts and obediently sat where they bade her. A waiter offered them a choice of champagne or lemonade.

Champagne was more than she'd hoped for from a provincial assembly. She rather liked the little fizz of fun that came with it. However, before she could grasp the glass, Uncle Smedley thrust the lemonade into her hand.

She bit back her annoyance, vowing to find her own drink when his back was turned. Sipping her lemonade, she leaned back and prepared to be ignored.

However, she reckoned without Uncle Smedley, who brought her a callow youth who could have been barely twenty years old. The boy asked her civilly to dance, and with the eyes of her family glaring at her, she could not refuse.

Arabella was not a great dancer. Despite knowing the steps, she always felt clumsy and disconnected. As a result, making conversation was doubly difficult. Somehow, she got through the ordeal. She suspected the young man was as relieved as she when the dance ended, and he politely conducted her back in the direction of her aunts. Bella was eight and twenty years old. She felt ridiculous being taken back to her family like some young debutante. But she allowed it since she could then go back to being a wallflower. Providing Uncle Smedley didn't make it his duty to drag unwilling dance partners to her all evening. Perhaps he would consider his duty done and retire to play cards or something.

However, before they even reached the wall, they came upon Aunt Sarah in conversation with a distinguished looking gentleman. Aunt Sarah halted Arabella by simply grasping her arm.

Her erstwhile partner, whose name she couldn't recall, effaced himself, as Aunt Sarah said, "Ah, my dear, allow me to present Mr. Tranter, who is visiting Blackhaven with his mother. Mr. Tranter, my niece, Lady Arabella Niven."

The man turned toward her, smiling. He had a soothing kind of smile and an unthreatening expression. And at least he was not twenty years old. Or sixty. He looked to be in his late thirties perhaps, and smartly dressed without any excesses of fashion. A gentleman without pretensions.

"How do you do," he said politely. "Lady Sarah tells me you have not been well."

"Oh, just a cough," she said hastily. "It is almost gone. And you, sir. Your mother is sick?"

"Oh, just a little convalescence. She heard such wondrous stories of Blackhaven's waters that nothing would do but that she must try them. Do you find them beneficial?"

"Well, they are inoffensive," Bella said doubtfully. "I've only been here two days, so I cannot really tell…"

"Would you grant me the honor of a dance, Lady Arabella?" Mr. Tranter asked kindly as she floundered into silence. "I know you will want to rest a little now, but perhaps the supper dance?"

With her aunt's eyes boring into her face, she could only smile and acquiesce. Returning to her seat with some relief, she sustained a lecture from her uncle on how to engage the interest of men, and another from Maria on how to dance without exhausting oneself. Arabella tried to think of her imaginary, peaceful cottage.

"Smile," Aunt Sarah hissed in her ear, and she saw with panic that Uncle Smedley was hauling yet another gentleman to talk to her. He seemed to be dragging his heels and when he came close enough for her to make out his expression, it was distinctly hunted.

This was utterly humiliating. Misery prevented her even hearing this latest victim's name.

Even worse, almost as soon as the man sat down beside her—on the very edge of the chair—her uncle bustled off again. He was clearly enjoying his duty. And if she failed to entice at least one gentleman to call on her aunts tomorrow, he would scold her mercilessly.

Her breath caught on a cough, which she managed to swallow down. The man beside her made some bored comment about the weather, to which she nodded, still trying to catch her breath. Aunt Sarah pinched her arm to make her respond.

"I believe it will rain," Arabella gasped. "I hope it will rain."

"Why?" the man asked, inevitably.

Arabella didn't know. She'd only said the first words that came into her head. "Variety," she managed stupidly.

The man's face twitched, as if he found her either mentally defective or just stupid. Aunt Sarah pinched her again more viciously, her irritation palpable and accusing. Around her, the chattering voices seemed to have grown louder, shouting over the music, and suddenly the whole situation seemed unendurable.

She almost jumped to her feet with some vague idea of reaching the cloakroom before she exploded into a fit of coughing.

"Excuse me," she gasped, and swung away directly into the path of two oncoming gentlemen. They halted at once. She tried to swerve around them, with a quick glance of apology, and froze.

The taller of the two gentlemen was familiar. In fact, his hard, saturnine face had haunted her waking thoughts at odd moments since she'd tried to pull him from the sea yesterday.

"You," she blurted in astonishment.

"You," he returned. "Escaping again?"

"Yes," she gasped, and seized his arm like a lifeline. Obligingly, he turned and began to walk with her away from her stunned family and the no doubt highly relieved stranger.

"Can I fetch you a fast horse?" he offered. "Prepare you a ship?"

This time it was laughter, albeit rather shaky laughter, that caught at her breath. "I wish you could. What are you doing here?"

"Looking for you."

"Liar. Is Captain Alban here, too?" The captain's presence would at least explain the upsurge of noise. Perhaps she hadn't imagined it after all.

"Oh, he's here." Although the doorway was crowded, he made a path for her without more than a couple of glances and then she was into the large foyer. It was hardly deserted. A few gentlemen stood talking there, and two ladies crossed from the cloakroom toward the entrance. But compared to the ballroom, it seemed like a haven of quiet, and she could breathe.

"Thank you," she managed.

"Are we leaving the ball?"

"Don't tempt me."

"A dull affair?"

"Worse." She cast him a quick glance. "For me," she added apologetically. "There is nothing worse than having people forced to talk with you or dance with you."

"Forced?" For once, he actually looked startled.

"The fault is in me," she confessed. "I don't enjoy such affairs. However, I can breathe again, so we had better go back in case my aunts think I have eloped with a stranger or been abducted."

Obligingly, he turned with her back toward the ballroom. "Then the fast horse and the ship are no longer required."

"I believe I'd settle for a glass of champagne," she said, as they reentered the ballroom.

"That is simple to arrange," he said, veering left to a table full of glasses, where he snagged one and presented it to her before lifting one of his own. "Your health," he toasted.

"And yours," she agreed cordially, and sipped the champagne, savoring the bubbles on her tongue. She no longer felt any desire to cough, and if her breathing was a little erratic, it was no longer unpleasantly so. It seemed to be just the excitement that came with this man who made her laugh without ever smiling himself. This man who'd kissed her for some reason she'd yet to fathom. She'd liked that, too.

"What now?" he inquired. "For purposes of enjoyment, should I return you to your family, or would you rather avoid them?"

"Avoid them," she said guiltily. "But it won't be possible. My uncle will be furious with me. Between him and my aunts, we shall be cornered in seconds."

"Nonsense. It's just like running a blockade."

She couldn't help the laughter bubbling up, and it turned out he was right. They evaded her aunts' original charge by merely walking in the other direction. A moment later, Uncle Smedley strode furiously in from the left. Arabella's companion veered into a throng of slightly rowdy young gentlemen and led her out the other side before doubling back around them.

Unhurriedly, he handed her onto a chair and stood slightly to one side, leaning his shoulder against a pillar. "You're on watch duty," he told her.

Since the dance had just ended, couples leaving the dance floor milled around the ballroom, blocking her view of everyone else.

"I was horribly rude to that man," Arabella said guiltily.

"What man?"

"I can't remember his name. But my uncle marched the poor soul up to me quite against his will. Which is somewhat unpleasant for both of us, don't you think?"

"If it's true," he said dubiously. "Though I don't see why you should be forced to talk to people you don't want to. Especially if they're rude and stupid enough not to appreciate the honor."

She smiled. "I like talking to you. You joke with a perfectly straight face."

"Who said I was joking?" He finished his champagne and bent to place the empty glass on the table beside her.

Over his shoulder, she saw both her aunts approaching. "Oh-oh." A quick glance to her left showed her Uncle Smedley almost upon them, skirting the other side of the ballroom as couples stood up for the waltz. "We are undone," she said ruefully, taking a last sip of the intoxicating champagne. The last ten minutes had been thoroughly enjoyable, but it was time to face the music.

"Nonsense," said her companion, straightening. He appeared to have taken in the situation at one glance, and now he held out his hand. "If you'd care to dance?"

Laughter surged once more as he drew her to feet, took the glass from her and set it beside his. Then, without looking right or left, he led her onto the dance floor and took her in his arms.

Instantly, she was reminded of how close he'd stood when he'd kissed her by the harbor wall. Warm blood seeped into her face, but the dance began and she followed him blindly.

"My uncle doesn't approve of unmarried women waltzing," she said breathlessly.

"Is he your guardian?"

"Lord no, my father is still alive, and besides, I am far too old to have a guardian."

"Then why worry about what he thinks?"

She regarded him curiously. "You have a novel approach to the world. Do you not care what anyone thinks?"

"No. If I ever did, I stopped a long time ago."

"I suppose it comes with your profession," she allowed. "But surely you must at least care what Captain Alban thinks?"

His lips twisted. "Up to a point that is unavoidable."

"I can't see them. Are they glowering at me?"

"I neither know nor care. Someone has taught you to waltz."

"Oh, I was taught all the dances. Waltzing is easiest in some ways since at least I can see my partner's face and not get him muddled with the gentleman next to him in the set." In other ways, such as the physical closeness, it was hardest. Not everyone was welcome in such proximity. This man was. Large, a curious mixture of safe and unsettling, he overwhelmed her.

"That is not always a blessing."

"So I'm told," she said ruefully.

He blinked. "No one can have objected to *your* face."

"Not directly. I look bored or stupid or frightened, apparently, and I don't smile enough."

"Not from here. If people bore you, don't dance with them."

"It would be unkind to refuse," she pointed out. "Even when they're forced into it. You see? Even you didn't refuse."

"I wanted to dance with you. It was my idea, if you recall."

The thought hadn't previously entered her head, but it struck her now that he was enjoying this as much as she. He liked her. The idea staggered her, and for a moment she could only gaze up at him, speechless.

"What's your name?" he asked.

"Arabella." Her wits had gone begging. She should have given him her surname, but he seemed to find nothing wrong in that.

"It suits you," he murmured.

"I don't know your name either."

He was silent, raising his eyes and gazing beyond her for a moment, before he turned her, dancing her forward and then back. "I'm afraid you're not going to like the answer to that."

"Why not?" she asked, intrigued. "What *is* your name?"

"Alban."

HER EYES WIDENED. He'd been right. It truly had never entered her head that he was Alban himself. Certainly, he'd never corrected her assumption that he was one of Alban's men. And so, he'd added deceit to the list of his crimes.

Worse, her family was clearly wealthy and utterly respectable. He'd done her no favors in anyone's eyes by dancing with her. But in truth, she'd looked so ill at ease and put upon when he'd entered the ballroom, that his first priority had been to get her away from the source of her distress. His second had been to give her just a little fun, to bring back her animation and make her eyes laugh as they'd done yesterday on the boat. To make her happy if just for a few moments, which was as much, in his experience, as one could hope for.

Well, she would still have had the fun when she asked to be delivered back to her tyrannical aunts. Or when she walked away from him. He even slowed a little, loosening his hold to make it easier for her.

But the gentle, hazel eyes were unreadable, beyond astonishment.

Unexpectedly, her lips twitched. Her breath caught, but on laughter. "Oh dear," she said shakily. "I'm dancing with Britain's hero."

Will had said something similar. Alban frowned now as he had then. "When," he asked abruptly, "was I heroic?"

"When you saved me from the combined onslaught of my aunts and uncle and the poor gentleman whose name I can't recall."

If he ever laughed, he'd have done so, then. Instead, he swung her around a little too dramatically for English ballrooms, and her eyes laughed up at him in appreciation. His throat constricted. He really had come here in the hope of seeing her. She'd intrigued him that much on their first meeting. When he'd first seen her in the ballroom looking so hunched and tense and hunted, so stiff in her elaborate ball gown, he'd given in to his urge to protect her. That was still there, but he wanted more. He wanted to gaze at her quiet beauty and suffuse it with passion. He wanted to know her. Perhaps it was the contrast, but those smiling eyes had just blotted out every pair of fine eyes that had ever seduced him.

This girl was hardly the seducing or seducible type. But he couldn't pretend he didn't want to try, for he did and with a strength he couldn't remember.

Perhaps she misunderstood his expression. Or perhaps lust stood out in his eyes too obviously.

She blurted, "I'm grateful for the rescue, but you may return me to them, or just let me go, whenever you like."

"I don't like," he said honestly. "Do you want to go back to them yet?"

She bit her lip. "No."

"Then stop worrying and dance."

"I never imagined a pirate dancing a civilized waltz at an English provincial Assembly."

"Piracy is only a secondary line of business. I am merely a trader."

"A *free* trader? My brother—my middle brother, Sebastian—fell in with some once on the south coast. He had a fine adventure, and my father won some excellent brandy. But I suppose I shouldn't tell you that."

"Not unless your father needs some more brandy."

"Seriously?" she said, awed. "Do they smuggle here, too?"

"All around the coast."

"Is that why you're here?"

"No, I told you. I came to see you."

"I mean, is it why you came to Blackhaven?" she said severely.

"No," he admitted, "I came to see an old friend who had some news for me."

"Bad news?" she asked with quick sympathy.

"I don't know yet. Have I got you into more trouble with your family?"

She thought about it, and smiled in a way that deprived him of breath. "I don't believe I care."

"That's my girl," he approved.

He was ridiculously disappointed when the dance ended, like some callow youth with his first crush. For in truth, although she was small and frail, she did fit rather comfortably into his arms, where he was all too aware of her delightful curves and the gentle rise of her breasts. The worst danger was in holding her closer, an urge that was increasingly difficult to resist.

He thought quite seriously about keeping her with him, at least until the end of the ball. He thought she would cooperate that far. But since he didn't truly want to ruin her life, he guided her instead toward one of the aunts who sat rigidly beside the uncle, trying not to cause comment by glaring at him. So long as they didn't glare at *her* in the same way, he would not object.

"Aunt Maria," she said in a rush. "Allow me to present Captain Alban. Sir, my aunt, Lady Maria Smedley. And Mr. Smedley, my uncle."

Smedley rose to his feet, outrage darkening his face. Ignoring him, Alban bowed to Lady Maria. "Ma'am. Thank you for lending me your niece, who has been most kind. I am acquainted with no one else in town." Apart from Will, but in the circumstances, he was sure Will would forgive the denial.

He could see the aunt dredging up his name from her memory. Her eyes were just widening with horror when he turned to her husband. "Sir."

Smedley's eyes were not entirely free of horror either, but mingled in there was a hint of awe. Perhaps Will wasn't so wrong about his heroic reputation. Which was quite funny, for he was hardly comparable to the late Lord Nelson. Or Lord Wellington. Either way, the man clearly struggled for something to say. Good.

Alban glanced once more at Arabella, lifting his eyebrows in silent question.

She said in a rush, "Perhaps you'd call on us one afternoon, Captain? We are staying at the hotel."

Both her aunt and uncle looked suitably appalled.

"Thank you, I will," he said, more to annoy them than because he'd any real intention of doing so. He inclined his head, closing one eye, and walked away, although not before he'd glimpsed her quick smile of response.

"Well," Will said, when Alban found him in the card room which opened just off the main ballroom. "That should put the cat amongst the pigeons."

"What should?" he asked, sitting down beside his friend and indicating he should be dealt in the game.

"I found out who they are," Will murmured. "They're the Duke of Kelburn's family. You've just danced with his eldest daughter."

Alban paused, his hand over his cards as he stared at Will. "Kelburn?"

"Precisely."

Alban picked up the cards. He hadn't thought of Kelburn in years. He'd only ever met the man once, and yet there had been a time when, young and furious, he'd hated him with a vengeance. Nick, his brother, had even called him the author of Alban's troubles. Which wasn't true, of course. Alban himself was the cause, and his own father had made it worse. He'd learned to live with that over the years, had become someone else far removed from his old world. In truth, he should never have dipped his toe back in by coming here, certainly not in pursuit of the Duke of Kelburn's daughter.

On the other hand, such a pursuit would make a fine revenge.

Chapter Four

"CAPTAIN ALBAN?" AUNT Maria hissed furiously. "How on earth did you meet such a man? Let alone get on such terms with him!"

"I went out for a walk yesterday and encountered him…near the harbor," Bella said as vaguely as she could. She was trying not to watch his receding back. "He was quite kind, I assure you."

"I'm certain he was!" Uncle Smedley all but exploded. "The Duke of Kelburn's daughter had just walked straight into his trap!"

Bella couldn't help her spurt of laughter. "Oh, it was nothing like that, I assure you. He didn't know my name any more than I knew his."

"You are an innocent," Uncle Smedley said with contempt. "A naive and foolish girl. You will have nothing more to do with him."

"You're probably right about that, Smedley," Aunt Sarah said, bustling over to join them. "But you needn't scold her, for I believe this has worked out for the best."

The Smedleys stared at her. "Even you could not wish such a suitor on our niece!" Aunt Maria exclaimed.

"Good gracious, of course not. But since she danced with Captain Alban, I've had two gentleman approach me to ask for introductions to her!"

Aunt Maria frowned, exchanging glances with both her husband and her sister. Mercifully, they all seemed to have forgotten Bella's presence.

"Why should they do that now?" Aunt Maria wondered.

Sarah waved her fan, enjoying her moment of worldly wisdom. "Either because Alban's distinguished her—he's spoken to no other lady so far—and this has given her some *cachet*. Or because she was comfortable enough with him to smile. You might have noticed she was much more animated dancing with him that any other point in the evening so far."

"Oh, we noticed," Smedley said grimly.

"Well, stop being so foolish about it then," Aunt Sarah snapped. "The reasons scarcely matter. Some men just have that knack of making ladies comfortable, of bringing out the best in their companions. The man must have charisma. And I'm sure Bella's much too sensible to like him beyond that. Or to read anything else into his attentions. If he has imparted some confidence to her, I for one am grateful."

Desperately, Bella looked around for a distraction from their unbearable conversation. She just hoped no one else could hear it. Unexpectedly, she caught the gaze of an extraordinarily beautiful woman in a gorgeous, dusky pink gown, who smiled at her and came instantly toward her.

"Lady Arabella," the lady greeted her. "We have met, so I hope you'll excuse my accosting you uninvited."

"Of course," Bella murmured, trying to place her. One didn't forget such beauty. "Lady Crowmore," she said in surprise.

Miss Kate Mere had been one of several debutantes who had quite eclipsed Bella during her first London season. She'd married Lord Crowmore almost immediately and speedily become the rage of the ton: beautiful, witty, and just on the verge of scandalous. If Bella had indeed met her, it couldn't have been more than once.

"Mrs. Grant, these days," the beauty said now, with a pride Bella was at a loss to account for. "I married the vicar."

"Truly?" Bella said breathlessly.

Mrs. Grant smiled and sat in the vacant seat beside her. "Go ahead and laugh."

"I wouldn't dream of it." Bella assured her. "Is Mr. Grant here, too?"

"Yes, and I shall be glad to present him to you. But do tell, Lady Arabella, how do you know Captain Alban? What can you give us to feed the legend?"

"Nothing," Bella said in surprise. "I met him by accident yesterday and had no idea who he was."

"And is he charming? Fierce and romantic? Or a bit of a clod with nothing to talk about except the sea?"

"Oh no," Bella replied, then shifted uncomfortably. "That is, he is hardly a chatterer, but he is funny—"

"Excellent," Mrs. Grant approved. "Then I rely upon you for an introduction."

Since Bella's aunts and uncle had ceased their heated debate, the surprising Mrs. Grant greeted them civilly and invited them to call at the vicarage.

"Vicarage?" Aunt Maria said, staring after her. "Kate Crowmore?"

"Kate Grant," Bella corrected. "She married the vicar."

BY THE SUPPER dance, Bella had already danced with a Major Doverton who commanded the local barracks, and sat out another with a scholarly young widower who was taking the waters to improve frequent headaches. Bella endured both these ordeals rather better than usual, probably because they had *chosen* to speak to her.

Mr. Tranter, the unthreatening gentleman with the sick mother, came to claim his supper dance without any outward signs of coercion.

"Would you like to dance?" he asked her. "Or shall we take a turn around the ballroom?"

Bella chose the latter. As they strolled, Mr. Tranter kept up an amusing commentary on the people they passed, and then asked her what she liked to read.

Bella stared at him in amazement. Such a question was so far from the normal small-talk of gentlemen to unmarried ladies, that she was temporarily stunned.

"Your aunt told me you were bookish," he said apologetically.

"She did?" It seemed very unlike Aunt Sarah to scupper Bella's chances with such an admission, but Mr. Tranter did seem to be the kind of man to whom one confided the truth—and the kind of man who did not object to a lady with more than two thoughts to rub together.

"Have you discovered the circulating library, yet?" he asked.

"What, here in Blackhaven?"

"Oh yes. It is just behind High Street. I would be happy to escort you and your aunts there, if you wish."

"Thank you, you're very kind," Bella murmured, just as her heart gave a sudden bump.

The unmistakable figure of Captain Alban was emerging from the card room door, ushering before him the beautiful Mrs. Grant. She had the most devastating smile imaginable and it was directed straight at the captain. Bella could imagine all too easily his straight-faced amusement, and something inside her began to hurt so much that she pressed her free hand into her body.

I'm jealous, she thought, stunned. Jealous of a stranger's attention to a married woman. Which was absolutely pointless. There never had been and never would be any contest between Bella and Kate Grant. She didn't want there to be. She just wanted to be…*different* to Alban.

Another two men followed him out of the room before Bella dragged her gaze free.

"Does he bother you?" Mr. Tranter asked, low.

"Who?"

"Captain Alban."

"Of course not."

"I only ask, because I saw you with him earlier." He seemed to hesitate. "Such a man may not know what is quite proper in polite society."

"I think he knows," Bella murmured. "I think he just doesn't care."

"Lady Arabella," came Kate Grant's distinctively lazy yet captivating voice. "Will you allow me to present my husband?"

Mr. Tranter made a quick movement, as though to encourage her onward, to pretend not to hear. But she'd already paused and now she turned deliberately to face Kate, Alban and the other two men. One of those was a thin, pale gentleman. The other, taller and more handsome, looked as if his leanness came from exercise rather than ill health. It was to this second gentleman that Kate gestured.

"My husband, Tristram Grant. And Mr. Conway. Gentlemen, Lady Arabella Niven."

Both gentlemen bowed to her, but as she gazed with some curiosity at the young vicar Kate had married, Bella was more conscious of Alban's gaze than of anything else. Somehow, it made her feel better that Kate's husband was present.

Remembering her manners, she introduced Mr. Tranter, who seemed to be already known to both the Grants and Mr. Conway. She thought their manner rather cool.

"Shall we all go into supper together?" Kate suggested.

From his tension, Bella knew Mr. Tranter was annoyed. He didn't want other company, which was flattering. Bella wasn't sure she did either. Kate was not someone she was ever likely to be comfortable with. She didn't even know if Alban and Conway were included in the invitation. But as the Grants led the way toward the supper room, she and Mr. Tranter could do nothing but follow.

"We don't have to sit with them," Tranter murmured. "You must choose."

During Bella's miserable London seasons, she doubted Kate ever noticed her. So she was surprised when the Grants kept to the plan and sat down with her and Mr. Tranter. Fortunately, Mr. Grant, who sat beside Bella and opposite his wife, was a likeable man and conversed with easy charm. Even more surprising was the banter which passed between the couple. It seemed Kate was not really anything like Bella had imagined.

As she picked at her food, which Mr. Tranter had kindly chosen for her, Alban and Mr. Conway joined them, sitting opposite Bella and

Mr. Tranter.

Mr. Tranter sat back, curling his lip as though he expected Alban to eat with his fingers, or even straight off the plate. "So, Mr. Conway," he said. "Are you a native of Blackhaven?"

"No, sir, though I don't live so far away either. Like so many, I came for the waters."

"And do you find them beneficial?"

"I feel much better than I did when I arrived," Mr. Conway allowed.

"As does my mother," Mr. Tranter agreed.

"There's no science in it," Alban said abruptly. "What makes you feel better is merely fresh air and relaxation."

"My friend, the town's physician, is of the same opinion," Mr. Grant said. "He is a man who needs evidence."

Alban cast him a challenging look. "Unlike the clergy."

Grant smiled good-naturedly. "I have enough evidence for my beliefs."

"So do I." Alban raised his glass.

"I must introduce you to my friend, Dr. Lampton," Grant remarked. "You would get on famously."

"Do you stay long in Blackhaven, Captain?" Kate asked.

"Just until my ship is repaired."

"Then I shall send you a card to our soiree," Kate said.

Alban glanced at her, clearly about to refuse without inhibition. But before he could speak, Mr. Conway said smoothly, "You can reach him at my house on Harbor View."

"Ah! Then you are old friends?" Kate said, clearly eager for more information.

"No," Alban said. "I never liked him." Without warning, his gaze came back to rest on Bella's face, intense, unsmiling, and yet curiously intimate, inviting her to share the joke. It deprived her of breath.

"The feeling is mutual," Mr. Conway retorted. "And you, Lady Arabella, are you in Blackhaven with your family?"

"Just two of my aunts," she managed, forcing her attention away from Alban. "And an uncle for a day or so. I don't believe the hotel is big enough to take all of us."

Kate laughed. "I don't think Blackhaven itself is big enough for your brothers! Apart from Lord Monkton, of course."

"Apart from Monkton," Bella agreed. Since her eldest brother had gone into politics like their father, he had become quite staid. Not to say self-righteous. He had scolded her at least as much as their father for refusing Sir George Beaton.

"Where is your home, Mr. Conway?" Kate asked. She had the enviable knack of making small talk sound interesting.

"A good three hours' drive from Blackhaven," Mr. Conway replied. "Wayfare House, near Roseley."

"Ah, I don't believe I've ventured so far, yet." Kate frowned. "But the name Roseley sounds familiar. Why is that?"

It was familiar to Bella, too. Lord Roseley was the absentee owner of Powmill, near the family home at Kelburn. And then, she had a distant recollection of a very brief meeting with a Lady Roseley in London, before Aunt Maria had dragged her away to meet some dreary heir. Not that she could recall the lady's face since it had been mostly a myopic blur.

"Perhaps you were acquainted with the late Lord Roseley," Mr. Conway said. "Or with Lady Roseley."

"Yes, I believe I am, slightly," Kate agreed, apparently pleased to have recalled. "Was there not some scandal in the family? A rebellious younger son forced to flee the law?"

"Something like that," Mr. Conway said evenly, although he shifted uncomfortably in his seat. "But I believe it all happened in Scotland." For some reason his gaze settled on Bella. "Your family also has land in Scotland, I believe?"

Alban turned his head and looked at Mr. Conway. Bella found his face unreadable. Did he know she was the Duke of Kelburn's daughter? She'd given herself no title, no surname. Would it make any difference to him?

And why did she care so much?

Bella took some food onto her fork. "Yes. Kelburn, in the Scottish Borders." She let the food slide off her fork again, for she had no appetite. "I've lived there mostly, although we also spend a lot of time at the estate in Sussex."

"I attended a ball in Sussex quite recently," Kate said to her. "About a year ago. You must have been there, too."

"Oh no, I was in Kelburn by then." Bella laid down her fork to avoid mangling the food any further.

Alban leaned forward, pushing a glass of sparkling wine across the table to her.

She took it, glancing up at him with a spontaneous smile.

He inclined his head with a hint of irony and stood up. "Please excuse me." With a slight bow to herself and to Kate, he turned and strolled away.

"Well," Mr. Tranter said into the astonished silence. "I suppose he isn't used to polite society."

"He is something of a free spirit," Mr. Conway allowed.

"He's not what I expected," Kate observed.

"What, were you hoping for a roistering Viking?" her husband inquired.

Kate raised her eyebrows. "I'm sure that's why he's left us, to go a-roistering. Assembly balls are too tame for…" She broke off.

"Pirates?" Mr. Conway suggested, just a little dangerously.

"Traders," Bella said, and sipped her champagne.

To her surprise, everyone laughed.

IT CAME AS something of a shock to Bella to realize she was almost enjoying herself. After supper, she spent some time with Kate and her husband, who turned out to be both funny and well-read. But if she hoped for any further encounter with Alban, she was disappointed. She wondered if he'd left the ball as soon as he left the supper table, but she refused to ask anyone.

With her poor eyesight, he could have been sitting on the other side of the room and she would have had little chance of seeing him. And with the understanding of his departure, the excitement seeped away from her evening of unexpected fun.

When she returned to her family, she barely heard Uncle Smedley's denunciation of Kate's lifestyle and morals. She thought it had been going on for some time before she finally noticed and stared at him. "Uncle, she's married to the *vicar*."

Smedley blinked in surprise. "I don't appreciate your tone, young lady," he blustered.

"No," Bella agreed. "I don't suppose you do. Excuse me." She stood up.

"Where are you going?" Aunt Maria demanded.

"To the cloakroom. I'll only be a few minutes."

As she hurried from the ballroom and across the foyer to the ladies' cloakroom, which was located close to the front door, relief washed over her. She'd enjoyed supper and her time with Kate, but her family made her feel smothered with constant disapproval. And she'd grown tired of always either agreeing or keeping quiet for fear of offending.

Fortunately, the cloakroom itself was quiet. A lady and her daughter were just leaving and curtseyed politely to her. She sank down on the bench where she'd changed her shoes and thought quite seriously about putting her outdoor shoes back on again and simply walking back to the hotel. She could send a message in to her aunts.

She sighed. Such behavior would only lead to a massive scold, which was scarcely worth the trouble for such a tiny gain. Somewhere, though, she was growing aware she would need to assert herself to make her life tolerable. And she would begin tomorrow by going to look at the cottage she'd inquired about this afternoon.

After a few deep breaths, she stood and brushed down her too-fussy gown. Glancing in the looking glass, she saw that the curl was already unravelling in her hair. She gave the loose parts a quick rake with her fingers to help the process along, then guiltily made her way to the door.

The foyer was empty, apart from a man about to leave the building. He paused, his hand on the front door, and her heart lurched, for it looked very like Alban.

"Lady Bella," he said, releasing the door.

She took a step nearer him, mainly to make sure it was truly him. "I thought you'd gone already. Are you going back to your ship?"

His lips twisted. "No, I'm going to get vilely drunk. Would you like to come?"

"I'm a poor drinking companion," she replied apologetically. "I've already had two glasses of champagne. One more and I shall fall asleep."

Rueful amusement softened his hard eyes. "You're not even offended, are you?"

"No. But I won't come."

"No. But then, even I wouldn't really have taken you to the tavern." His tone was sardonic, his stance curiously restless.

Impulsively, she came nearer yet, close enough to touch him, and for an instant, she read pain in those hard, turbulent eyes. Then his lids closed down like hoods, and when they lifted again, his expression was merely predatory. As it had been before he kissed her at the harbor. Her stomach gave an excited little lurch.

His gaze dropped to her lips. "You should stay away from me."

"My uncle says you're dangerous," she admitted.

"I am. And I want you, Bella Niven, in spite of everything."

Heat surged through her body, burning her cheeks. She seemed to be rooted to the spot. Slowly, he raised his hand and brushed two fingers across her lips. A tiny gasp fell from her, of shock and a need she barely understood.

His gaze lifted once more to her eyes.

"In spite of what?" she managed.

"Avoid me like the plague," he said huskily, bending his head.

The breath seemed to leave her body, for she knew he meant to kiss her again. Everything in her leapt toward him. His fingertip pressed lightly, parting her lips.

And then a surge of noise from the ballroom told her the door had opened. Instinct propelled her backward. It didn't feel like shame. She just didn't want anyone else sullying such a moment. A party of local people emerged into the foyer, talking loudly. Beside her, the door shuddered on its hinges, and she realized she was alone. Alban had gone.

She walked slowly back to the ballroom, churned up by the peculiar encounter which had left her feeling both exhilarated and disappointed.

He wants me, she thought in wonder. *He wants me.*

She wasn't as naïve as everyone thought her. She knew perfectly well he wasn't proposing marriage to her. Even a *respectable* trader captain had no hope of marriage with a duke's daughter, and in Alban's case, she suspected he was not a marrying kind of man.

She should probably feel insulted, she thought as she made her way around the edges of the dance floor in the vague direction of her family. But in truth, she didn't. She felt warm and curiously powerful, and knew it was time to set in motion her own plans for independence.

Chapter Five

Alban, who'd got bored drinking alone before he'd got anywhere near the desired state of total oblivion, rose early the morning after the ball, and quietly let himself out of Will's house.

He knew what he had to do. He would ride out to Roseley, look in on Nick's children and see that they were safe and well fed. And then he'd find old Johnstone, the solicitor—or his successor—and find out his legal position with regard to the children.

Not that he had any intention of coming home, whether or not he could. On the contrary, as soon as he put these wheels in motion, he meant to return to his ship. According to Barnaby, his capable lieutenant and navigator, repairs were going well, so *The Albatross* could be back in the water tomorrow, or even later today.

At all events, Alban had had enough of Blackhaven. It was past time to leave, for his wits were clearly addled. It was not remotely like him to begin falling for a respectable, sickly lady, no matter how beautiful, sweet, and funny she might be. That she was the Duke of Kelburn's daughter merely put the icing on the cake of his folly. Vengeance might have been amusing, of course. It certainly provided him with an excuse to pursue her. But he'd known last night at the Assembly Room door that he couldn't hurt her, so there was only one thing left for him to do.

He was familiar with the pangs of regret and loneliness. He knew from experience that they would pass. So, he merely ignored them as always, and strode out to the livery stable where he'd arranged the hire of a horse for the day.

Here, he was introduced to Pegasus, a decent looking animal reputed to be fleet of foot, already saddled, bridled, and ready to go. He was just about to mount when a woman's voice filtered through to him. Bella Niven had clearly got too far under his skin, for it sounded just like her.

"I can see he's a very nice pony, and I do not wish to insult him," she said gravely. "But you must admit he is fat, elderly, and indolent. I suspect it will take us until midday to get out of Blackhaven, and I need to have *returned* from my errand by then."

Alban lowered his hands from Pegasus's saddle and turned to gaze across the yard at the woman, the pony, and the stable employee who was clearly trying to fob her off.

"Well, without notice, ma'am, there's no other suitable mount available."

She looked small and insignificant in the old travelling cloak he had first seen her in. But she was wearing spectacles. Clearly, she had managed to extract them from whichever aunt had confiscated them. So today she could see. She was in no obvious danger.

Alban knew he should walk away, keep to his original decision. Instead, he turned to the groom who'd presented him with Pegasus.

"You," he ordered as the man began to walk away. "Make sure the lady is given a suitable mount and take the donkey back to its stable."

Immediately looking worried, the groom began to jog across the yard while Alban vaulted into his saddle.

But it seemed he'd misjudged Lady Bella.

"The brown mare there will be quite adequate," she said firmly. There was no stridency, no threat in her voice, but she did not back down when the employee tried to stare her out. Belatedly, he obviously came to the conclusion that she was not of the rank to be trifled with, and snapped at the approaching groom to saddle Betsy.

Interesting. They would have fallen over themselves to give Lady Arabella Niven whatever she wanted immediately. She wouldn't have had to fight for it. So, clearly, she had not divulged her identity. What was she up to?

He truly had meant to ride straight past her. Instead, he walked Pegasus across the yard until their large shadow fell completely across her.

She glanced up. Her eyes widened with surprise and her hand rose as though involuntarily, pressing into the base of her neck. Her color heightened, and yet her smile was spontaneous and open. And God help him, she was even more appealing in the spectacles.

"Captain Alban."

"Ma'am," he returned gravely, preserving her anonymity. "You would appear to have no attendant with you."

"That is true." She gave another quick, fugitive smile. "It is another escape."

"One a day is a decent average." He didn't have time to escort her on expeditions of pleasure. Nor could he take her with him. On the other hand, he didn't know how far she planned to go without protection of any kind. "In which direction do you plan to ride?"

"Toward Silton." She hesitated, then added. "I'm meeting someone there. A solicitor."

He made a last effort to talk himself out of it, reminding himself of his decision last night and all the reasons behind it. But in the end, he knew he'd never meant to do anything else from the moment he'd seen her here alone.

"I'm going in the same direction. Allow me to escort you."

He thought her fading flush returned, but he couldn't be sure, since a brown mare was led from the stables at that moment and she moved toward it. Alban cast a critical eye over the animal and decided she would do. It appeared the duke's daughter also knew her horseflesh.

Although she hadn't answered him, he held the impatient Pegasus in check until the groom boosted her into the saddle. Beneath the cloak, he saw that she wore a rather fine, burgundy riding habit, but she drew the cloak around her again immediately. She wished to remain incognito.

"You know the country better than I," she observed as he took the right fork out of town. "I had to ask for directions."

"What makes you think I didn't? What are you up to, Lady Bella?"

Endearingly, she didn't dissemble in the slightest, merely said, "I have your word you won't speak of this to anyone just yet? Even if you believe it is for my own good?"

"Of course you have my word. For what it's worth."

Ignoring that, she said in a rush. "I am going to look at a cottage near Silton. It sounds ideal for my purpose, and I feel I could manage a house much more easily than a yacht."

He nodded. "And the solicitor is meeting you at this cottage?"

"Precisely. So you may leave me comfortably in his care. I daresay we will return to Blackhaven together."

"Won't that give away your purpose before you're ready? Or by the time you sign the contract to take the cottage, will you no longer care for secrecy?"

"I haven't decided yet. If I don't want it—and I would be foolish to immediately take the first I see without at least thinking about it very carefully—I wouldn't want to be prevented looking at others."

He nodded, but regarded her with some curiosity. "If they could prevent you looking, couldn't they just prevent you living in it?"

She thought about that. "I don't believe they could. If I had a home to defend, I could dig my heels in quite forcefully. I don't believe even my father would order the servants to carry me out."

"What of your brothers?"

"I suppose they might do it themselves," she allowed. "But I have other ways of dealing with brothers."

"I'm sure you do," he said, amused. "In fact, I'm beginning to think you have ways of dealing with everyone. How did you persuade your aunt to return the spectacles?"

She flushed a little, as though just remembering them, and touched one nervous finger to the metal bridge across her nose. "I saw them in Aunt Sarah's bedchamber and just picked them up. They are mine, after all."

"Of course they are. And it would be a shame to take your cottage if you couldn't actually see the woodworm. Or the mice."

"I am persuaded it has neither," she said firmly, urging Betsy to a trot, and then a canter. He left the road, cutting across the countryside, heading for the valley that passed between the hills, and she followed him trustingly.

For a little, they galloped hard, allowing the horses their heads. Her smile of pure pleasure delighted him. He wondered if he'd ever tire of watching her ever-changing expressions, and something deep within him began to ache.

They slowed over the more difficult ground that led up to the rise, and she paused to look back at the view spreading down to the sea.

"I wish I could paint," she said with a sigh.

"You're just appreciating your spectacles."

She laughed. "I am. The world is so much more *imposing* when it's sharp."

As one, they rode on and rejoined the road. The cottage she'd arranged to look at was easily found on the edge of Silton, for a small, balding man stood outside the garden gate consulting his pocket watch in an anxious kind of way.

"Mr. Morley," she said in delight. "Oh, the house is charming!"

The house was tiny. Just looking at it made Alban feel trapped. But it was pretty, with a small, neat garden at the front.

"Mrs. Nieve," the blading man said, bowing slightly. He looked relieved. "I'm so glad your husband has accompanied you. My name is Morley, sir."

Alban, who had just dismounted, reached up to help Bella, who was blushing a fiery red. Her mouth was open, clearly ready to disabuse Mr. Morley about their relationship.

"Nieve," Alban informed him, while he raised one eyebrow for Bella's benefit.

She closed her mouth and allowed herself to be lifted from the saddle. He tied their horses to the garden fence, which looked too frail to hold them if they chose to wander.

"This way, if you please," Mr. Morley said, hurrying up the garden path.

"Nieve?" Alban murmured, ushering her after him.

"Well I was about to give my own name when it struck me he might recognize it, so I stopped half-way."

"Very discreet," he agreed.

"Are you laughing at me, sir?"

"You know I never laugh," he assured her, and they followed Mr. Morley inside.

To Alban, it looked dark, even with the shutters thrown wide. It had a small parlor and dining room and a decent sized kitchen with a tiny alcove for the maid. Upstairs were two bedchambers and a box room.

"I'll leave you to look around for five minutes," Mr. Morley said, glancing at his fob watch once more. "And then I must lock up and be on my way."

"Ah. Are you returning to Blackhaven, sir?" Bella asked.

"Gracious, no. I have business at Gorse Farm. Excuse me." He bustled off again.

Alban peered out of the bedchamber window. The view was obscured by trees. "What would you do here by yourself?" he asked. "After the novelty of solitude had worn off."

"I would write my book," she said, surprising him all over again. "Maybe several books."

"What kind of books?" he asked, shifting restlessly.

"I am writing a history of my family, going back to the fifteenth century. It's quite a fascinating story! They were a wild lot, not in the least like my contemporary family!" She paused. "Well, except Seb and Harry perhaps. My younger brothers."

"You must tell me more about it. Would you be comfortable here?"

"It's cozy," she said enthusiastically. Then her shoulders fell. "It's rather gloomy, isn't it? And the rooms are quite cramped, don't you think?"

"Yes, I do," he said, relieved, for he didn't like to think of her living here. "There will be more suitable houses for you."

"It's true I've only just begun my search," she said, clearly disappointed. "But the longer I take, the more likely I am to be found out and stopped."

"Does it have to be around Blackhaven?" he asked, walking to the door and holding it open for her.

"No," she allowed, passing him into the tiny hallway. "It could be anywhere. But normally I'm only ever in Kelburn or Sussex for long periods of time, and though I have much more freedom to look there, everyone knows me."

"Thus defeating the object."

"Exactly," she said, with a quick smile for his understanding.

He led the way down the narrow stairs and out the open front door, where Mr. Morley awaited them tucking away his timepiece.

"What do you say, Mr. Nieve? Shall I have my man call on you with the contract?"

"No, I'm afraid it won't do for us," Alban said.

"But thank you for your time," Bella added quickly.

Mr. Morley sniffed. "Then I bid you good morning." He bowed stiffly and hurried away.

"And this is where we part company, Mr. Nieve," Bella said lightly. "Thank you for your escort and your opinion."

Alban, untying the reins from the fence, made no effort to stop Pegasus munching the nearest flower head. Perhaps it was relief to be out of the dark little house, but he was very aware of the fine day and his desire to enjoy it in her company. Of course, a young lady galloping around the countryside unaccompanied would cause comment, but his motive wasn't entirely chivalrous.

"If you wish to prolong your escape, my business is further west," he said. "You wouldn't be back by midday, but if we travel fast, we should be back in the earlier part of the afternoon."

She searched his eyes with a hint of anxiety that slowly cleared. "I didn't say when I'd be back," she admitted. "And if I return now, they'll make me go to the pump room and drink water."

"I can give you brandy to lace it with," he offered, bending to boost her into the saddle.

A gurgle of laughter escaped her lips. "I believe you would!" She stood on his joined hands and landed neatly in the saddle.

He handed up the reins. "Champagne would go flat."

"True, but brandy would color the water."

"Hmm. Have you ever tried Holland gin?"

"That is not a respectable drink for a lady."

"Neither is brandy. Certainly not in the middle of the day. One thing before we go."

The humor died from her eyes leaving them serious and perfectly trusting. His stomach twisted. "Like yours here, my business is private," he said shortly.

"I think we can rely on each other," she replied, her voice steady.

He kicked Pegasus into motion.

THE COUNTRY WAS wild and varied, from rocky hills to forest tracks and rushing streams that had to be jumped or forded. For Bella, nothing in the world had ever been quite so exciting as riding with this man, presumably upon his secret business. Curiosity as to what this might entail sent pleasurable little frissons up and down her spine as they galloped. She felt almost as if she were in a novel, and not a terribly improving one. One that was fun and a lot more thrilling than real life. Perhaps because he rode fast over the difficult terrain without either criticizing her seat or worrying that she would fall off.

And yet, even breathless from the horses' speed, they still managed to hold conversations of the kind she most enjoyed and rarely found. Although he never laughed out loud, he replied in kind to all her humorous observations that normally passed unanswered or produced a retort that she was talking rubbish. He never once asked *what are you talking about, Bella?* In fact, she rather thought he enjoyed her company almost as much as she enjoyed his. And once or twice she caught an arrested expression in his eyes, as though this fact surprised him.

After a couple of hours of mostly hard riding, he slowed and at the next fork in the road, turned left, following a muddy signpost to Roseley.

"There's a respectable inn just on the edge of the village," he said. "I propose you rest there while I conduct my business."

"I *would* like coffee," she confessed. "And breakfast."

"There's a private parlor. Or at least—" He broke off with an impatient shrug.

She was sure he'd been about to say, *at least there used to be.* As if he had some long-standing connection to the place. Bella wondered if there would be other pirates there. Of the more obvious, cutlass-wielding variety, perhaps.

Smiling, she turned her head to share the joke with him, and found him staring beyond her head into the wood. For the first time that day, he reached out to take her bridle and brought both of their horses to a standstill.

While she frowned quizzically, he never took his eyes off the wood. Releasing her bridle, he urged his horse in front of hers, and then beside it, facing the other way.

"If I say the word," he murmured, "don't hesitate. Dig in your heels and ride hard along this road. I'll find you at the inn."

Her lips parted in shock. It was all she could do not to drop the reins immediately and clutch her lurching stomach. They were in *real* danger here. Suddenly, the adventure wasn't quite so comfortable, particularly not when he drew something from his saddle bag nearest her. A pistol.

Her breath caught, but this was no time for coughing fits of any kind. She tightened her grip on the reins, but knew instinctively she could never leave him here alone to face whatever this danger was…

"Come out," he called clearly, although he kept the pistol hidden between them. "I can hear you crashing about like elephants."

"We are *not* crashing about!" exclaimed an outraged and childish voice, closely followed by a boy of perhaps eight summers, leaping out of the wood. "We are *creeping*. And you must have ears like a dog to hear us!"

The boy wore a torn suit of what had once been decent clothes. His face was almost as muddy, and his hair was wild and unkempt. Behind him came a smaller girl in a grass-stained dress with her tangled hair tumbling half over her face.

A pair of urchin children if ever she'd seen them. And yet the boy hadn't spoken with a local accent of any kind.

Discreetly, Alban un-cocked the pistol, though he didn't yet put it away.

"Clearly my hearing is better than my eyes," he observed. "For I put you both at three feet taller."

"We climbed the chestnut tree," the girl said proudly. "To try and see you better."

"Why?" Alban asked.

"We'd like to st… *borrow*," the girl corrected, glaring furiously at the boy who'd just nudged her sharply, "your horses. Or perhaps just one of your horses, then you could share and so could we."

Definitely not local laborers' brats, or even gypsy children.

"Why, where are you going?" Bella asked.

The two children halted, exchanging glances. "We can't quite agree on that yet," the girl confided. "I want to go to London to find Mama, but he wants to find our uncle, which is silly, even if he is older than me, for we don't know where my uncle is, and we *do* know where Mama is."

"You're running away," Bella said, impressed. "Do you live around here?"

Again, the boy nudged his companion, and this time she closed her mouth with a defiant gesture.

"Oh, don't worry," Bella assured them. "I'm a stranger here myself and quite given to escape, too, although a little less drastically than you. So far." She peered at them. "Are you hungry? You look hungry."

"We're saving our breakfast," the boy said, patting the little bundle he carried.

"What for?" Alban asked.

"Supper," the boy said ruefully. "We don't have any money, so we can only eat once a day until we find my uncle."

"Or Mama," the girl added.

"I can see you have a dilemma," Alban said. "Why don't you come to the inn with us and discuss it? We're having breakfast there and you can share."

The children's eyes both lit up for an instant, but they exchanged glances, and the boy sighed. "We can't. They'll tell Jenkins."

"Who's Jenkins?" Alban asked.

"I don't really know," the boy said. "But we're bidden to obey him."

"Bidden by whom?"

"By Rad…my stepfather." He grimaced. "And by Mama, which is one reason I don't think we should go to her in London."

"But our uncle is probably in London, too," the girl pointed out.

"You can't possibly know that!" the boy exclaimed.

"You can't know that he isn't," the girl retorted.

Bella threw up her hand. "Peace! We refuse to share our lunch with warring runaways. If you won't come to the inn, let us move into the trees and we can break our fast al fresco style. We may sit on my cloak and be quite comfortable."

She cast a quick glance at Alban to see if he would go along with this. It didn't matter if he wouldn't. She couldn't leave these clearly quite determined children to run into the world alone, and she had every intention of helping however she could. To her surprise, Alban's pistol had already vanished and he was dismounting.

"Take us to your favorite hiding place," he commanded.

The children regarded them speculatively before exchanging glances. Finally, the boy turned and led them back into the woods.

With Alban's aid, Bella dismounted, too. "Thank you," she breathed. "Who knows what might befall them if they keep to their plan."

Alban said nothing. His face was unreadable, but his attitude seemed grim. She supposed he had seen plenty of the worst the world had to offer.

"Here," the boy said at last, pausing by a hollowed out oak tree. "We hide inside it, sometimes. Or shelter there from the rain."

"Excellent," Bella approved, unfastening her cloak and spreading it on the ground. "This is what I brought for my breakfast." While Alban tied the horses, she retrieved her parcel from the saddle bag and spread it out—a half loaf of bread, two apples, some strawberries, half a cheese, and a flask of water.

The boy swallowed. "You've got more than us," he said enviously.

"We're bigger. But since we're going to eat at the inn, you can have what you like from this."

After an instant, the boy seized the loaf, tore off a chunk and broke it in two, shoving one half into the girl's eager fist.

"My name's Arabella," Bella told them. "And this is—"

"Nieve," Alban said sardonically, sitting down beside her on the grass rather than on her cloak. "Apparently."

"I'm Leo," the boy said. "My sister is Florrie."

Alban didn't say anything.

"How old are you?" Bella asked.

"Eight," Leo replied. "Florrie's nearly seven, but she's clever for a girl."

Bella nodded. "One of my brothers is clever, too. For a boy."

Florrie laughed, though Leo looked slightly bewildered.

"Never mind," Alban said, pushing the strawberries toward the boy. "We are doomed never to be taken seriously by the fairer sex. Why are you running away? Just looking for adventure, or is someone cruel to you?"

"Jenkins will beat me if I hide too long," Leo said with a shrug. "But mostly we're just hungry."

"They don't feed you?"

"They forget," Florrie said, "and the new cook won't let us in the kitchen. And sometimes we're too naughty and have to miss dinner."

Beside her, Alban had gone very still. It seemed to betoken outrage, which might have been incongruous in a man of his reputation, but made her like him all the more.

"Does your mother know this?" he barked.

"She doesn't know anything," Leo said.

"But she wouldn't like it?" Bella asked anxiously.

"Oh no," the children said together, although Leo looked slightly dubious.

"Well, I might have a better plan," Alban said, "if you can be brave for another few days."

"What plan?" Leo demanded with suspicion.

"Don't go to her or your uncle—you'd find it too hard, anyway with no money or an adult companion. Get them to come here."

The children gazed at Alban in consternation. "How?" Florrie asked.

"Write her a letter."

Their faces fell. "Jenkins won't let us," Florrie said. "He tears them up and threatens to beat us."

Appalled, Bella could only gaze at them in pity. Obviously, this Jenkins was enjoying the easy life here away from supervision and didn't want his neglect reported—at least until he could clean the children up, presumably, and accuse them of lying if they told the truth about his treatment.

"Write a secret letter and give it to us," Alban said in a hard voice. "I'll see your mother gets it. Tell her everything."

Florrie's eyes brightened, but her brother was glowering. "She won't believe us."

"Oh, she'll believe you," Alban said grimly. "I'll vouch for you."

"Do you know her?" Leo asked, surprised.

"No," Alban said shortly.

"In any case, she'll believe me," Bella said determinedly. Sometimes it was useful to be a duke's daughter. "Who is your mother?"

The children exchanged glances once again. "You'll really post a letter to her?" Leo asked with a hint of eagerness behind the doubt. "And maybe one to my uncle, too?"

"I can try and find him for you," Alban said.

"Mrs. Radnor," Florrie said in a rush. "Our stepfather is Mr. Julian Radnor. And my brother is Lord Roseley."

Chapter Six

ROSELEY AGAIN. ACCORDING to Kate Grant, there had been some kind of scandal in the family, which immediately made Bella more protective of the children. This youthful lord was presumably the son of the Lady Roseley she had once met.

To Bella, it was inconceivable that anyone would leave their children with no care but an apparently brutal keeper. That a young baron and his sister should be kept in such conditions boggled the mind.

She glanced at Alban, who didn't look remotely impressed by the title. She couldn't be sure he'd even heard, for he was gazing off into the trees, his face in profile calm and unreadable.

She said brightly, "Lord Roseley? I believe we might be neighbors in Scotland." Although the Roseleys were never there. For as long as she could remember, Powhill had been rented out to a series of people her father disapproved of. She certainly couldn't recall ever meeting any of the family up there.

"I've never been there," the boy said dismissively. "My father never cared for the Powhill place."

Abruptly, Alban sprang to his feet.

"Did you know our father, then?" Florrie asked Bella. "Or our mother?"

Bella frowned, trying again to recall anything about the lady she'd once spoken to, who might have been their mother. "I believe I met your mama in London several years ago. But it was a short meeting." When Maria had dragged her away, hadn't it been when she'd mentioned Scotland? "Do you know," she said slowly, "I think our families might have some sort of feud?"

"Oh, that will be my uncle's fault," Leo said cheerfully. "He's an outlaw, like Robin Hood."

"Goodness," Bella said, startled and beginning to lose a little hope in the uncle as more than a figment of the children's lonely imaginations. The poor things needed a hero. "What did your uncle do?"

"He helped a prisoner to escape the law and had to flee the country," Leo said with pride.

"Oh dear," Bella said. "Then he will be hard to find!"

"My father always said he would come home."

"But then maybe he wouldn't be the best person to care for you," Bella suggested. "In your mother's absence, I mean."

"Nonsense," Leo retorted. He cast her a quick grin of apology. "That is, I don't believe he is a bad man. The wicked duke was going to hang a poacher—or send him to be hanged or something. The poacher was one of our people and my uncle spirited him away under the noses of three guards! I expect he killed them," Leo concluded with relish.

Alban had his back to them, but his shoulders shook as though he might actually be laughing. Bella didn't feel very amused. The wicked duke of Leo's tale could easily be her father.

"Let's hope not," Bella she hastily, "though I'm sure they deserved it."

"Oh yes," Leo agreed. "But the wicked duke was furious, and so was my grandfather, who threw my uncle out of the house." He shrugged. "To be fair, he had to go or he'd have been arrested. But my grandfather was so angry, he didn't give him a penny, and he forbade my father to have anything—"

"Who told you all this?" Alban interrupted impatiently, swinging back to them.

"My father," Leo replied in some surprise. "And old Mattie."

"Who's Mattie?" Bella asked.

"Our nurse," Florrie replied. "She died."

There seemed to have been a lot of death in these children's lives.

Now, apparently, they had no one except a neglectful mother, an unkind stepfather, and a criminal uncle.

Alban gazed at the children for another moment, as though he were thinking of something else entirely. Or wanted to. Something was bothering him, she realized. Well, the plight of these children bothered her, too.

"We need a plan," he said abruptly. "And the first stage is for you to go back to the house and write letters for us to post."

"But we might not be able to sneak out again," Leo said uneasily.

Alban considered it as he walked back to them and offered Bella his hand to rise. The children sprang up. Like a plague of locusts, they'd left nothing but a few crumbs. Alban lifted Bella's cloak and shook it out before flinging it carelessly over one arm.

"I don't think you'll need to sneak," Alban said at last. "I think I should have a word with Jenkins."

"Oh no," Florrie said in alarm. "He's huge! He'll hurt you."

"I guarantee he won't," Alban said. "Lead on."

Excited and somewhat awed by the idea of anyone standing up to Jenkins, the children skipped ahead, talking in low voices. Clearly, they suspected Alban might change his mind when he met the man in person. Bella thought they were wrong. And she had a few things to say to him herself.

But either way, this was *wrong*. The children should not be living with people they held in fear and loathing.

"I've been thinking," she said to Alban. "I should take that cottage in Silton and the children can live with me there until their mother comes home."

Alban stared at her. Although she couldn't remember taking his arm, her hand was tucked warmly into the crook of his elbow.

"Don't you think it a good idea?" she said, disappointed.

"No. No, I don't. To begin with, you don't know them or their family, and then, legally, you can't just take children away from their homes."

"But they shouldn't live in their home like that, not when they're *frightened*. They should never be frightened."

A frown twitched down his brow. "Who frightened you?"

Flushing, she waved one dismissive hand. "Oh, everyone who raised their voice. I was a timid child, which annoyed my father excessively. However, we are not talking about me, but about them. They are neither fed nor clothed nor washed! And probably don't want to be by anyone who frightens them."

"That's why we're going to see for ourselves."

Bella remained unconvinced, but obviously they should have a look before coming to any decisions at all. The children could be making up stories, about some of it at least.

It wasn't far to walk. The children led them to the edge of the wood and through the hole in a fence into a formal, well-tended garden. Bella, who'd expected a neglected estate surrounding a crumbling old house, glanced at the children and felt like scratching her head. More than one day of rolling around in forest mud had led to their present appearance.

As they approached the manor house, Florrie and Leo fell back to walk between them. Florrie almost seemed like a little dog hiding in Bella's skirts.

"So how would you normally go into the house?" Alban asked casually.

"Through the side door and up to the nursery," Leo replied.

"And where would I find Mr. Jenkins?"

"At this hour, probably in the kitchen," Leo said.

"Who's your favorite among the servants here?" Alban asked unexpectedly.

"Molly," Florrie answered at once. "She's the kitchen maid and she slips us food when Jenkins—and the cook—aren't looking. She has a kind smile."

Alban nodded and glanced at Bella. "Could you bring yourself to go with them? And supervise the letter writing?"

She understood at once that though he'd never insist, he wanted to know the true state of their living conditions. And perhaps he wanted them all out of the inestimable Mr. Jenkins' way.

"Maybe I should be with you," she said doubtfully. "I could threaten him with my father."

Alban blinked. "Trust me. I'm more frightening than anyone's father."

It was easy to forget who he was. And the children didn't appear to be frightened of him either. No doubt it was something he'd learned to turn off and on for purposes of disciplining his men and scaring the enemy…whoever the enemy happened to be that day.

The children settled the matter by tugging at her hands. "Be careful," she begged Alban and allowed herself to be dragged away from him across the lawn and down the side of the house.

IT WAS A long time since Alban had been anywhere near this house—more than twelve years, in fact, several weeks before the events in Scotland which had led to his exile. Although he'd learned long ago to squash homesickness and nostalgia with utter ruthlessness, he couldn't prevent the strange prickling of his skin as he approached the house. As if he were going to meet his past. Or someone else's past.

Nick had told his children about him. That meant something to Alban, more than he'd ever admit. But Will had been right to inform him about the children's situation. This was something he would not tolerate, and never would have, even if Nick had vilified him or never spoken his name.

He chose not to use the front door. He wanted to observe this Jenkins character in his natural surroundings. So, he walked around the house in the opposite direction to Bella and the children, until he came to the kitchen steps.

He strolled down the stone steps, listening to the droning male voice and the raucous laughter, which both seemed to belong to the same man. The stale smell of tobacco smoke and ale mingled with the fresher scent of cooking beef.

Inside, three men lolled at the kitchen table. A plump woman of middle years was chortling as she rolled out pastry. Behind her, a maid was stirring pots above the fire. Another maid sat, giggling, in the lap of a large, florid man in a buff-colored coat. A somewhat older man, similarly dressed, looked to be three sheets to the wind. The youngest of the three males wore livery—a footman, clearly—although his coat was open and his necktie loosened.

All of them turned their heads as he entered in the kitchen, their mouths lolling in surprise.

"Lord Roseley's residence, I apprehend," Alban drawled.

"Mr. Radnor's, as it happens, though what's it to you?" the large man said rudely. "Who in hell d'you think you are just walking in here without a by-your-leave?"

"I don't need your leave," Alban said flatly. "Jenkins, is it? On your feet, man."

Jenkins stood up so quickly the maid tumbled off his lap on to the floor. However, there was clearly more aggression than obedience in his action.

"You can't give me orders!" he blustered.

"Oh, I can. I'm a friend of your mistress's, looking in on her behalf. Where is the young lord and his sister?"

"In the nursery, of course," Jenkins said, frowning as he tried to get his head round this sudden intrusion.

"Being taken care of by whom?" Alban barked.

"By the nursery maid, of course," Jenkins said. He pointed at the girl who'd been in his lap and was now climbing unsteadily to her feet. "That's Lily there. She just nipped down for a cup of tea. They keep her on her toes all day, little varmints."

Alban didn't even think about it. He swung hard.

Jenkins was a large man and he went down like a felled tree.

The maids squealed. The other men leapt to their feet, but Alban had no intention of giving Jenkins the chance to retaliate. He leapt on to him, struck him again, then hauled him to his feet, shaking him like a rat.

"That's for lying, you filthy wastrel. And *that*—" Alban struck him a third time across the open mouth—"is for your so-called care of Lord Roseley's children." He swung on the other two approaching, glowering men. "Sit down!" he thundered, and they did, so quickly that the footman sat on the knees of the squealing maid from Jenkins's lap.

Alban flung Jenkins from him. "Where is Molly?" he demanded, without even looking to see where Jenkins fell, though he heard him land on the floor again.

The little maid who'd been stirring the pots nearly jumped out of her skin with fright.

"Her!" cried the other maid, shoving the footman off her so she could point triumphantly at the kitchen girl.

"Come here," Alban barked, and the girl did. Her legs shook, but she met his gaze with conscious bravery. He inhaled, searching for any sign of strong drink. Finding none, he looked deeper. Behind the fear was simple kindness. No doubt she was frightened of Jenkins, too.

Alban nodded. "From now on, you are in charge of the children. No one touches them but you. You'll see them washed and dressed and fed properly three times every day. That will not happen in here, but in the nursery which you will keep clean and tidy. Understood?"

"She's my kitchen maid!" the cook expostulated.

"Use *him*," Alban said, flicking one contemptuous hand at the footman. "Clearly he's got nothing else to do. As for you." He glared at the third man, and then at Jenkins who was sitting up and shaking his clearly woolly head. "I think it would be best if you stuck to outdoor duties. You're clearly unfit for a gentleman's house."

Jenkins stared at him, fury and aggression beginning to return as he realized his utter humiliation.

Alban held his gaze and spoke with ice in his voice. "And you, filth. If you lay so much as one finger on those children again, I'll have you tried and hanged before your master even hears of the mess you've made here. Don't imagine I won't know, for I'll be back. Tomorrow. Now clean up this pigsty. It isn't fit to cook in. You have ten minutes, and then I want you all outside in the yard. All the servants. Molly, go to the nursery and introduce yourself to the lady you'll find there."

He turned on his heel and walked up the steps.

"Next time, I'll have the pompous little shit," Jenkins muttered audibly to his cronies. "Next time, I'll hit him so ha—"

"Next time," Alban interrupted, "if there has to be a next time, I'll simply shoot you. Ten minutes. Don't waste it."

BY THE TIME Molly the kitchen maid appeared in the nursery, looking bewildered, the children were seated together at a desk composing a letter to their mother. Bella was relieved that Leo at least could write.

She had managed to wash their hands and faces and combed out their hair. Though quite mutinous at first, they quickly cooperated, laughing, when she turned it into a jest by pointing them at the looking glass before and after.

"Gentleman said I should come here, ma'am," the maid said, bobbing a nervous curtsy. "I'm Molly the kitchen maid, but he says I've to work here, now."

"No one's caring for these children," Bella said severely.

"I know, ma'am. Sorry ma'am. I slip them some food when I can, but Mr. Jenkins and Cook are something strict."

"You mean they're eating—or selling—all the food that should be for the children!"

Molly bowed her head. "Wouldn't know about that, ma'am."

"Don't cry, Molly," Florrie said anxiously. "We said we liked you best, and you don't need to spend much time in the kitchen at all now."

"If Mr. Nieve gets around Jenkins," Leo said gloomily.

"Well, I'm not sure he's got round him exactly," Molly said judiciously. "More like over the top of him. Are you really friends of her ladyship? I mean Mrs. Radnor."

"They met in London," Leo said, returning to his letter.

"Do you have little brothers and sisters?" Bella asked Molly.

"Why, yes, ma'am—"

"Then look after these two as if they were your siblings," Bella said. "It should only be for a few days until their mother comes, but you should take them out to play and go for walks, and protect them. And don't let that man who beats them anywhere near them. If there's any trouble at all, you must bring them to me at the Blackhaven Hotel. Now, perhaps we could take these dirty dishes down to the kitchen and fetch a broom and a mop."

"Oh, *I'll* do that, ma'am," Molly said, hastily taking from her the slightly furry plates she'd discovered earlier, and adding them to a few more. "If you could just get the door for me…"

Bella obliged. But in the doorway, the girl hesitated. "Who is he?" she asked bluntly. "I can see he's a gentleman but he's…" She took a deep breath, then looked Bella defiantly in the eye. "Rough."

"I certainly wouldn't offend him," Bella agreed. "He's Captain Alban."

The maid's eyes widened in instant recognition, and she walked out the door as if sleepwalking. An instant later, she glanced over her shoulder, a whole new set of questions clearly hovering. Bella gently closed the door on her and turned back to the children.

Leo had completed his letter to his mother and left it lying at the side of the desk while he worked on his uncle's.

"Did you tell her everything?" Bella asked.

"Everything we told you," Leo said. "Read it if you like."

She did, and was immediately touched by the attempt at a grown-up tone. Leo clearly bore a grudge against his mother, perhaps for leaving them here, perhaps for choosing her new husband's company over theirs. But his longing and affection still came through, although he ascribed them hastily to Florrie whose message he'd transcribed faithfully.

If that doesn't bring her, nothing will, Bella thought.

Leo's letter to his uncle was shorter and he didn't invite her to read it. While he signed it, folded it, and inscribed his uncle's name, she looked out of the window onto the kitchen yard. Alban had the grubby servants lined up there and seemed to be laying down the law. A huge man with a black eye and a scowl stood to one side as though not really part of them. Molly stood between a fat older woman and a somewhat blowsy young girl.

Leo presented her with both letters, but his gaze was on the yard below.

"Jenkins isn't saying a word," he said, in some awe. "Has he got a black eye? And a fat lip?" His mouth fell open. "Did Mr. Nieve *hit* him?"

"Oh, I shouldn't think so," Bella said hastily. There was no sign of a fight about Alban that she could see. But it was as well they knew who he was. They were less likely to defy him. "But remember, if there's any trouble at all, Molly must bring you to me. She knows where to find me. But I'm sure your mother will come and sort everything out in just a few days. You're better here with Molly than running away."

She glanced down at the letters in her hand, one inscribed to Mrs. Julian Radnor in South Audley Street, London, the other simply with a name. The Honorable Alban Lamont.

She blinked, assuming she had read it wrongly. "What is your uncle's name?"

"Alban. Alban Lamont."

She let her hand fall, hiding the letters in the folds of her gown. *No wonder he cares what happens to them…*

He'd always been coming here. This was the business he'd always meant to attend to, though initially with her safe in some inn and none the wiser.

SHE EMERGED INTO the yard just as the servants were being dismissed about their business. To Bella, they seemed a trifle bewildered, but there was something in Alban's manner that commanded obedience, even from servants who were not his own, who were, in fact, complete strangers to him. Perhaps the fact that he'd grown up here had imbued him with some invisible authority. Or perhaps years of commanding rough seamen had simply taught him how to gain obedience from anyone. Through fear if nothing else.

He turned as she approached. "Will the girl Molly do?" he asked.

"I think she's kind. But she's too used to obeying this Jenkins for me to be entirely comfortable leaving the children here."

He glanced unerringly up at the nursery window, where the children's grinning faces could be seen pressed against the glass. Molly's more serious face loomed behind. Bella waved.

"I know," he said.

She drew in her breath. "Maybe we should take them with us."

"I can't, for any number of reasons," he said abruptly. "And neither can you."

"I can find ways around my family when I need to," she said defensively.

"I believe you. But there is a feud between your family and theirs that spiriting away their children would not help."

"You mean it would be misconstrued. And the children stuck in the middle."

"We've done what we can here," he said abruptly. He lifted his hand to the children at the window as he began to walk out of the kitchen yard. "I'll keep my eye on them until Mar…their mother returns."

Bella hurried after him. "Do you think she will?"

"She'll at least send for them."

"Leo wrote very well." She handed him the two folded letters, which he took without a word and slipped inside his coat.

He began to walk faster, so that she had to trot to keep up with him. Noticing, he slowed. "Sorry. I don't like this place."

Bella didn't believe that was strictly true. She suspected being home tugged his emotions in so many different directions that he found it difficult. But he hadn't even told her his real connection to the place, so she would never bring it up.

Instead, thinking more exercise might help him to feel better, she offered, "We can run, if you like. Once we're into the wood, of course, out of sight from the house, and can preserve our dignity."

He cast her a surprised glance, and then his eyes began to gleam. "You are good for a man's soul, Arabella Niven. And I shall hold you to the offer."

He did. Almost as soon as they entered the wood, he seized her hand and bolted. With a breath of laughter, she ran, too, but he was so clearly holding to a slow pace that she tugged her hand free and darted past him into the trees, swerving to avoid obstacles and find new paths. Although he always caught up with her easily enough, she was smart, racing in circles to avoid him and forcing him to change directions.

Inevitably, however, she tired first. As he shot passed her, she took the opportunity to slow to a halt, leaning against a tree to catch her breath. It had been years—too many years!—since she'd run like that, and she was no longer as spry as a child.

What she didn't expect was for him to double back and loom over her before she even noticed he'd changed direction.

"Bella." He frowned, throwing one arm around her waist. "Bella, I'm so sorry. Sit and rest—"

"I don't need to," she said breathlessly. "I'm fine. Just not used to running."

His supporting arm was hot at her back, holding her too close to him while his impatient fingers tipped up her chin so that he could search her face, presumably for signs of illness. Although her breath was quick and uneven, it didn't wheeze. No coughing fit threatened to drown her.

"I don't believe you're ill at all," he said in wonder. And with no further warning, he dipped his head and kissed her.

Perhaps because she'd wanted this so much ever since his last shocking embrace at the harbor, she let out an inarticulate squeak of triumph. But this was nothing like the quick, hard kiss he'd given her then. This was long and unhurried, exploring her mouth with slow, gentle caresses that seemed to curl her toes. Heat suffused the pit of her stomach, which seemed to host a thousand soaring butterflies.

One of her hands was trapped between their bodies, but she flung up the other to cup his rough cheek while she opened her mouth to his onslaught. Against her trembling body, every inch of his was hard, male, and exciting.

"Hit me," he groaned into her mouth. "Slap me. Hard."

Bella couldn't think of anything beyond the amazing kiss. "Why?" she managed.

He released her lips, but only just. Carefully, he removed her hazy spectacles. "Because if you don't, I might just take you against this tree." He pushed with his hips until the rough bark dug into her back.

Nothing in the world had ever been as thrilling as his kisses, or the pressure of his hips, and the ever-growing hardness between. Because his lips were so close above hers, she reached and took them back.

She was lost, drowning as his hand trailed down her throat and closed over her breast. Delicious weakness suffused her, and yet the confused desires pulsing within her were powerful, demanding, overwhelming her.

"Don't let me be a cad," he whispered against her lips. "Not to you."

"*Are* you a cad?" she wondered.

"Oh yes." His lips sank into hers once more while his hand cupped and caressed her breast so sweetly that she pushed into it.

"I expect it comes with the profession," she said shakily when he raised his head for breath.

"No," he said ruefully. "It comes from my nature. And it's taking advantage of yours."

With what seemed a massive effort, he tore his body away from her, turning her, and walking with her back toward the main path. She was glad of his arm still around her waist, holding her upright.

"I suppose it was most improper," she managed.

His lips twisted. "It still is. But in a moment, if the horses are still where we left them, I'll put you in the saddle and propriety will be restored."

Her heart still beat frantically. "Why?" she asked, hearing the desperation in her own voice.

He squeezed his eyes shut, walking on, it seemed, purely from instinct. "Don't tempt me anymore, Bella, I'm being good now."

A horse snuffled through the trees, and he opened his eyes once more, veering toward it. When they found the horses, which still stood cropping grass and leaves where they'd left them, he took her forgotten spectacles from a hidden pocket in his coat and polished them on his handkerchief before returning them to her nose.

"Thank you," she managed.

He swooped and pressed a quick, soft kiss on her lips. But then he was as good as his word, boosting her into the mare's saddle with perfect courtesy before mounting Pegasus.

"It's midday," he said, glancing up at the sun as they emerged back onto the road. "We'll have to hurry."

She was glad of the speed to dissipate any awkwardness. She would have hated that after the delicious interlude in the woods.

ALTHOUGH SHE REFUSED to dwell on his kisses—at least until she was alone—she couldn't think of anything except him, and by extension the children they had left at Roseley. He obviously cared for their wellbeing, although not enough to actually stay there with them. But then "Captain Alban" couldn't just stay in Roseley House without revealing who he actually was, and that could easily lead to his arrest. What use then would he be to the children?

It had churned him up to be there. She had sensed that before she even understood why. In some ways, perhaps his anger with the staff had been a relief, a means of dealing with his unwanted emotions as well as the intolerable situation in which he'd found his brother's children. Had he loved his brother? Missed him? Or did he hate his family for his banishment?

She was sure now that her father had to be Leo's wicked duke. Mr. Conway had known it, too, which was why he'd brought the subject up at supper last night. She wished she could recall details of what had happened between her father and his at Kelburn. But no one had told her about it and she'd never asked. Although…

Now that she dredged it up, she did remember a lot of shouting about a poacher and how someone or other—Lord Roseley, perhaps—might as well have spat in the duke's face. She'd stopped listening at that point, although she vaguely recalled feeling relieved when she'd discovered the poacher had escaped. She'd been about sixteen years old.

Her father had never spoken of Lord Roseley after that. She'd even been prevented from conversing with young Lady Roseley, encountered by accident at some London party. And no one had ever mentioned the younger son. Or at least, she hadn't paid enough attention to hear. She'd just wanted the shouting to stop.

But now, galloping across the rugged country beside him, a faint memory stirred. Of standing in the schoolroom with her younger sisters, being told off by the governess for her poor deportment. In fact, she suspected she had been clumsier and more nervous than usual because her father's furious voice had filled the whole house, along with that of an angry stranger. And as she'd stood miserably in the schoolroom, Edmund Burke's *Reflections on the Revolution in France* balanced precariously on her head, she'd seen a dark young man bolt furiously along the path in front of the window.

She'd only ever seen the back of his head. Wild, black hair, a tall, lean back and long legs. Every inch of him had screamed with tension and anger. And yet the way he'd dragged his hand through his hair had seemed to hold utter despair. She'd felt an instant's pity before the relief set in. He'd been the other shouter. With him gone, her father would quieten down. For a little at least.

Had that young man's back belonged to Alban Lamont? She couldn't ask him, and there was no real reason to imagine so. Except that few people were ever prepared to shout back at her father.

They had reached the coast, and beside her, Alban drew rein, bringing Pegasus to a halt. She pulled up beside him, letting Betsy snort and blow while she and Alban gazed over the sea.

"Everything seems possible when you look out to sea," she observed. "I wonder why that is?"

It was a stupid thing to have said aloud, and she immediately bit her lip. But Alban only said, "Because you don't know what's on the other side. It could be anything. And because it's bigger than you and all your little problems."

She turned her head, gazing now at his profile. "Is that what it does for you?"

"Once, perhaps. Maybe still." He met her gaze. "Mostly, it makes me a good living."

"Are you really a pirate?"

"I might have committed the odd act of piracy. It's easier in war time and one side or the other is always pleased with you. Mostly, I just trade."

"How did you come to this life?"

He shrugged. "I learned to sail with fishermen and then with a merchant captain. I traded a little on the side and eventually bought his ship."

"*The Albatross*?" she asked.

"No, I bought her later, once I'd sold *The Maid*. And then in time, I acquired the others."

"How many ships do you have?"

"Four. Why?"

She smiled apologetically. "I'm curious. Your life seems exciting to a mere landlubber."

"Sometimes it is," he admitted. "But whatever anyone tells you, it was never heroic. Don't imagine I'm something I'm not."

She pulled her gaze free. "I'm not a child, Captain. Nor was I ever given to hero worship."

She could almost see the sardonic twist of his lips as he urged Pegasus back into motion. She didn't quite catch what he muttered into the wind, but it sounded like, "And now I'm perverse enough to wish you were."

Chapter Seven

BY ILL-LUCK, SHE and Alban entered the hotel just as Uncle Smedley strutted across the foyer. Inevitably, he saw her at once and, scowling furiously, increased his pace.

"Oh dear," Bella said nervously. "We should say goodbye now." She halted, spinning to face him and thrusting her hand very briefly into his. "Thank you, Captain Alban," she said as brightly as she could, and turned her back on him just as Uncle Smedley was upon her.

"There you are!" he exclaimed. "What in the world do you think you're about? In here, Arabella, now."

Since he took her arm and she had no desire to be dragged anywhere in front of Alban—although she hoped fervently the captain had already left the hotel—she walked across the foyer with her uncle. There was a small reception room to the left, where Uncle Smedley clearly meant to scold her. She'd get it over with and then face her aunts. She supposed, drearily, that they would all shout. But perhaps she could shut them out by remembering the plight of the Roseley children… or the delight of Captain Alban's kisses.

"What is the matter with you?" Smedley demanded, without even closing the door. "Sometimes I think you must be a changeling, you show so little concern for your name, your conduct or any common sense!"

"Maybe I am," she said vaguely. "My father always thought so."

Uncle Smedley's scowl darkened further with suspicion. "Are you trying to be insolent?"

"No," she said in surprise. "I am truly sorry for worrying you all, but I left a note for my aunts—"

"A note saying nothing," Uncle Smedley fumed. "Besides, what use is a note when eligible gentlemen call upon you and you aren't here to receive them? Are you so lost to what you owe your family that you'll play fast and loose with even this last chance? Don't you understand what has been done for you? Are you so idiotic—"

"Lady Arabella," interrupted a quite different voice from the doorway.

In despair, Bella turned her eyes upon Alban, who must have heard everything. She really didn't want to be so diminished in his eyes by this revelation of how her own family regarded her.

His face gave away nothing. He said coolly, "I know you wished to lie down. Might I escort you to your aunts?"

"Oh no," she said, flustered. "That is, I…"

His lip twitched. To her amazement, his eyes were laughing, inviting her to share a joke she hadn't yet seen. His head jerked very slightly in the direction of the foyer, and she understood at last that he'd engineered her escape from Uncle Smedley. An escape she'd almost sabotaged by rejection.

Her breath caught on hysterical laughter, or the surging cough, perhaps. "I will just go up," she said. "But I will not need your escort… thank you…" Since he'd stepped into the room, she drifted past him and out the door. Although she felt his gaze upon her, she dared not look at him. Or at her uncle who seemed to radiate stunned fury.

Bowing, Alban closed the door behind her.

"Sir, I take your interruption very ill," Smedley began, his voice booming from inside the room.

Bella didn't want to hear this. But at least the foyer was empty, save for the young man busy at the desk.

"I take your entire manner very ill," Alban snapped. "A gentleman would not speak to a naughty child the way you address that gentle lady."

Bella's lips parted in shock. Her foot, already raised to walk, simply slipped back to the floor. Astonishment seemed to have frightened off the rising cough.

"I am that gentle lady's uncle!" Smedley blustered.

"I don't care if you're her fairy godmother," Alban retorted. "You'll mend your manners around her."

"Manners!" Uncle Smedley spluttered. "Am I to be lectured in manners by a damned pirate?"

"Trader," Alban said sardonically. "And yes, apparently so. I don't want to have to do it again. Good afternoon."

Bella fled across the foyer with no signs whatever of breathlessness. She didn't glance back at Alban as he emerged from the room, but her heart was singing because he'd defended her from her own family. And what was more, he hadn't done it from pity but because Uncle Smedley truly had been in the wrong. He had no right to speak to her like that. None of them did.

And with that new warm knowledge, she somehow gained the strength to face her aunts without any qualms at all.

THE MEANING OF her uncle's complaints about her not being present to receive eligible gentlemen, soon became plain. Mr. Tranter, her partner from the ball, was discovered drinking tea with her aunts in the sitting room.

Bella, still buoyed up by her day's adventures and by her new personal discovery, greeted her visitor with unaffected pleasure. Which seemed to mollify her aunts for the present at least, although Aunt Maria peered at her as if searching for signs of fatigue or ill health.

As they made easy conversation, she found herself warming to Mr. Tranter as a most pleasant companion. She agreed at once to walk with him to the circulating library the following morning, and from there, perhaps, looking in at the art gallery.

"I'm so glad I caught you this afternoon," he said warmly as he took his leave. "I so enjoy talking with you."

"There, he likes you!" Aunt Sarah exclaimed with glee as the door closed behind him. "And it's so nice to see you making an effort with someone."

"I wasn't making any effort," Bella said in surprise. "I think he is a kind man who is a little lonely."

"Oh, but Bella, you're wearing the wretched spectacles!" Sarah exclaimed.

"They help me to see and make me feel better," Bella said.

"Well, they don't make you *look* better, so until you have a husband who can see beyond your outward appearance, you had better give them back to me."

Bella took them off to keep the peace, but placed them absently in the pocket of her riding habit. "Why, are we going out?" she asked.

"You haven't taken the waters today," Aunt Maria reminded her. "Go and change and we'll walk round to the pump room now."

It seemed a small price to pay for avoiding the scolding she'd so fully expected, so Bella dutifully changed into a day gown, and, with her spectacles in her reticule, set out with her aunts.

IT WAS FULLY dark by the time Alban stepped into the tavern. He ordered brandy—one could always, it seemed, get decent French brandy in Blackhaven—and turned to survey the other shady patrons.

Mr. Tranter blended in fairly well, interestingly enough, except that, catching Alban's eye, he raised his mug of ale to him. Alban thought. He was getting bored with merely threatening people, was spoiling in fact, for a fight. He should probably have just nodded back, finished his brandy and repaired to Will's house. But curiosity won, as usual.

Swiping up his glass, he walked around the shoving contest in the middle of the floor, and took the stool opposite Tranter.

"Not spending the evening with your mother, I see," he said mildly.

"Mothers are like ships," Tranter said, raising his mug once more.

"Both may be abandoned for a few hours with impunity."

"Well, I'll be joining my ship in the morning," Alban said. "When will you be joining your mother?"

Tranter's half-smile faded. "I don't catch your meaning."

"Yes, you do. Your mother's been dead for ten years. I really think she's beyond the power of even Blackhaven water to revive."

Tranter laughed. "Where did you hear that?"

"From the vicar, oddly enough."

Tranter curled his lip. "From the vicar's wife, you mean. She'll cause any trouble for me that she can. Just because I once rejected her advances."

Alban allowed himself one contemptuous glance. "What trouble could lack of a living mother possibly cause you?" he wondered. "Of course. It would take away any valid reason for your skulking in Blackhaven, where the rich, sick, and stupid come to be cured. Of course, the waters can't cure stupidity, which is your good fortune."

"You're making no sense to me, *Captain*," Tranter said coldly.

"You needn't sneer. I *am* a captain. I just thought I would tell you, as one bastard to another, that the ladies of the town are likely by now to be as aware of your true situation."

"And what would that be?" Tranter asked belligerently. Perhaps he wanted to see how much Alban actually knew, perhaps he was trying to be intimidating.

"That of a poor but greedy man who preys on wealthy women."

"Not very successfully if I'm still poor," Tranter retorted. He sat back, gently swirling the dregs of ale at the bottom of his mug while he met Alban's gaze. He smiled. "What if I had a proposition? One that would help us both."

"I'm listening," Alban said steadily.

AT THE PUMP room the following morning, Bella was glad to encounter Mr. Conway, whom she'd met at the ball in company with Captain

Alban. Her impression had been that they were old acquaintances, in which case he knew all about Alban's true identity, and what had happened at Kelburn twelve years ago.

Mr. Conway sat by Bella and her aunts for a little to make civil conversation. He seemed somewhat curious about Bella, so it was natural enough for her to return his questions, especially when her aunts moved to converse with a lady of around their own age.

"So, you are not living at home just now, Mr. Conway?"

"No, it is more convenient to stay in Blackhaven than to travel from Wayfare every day for the waters."

"Of course it is. I imagine it would defeat the object of convalescence. I suppose you will have known the late Lord Roseley very well?"

Mr. Conway cast her a closer glance. "I grew up with him and his brother."

She took a deep breath. "Forgive my asking. It's just that I can't quite remember…What *was* the scandal about the younger brother?"

"There is no mystery about it," Mr Conway said easily. "Someone from his lordship's Scottish estate was arrested for poaching on… someone else's."

"My father's," Bella suggested.

Mr. Conway's face relaxed. "Indeed. Lord Roseley's younger son took exception to the arrest and took it upon himself to free the prisoner. After which, they both fled and no one has seen him since."

"No one," Bella repeated vaguely. "You were their friend… I suppose you know the current family well?"

"The present Lord Roseley is a child, but I am acquainted with his mother."

"And his stepfather?"

"I'm afraid I don't have that pleasure. He is in trade, I believe." It was spoken with the gentleman's natural disdain for a man who was not born of gentle stock but made, rather than inherited, his own money.

"What a coincidence," Bella murmured.

"Come, Bella, drink up," Aunt Maria said impatiently, looming over her. "There's no point in coming if you don't drink."

"No point," she agreed, though she obediently finished her glass. "Good morning, Mr. Conway."

"Good morning, Lady Arabella. Ladies."

Mr. Conway had told much the same story as Leo about Lord Roseley's black sheep, and yet Bella had the feeling he was holding something back.

Outside the pump rooms, they were met by Mr. Tranter, who escorted them to the circulating library. This seemed to be more of a meeting place than a reading place, and there wasn't a great deal of history. However, she did find the first volume of a new novel by the author of *Sense and Sensibility* which she had read and loved last year. Armed with *Pride and Prejudice*, she rejoined her aunts and Mr. Tranter who were seated on chairs by the door gossiping together.

Mr. Tranter was, she thought, a bit of a chameleon. He seemed to change his manner just a little, according to who he was with. Which was an excellent talent, although she wasn't sure she quite liked it. However, it made him pleasant company, and she was happy enough to accept his escort to the art gallery.

Bella found several of the pictures to her taste, and was soon imagining her favorites on the walls of her fictional cottage. However, in her fantasy now, there seemed to be a shadow in the doorway, a shadow whose opinion she sought as to the balance of the painting.

Hastily, she blinked it away before the shadow grew a face. She knew whose it would be.

"Do you go to Mrs. Grant's soiree tonight?" she asked Mr. Tranter hastily.

He sighed. "Sadly, no. I have not been invited. Mrs. Grant is pleased to disapprove of me."

Bella blinked in surprise. Considering Mrs. Grant's own reputation, and her avid pursuit of an introduction to such a shady individual as Captain Alban, this was difficult to believe.

"I'm sure you must have misunderstood her," Bella said consolingly.

"No, I don't believe so."

"Then how did you offend her?" Bella asked, then blushed. "Forgive me, it's none of my business."

"I don't mind in the least. It has to do with an incident several years ago, when Lady Crowmore, as she was then, saw fit to interfere in what was, to me, a serious matter of the heart. I wished to marry a certain lady, a friend of Lady Crowmore's. I was slandered to the lady's father and we were torn apart."

"But why would she do such a thing?" Bella demanded, inclined to remember the haughty young London lady of fashion rather than the friendly vicar's wife she'd met at the ball.

"It's not my place to guess," Mr. Tranter said uncomfortably.

"I am discreet, sir, and make my own mind up."

"Then it's my belief she disliked me for preferring my own lady to her."

Bella closed her mouth. "That would be very…spiteful," she observed.

"Let us speak of something else."

Bella was glad to, for she'd rather warmed to Kate Grant at the ball and didn't want to see her as the selfish, malicious person Mr. Tranter portrayed. She felt for his loss, but providing she knew no more, she could still put it down to misunderstanding.

As she glanced around the gallery in search of fresh inspiration, she saw a carelessly dressed man with hair half-swept back from his forehead, staring at her. Hastily, she looked away. However, the man immediately left off his conversation—or had it been a quarrel?—with the gallery proprietor, strode straight toward her, and stopped directly in front of herself and Mr. Tranter.

His intense eyes seemed to devour her. "Forgive me, madam, but you have such an interesting face, I wonder if I could paint you?"

Flustered, and not a little astonished, Bella opened her mouth to refuse, but Mr. Tranter spoke first.

"Certainly not. Do you mistake Lady Arabella Niven for some

woman of…lesser class, shall we say?"

"You can say anything you like," the artist said amiably. "I don't care about her class. It's her face I want. Here." He delved into his coat and came back with a card. "Here's my studio. I can paint you there, or in your home, or any other place of your choosing. I take commissions, of course, but I'd paint *you* for nothing."

"You're very kind," Bella murmured, taking his card. "But I don't think—" She broke off, for with a quick bow, the artist simply turned away and strode back to resume his argument with the proprietor. "What a strange man," she said, amused.

"You are too tolerant of such riff-raff," Mr. Tranter said. "A lady in your position need not put up with these impositions. Your heart is too kind."

"Actually, I believe I am flattered," Bella said mildly.

AFTER SUCH A tiring morning, Aunt Maria was inevitably anxious to take Bella back to the hotel to rest. Bella cooperated without demur, even when Aunt Sarah tried to bribe them with a trip to the ice parlor. Aunt Sarah seemed to imagine that this was where they would encounter more of Bella's so-called admirers. Without her spectacles, Bella doubted she would recognize them. Or anyone else.

"Can't you see she's exhausted?" Aunt Maria scolded her sister. "We need to get her home and rested before the coughing fits start again. And if we are to go to the vicarage this evening, rest is vital."

"I'm suggesting she sit down an eat an ice," Aunt Sarah exclaimed. "Not climb a mountain before luncheon!"

"In truth, I would like to go back," Bella said apologetically. "Let's have the ice tomorrow. It will be something to look forward to."

Aunt Sarah sniffed. Aunt Maria bore her off in triumph.

In fact, Bella did not feel remotely tired. But dissembling seemed the simplest way to be at home if Captain Alban called, and surely, he would. Even if she read too much into yesterday's kisses—her heart and stomach seemed to plunge together at the very memory—he must know how anxious she was to hear any further news of the Roseley children.

She ate a light, cold luncheon with her aunts in their sitting room. Since the older ladies were bickering, she was more than happy to change the subject as soon as they relapsed into hostile silence.

"Aunts, do you remember His Grace's quarrel with Lord Roseley? What was it all about?"

They both looked surprised. Aunt Sarah stopped chewing.

Aunt Maria frowned as though searching her memory. "Poaching. Roseley owns Powhill, though he rents it out now. One of his people poached a deer from Kelburn—or was it grouse?—and was sent to the magistrate. Roseley's younger boy pled for his release, said he'd been with the culprit and hadn't realized they'd wandered off Powhill land. Took it very ill when His Grace refused to budge on the matter."

"No, there was more than that," Aunt Sarah intervened. "The Lamont boy swore it was he who shot the animal and not their tenant."

"Was it true?" Bella asked breathlessly.

"I've no idea. His Grace didn't believe so, said it was the boy's way of getting his man off because he knew Kelburn would never prosecute him." Aunt Sarah's frown deepened. "He was a bit of a Jacobin, was he not?" she said to her sister. "Held very radical principles and wouldn't keep them to himself. At any rate, he had a huge row with His Grace, after which he went and freed his man, assaulting the guards to do so. His Grace was furious all over again and went storming over to Powhill, threatening Roseley with all sorts of retribution."

"The Roseley boy fled with his poacher," Aunt Maria recalled. "Or his father got them out of the country. At any rate, no one ever saw the younger son again. They believe he's dead, which isn't surprising with the war and everything else. And of course, Roseley and Kelburn never spoke another word."

Bella could imagine it only too well. Taken together with her glimpsed memory of the young man storming away from his quarrel with her father, when he must have tried to take the blame himself…

She felt for him, for his anger and his burning sense of injustice. The man he'd freed would have faced a terrible punishment for a trivial crime, one that should not have impacted anyone at Kelburn at all. But everyone took poaching so seriously.

And so, Alban had been flung out into a dangerous world at barely eighteen years old. Somehow, he'd thrived and become the trading captain of today, harsh, cynical, and utterly careless of convention. Yet surely that idealistic boy still lurked within the façade. His eyes still smiled even if his lips didn't.

Hastily, she caught up on her aunts' continued conversation and was just in time to reject Aunt Maria's suggestion of lying down in bed. Instead, she curled up on the window seat with her library book.

The afternoon seemed interminable. Major Doverton called, as did another gentleman with whom she'd danced at the ball, but of the captain there was no sign. Not even in the street when she glanced down at the High Street traffic. Although she glimpsed Mr. Conway once, Alban was not with him.

His absence made her restless, discontented, and yet she had no real reason to expect him. He'd made her no promises, no offers except to try not to seduce her. And she'd gone on kissing him. Perhaps she'd been too forward, given him a disgust of her… But in truth, it didn't matter. She knew Captain Alban was not the kind of man who married women like her. She should just be grateful for his friendship.

Only friendship didn't normally come with kisses like those.

He was just toying with me for his own amusement. That had more the ring of truth. Only he was not truly a bad man and so he'd stopped short of seduction. Not that she would have permitted such an outcome, of course …would she?

Oh dear, this is a whole new side of myself I did not know existed. I seem to be very brazen. And very silly. No more. We like each other and that must be where the matter stays.

Must it? whispered the dreamy voice in her head. *He is Lord Roseley's son. It would not be such an unequal match.*

She tried to thrust the thoughts aside, cram them into a closed box in her mind, along with the shadowy figure who stood in her cottage doorway admiring her painting of Blackhaven Harbor.

She couldn't ever remember feeling so wound-up, so tense—at least not with this strange, warm pleasure behind it.

By the time the dinner hour approached, she knew he would not come. Disappointment was intense and difficult to accept, and she prepared somewhat listlessly for dinner and the vicarage soiree.

In fact, even her aunt's grumbled.

"A musical soiree," Aunt Maria said discontentedly. "At a country vicarage? It will be appallingly dull and painful on the ears."

"Oh no," Sarah said. "It's not to show off local accomplishment, or lack of it. Apparently, Mrs. Grant has discovered an extraordinary singer somewhere or other.

Aunt Maria sniffed. "I'm not sure it's quite proper in a vicar's wife to be promoting theatrical people."

"Well, she is still Kate Crowmore," Sarah said wryly.

"If she weren't, I wouldn't risk going," Maria retorted. "At least she always had impeccable taste. But even so, what manner of musical discovery can she possibly have made in this backwater?"

Bella didn't really care. She welcomed the event as a distraction, but remembering Alban's face when Kate had issued her invitation, she knew he wouldn't be there. It was only as they walked round to the vicarage that she realized how out of character it was for her to welcome a social occasion for any reason. Perhaps it was the knowledge of her spectacles, carefully stored in her reticule, that gave her confidence.

She put them on while trailing after her aunts across the vicarage hallway to the drawing room. As a result, she could see beyond Kate's welcoming figure to the other guests, most of whom she recognized as local gentry or town worthies, with a few visitors like herself thrown into the mix. She saw Mr. Conway at once and, to her surprise, the artist who'd accosted her that morning. His face lit up most flatteringly when he caught sight of her.

"Delighted you could come," Kate said warmly. "I was just about to introduce Mrs. Gallini, so this is perfect timing. I've saved you the best places at the front."

"Is she loud?" Aunt Sarah asked dubiously, holding back.

Kate's lips twitched. "Powerful," she allowed. "But you won't regret hearing her clearly, I promise. Let me just present Lord Tamar who is staying in Blackhaven for the summer."

Astonishingly, Lord Tamar was the artist. He bowed to all three Niven ladies, in a haphazard kind of way, and took his seat next to Bella.

"You look different," he said abruptly.

"That will be the spectacles," she said. She could feel Aunt Sarah's furious glare on the other side of her face.

"I like them," he said unexpectedly. "Another aspect of you—less unworldly and angelic. I should like to paint you with and without."

"I can't think why you want to paint me at all," she said, frankly.

"Because you're the Duke of Kelburn's daughter," Aunt Sarah snapped below her breath.

She may or may not have intended Lord Tamar to hear, but he retorted instantly, "So are you, ma'am, but I haven't offered to paint you."

Aunt Sarah glared at him in outrage, but to Bella's surprise, the artist was neither apologetic nor rude. He merely grinned in a disarming kind of way and said thoughtfully, "Yet."

Bella laughed, and then Kate was calling for their attention to introduce a plump, pretty young woman as Mrs. Gallini.

Bella liked music, but she hadn't expected to be more than mildly entertained by Kate's "discovery". As it turned out, Mrs. Gallini's talent was exceptional. Both powerful and unusually sweet in tone, she imbued every line with emotions that tugged at the heart, through both grief and laughter. Bella was able to lose herself in the music, forget about her aunts, the peculiar Lord Tamar, and all the other guests.

She applauded with enthusiasm when Kate finally rose to thank Mrs. Gallini.

"We'll have some refreshment now," Kate added, "but you'll be glad to know that Mrs. Gallini has kindly agreed to sing one more song for us this evening." She smiled as the door opened, and moved quickly down the room. "Why, Captain, we'd quite given you up."

Bella couldn't help it. Her head jerked around before she could stop it, and there, strolling into the room was the unmistakable figure of Captain Alban. Blood rushed into her face, making her ears sing and her heart race. Quite suddenly the evening was perfect.

"Well I'll be damned," she heard Mr. Conway murmur in the row behind. "How on earth did your wife persuade him to come to such an event?"

"A certain lady's name, I believe," Mr. Grant replied, even more quietly, before he stood and walked across the room to greet the late arrival. But Kate had heard him.

Me? My name? He does *like me…!*

"I see," Lord Tamar said beside her. "So that is the lie of the land."

"I beg your pardon?" Bella said distractedly.

"Now I *have* to paint you. Can you bring him, too?"

Bella rose in response to her aunt's hand under her elbow, dragging her gaze back to Lord Tamar. "You must ask him, sir, not me," she said firmly as Aunt Sarah tugged her in the opposite direction.

"Is he really Lord Tamar, or has Kate Crowmore been taken in?" Aunt Maria wondered.

"Why wouldn't he be Lord Tamar?" Bella asked, trying very hard not to look around for Captain Alban.

"Because no one's seen anyone from his family for years. The estate was ruined decades ago, long before this marquis succeeded to the title. He and his siblings live in the ruins of their old castle in Devon, and get up to all sorts mayhem. You may think he's eccentric and amusing, Bella, but trust me, he is not an eligible choice in the marriage mart!"

"Oh no," she agreed. She was barely listening. Glasses of wine and lemonade had been set on tables at the side of the room, along with canapes and little cakes, for guests to help themselves. Bella was grateful for the lemonade thrust into her hand by Aunt Maria. It gave her something to do while she waited for Alban to notice her.

This was ridiculous. She was eight and twenty years old, long past the age of school-girl crushes. In fact, even when she'd been the correct age for them, they had largely passed her by. She'd been more interested in books than young men, and the few who had impressed themselves upon her notice were quickly dismissed. It was difficult to sustain incipient infatuation when the object of it paid one no attention whatever.

She hadn't missed them, hadn't begrudged her younger sisters their social successes and brilliant marriages, for she'd long known that the world of love and marriage, in whatever order, was not for her. Even the few offers of marriage she had received had been untempting in the extreme, made as they were by unlikeable gentleman more interested in her father's wealth and power than in her. Not that she blamed them for that, but she refused to swap the possibility of contented spinsterhood for the certainty of a miserable marriage under the thumb of an unpleasant man. It was the only duty she'd ever shirked, for her family already had all the influence and all the riches they would ever need.

Captain Alban was the only man she could ever recall affecting her this way. Of course, he was the only man who had ever kissed her, but more than that, he seemed to see her as Bella, and to *like* what he saw. She didn't need to hide or pretend, or dredge up suitable topics for stilted conversation. He was fun, exciting, and different…

And I have to pull myself together. What is the matter with me?

It was torture to keep her eyes from straying, but she forced them ruthlessly to pay attention to Mr. Marlow and his shy daughter Catherine. A little later, she met a very amiable young man called Bernard Muir who told her with a grin that she was better off with her lemonade than risking the wine, for Grant bought only the inferior type that paid duty.

"Are you in the market for some that doesn't?" someone asked, reaching around him for a glass of wine. Alban, looking as saturnine and handsome as ever in his black coat and snowy white but carelessly tied cravat.

Bella met his gaze with something almost like fear. Until his lips and eyebrows quirked together and she found herself smiling.

"Depends who's asking me," young Mr. Muir said warily.

"Sensible answer," Alban allowed, dragging his gaze from Bella with apparent reluctance. "Although it might leave a cloud of suspicion over your head."

"But no evidence," Mr. Muir argued, thrusting out his hand. "You're Captain Alban, aren't you?"

"I am," Alban admitted, giving the briefest of handshakes. "And I'm afraid I've come to steal your companion away."

"You missed most of the performance," Bella said a trifle breathlessly as they strolled around the room.

"I missed you," Alban replied. "I like your hosts—for a vicar and his wife—but I feel like a barbarian specimen at such affairs. Or a wild beast for people to gawp at and poke sticks at if they dare."

"I shouldn't think they would. Dare, I mean. Have you been back to Roseley?"

"Briefly. The children are well and being regularly fed. I'll go back tomorrow, or send someone else."

"You are busy?"

"I've had word *The Albatross* is fully repaired at last, so I'll be riding on to Whalen tonight."

Her heart stood still. "Are you sailing? Away, I mean?" She tried to drag her eyes free of his gaze, since they no doubt gave away everything she should hide, but he held them.

"I have no business here," he said abruptly. "With you."

Now her eyes fell easily because the pain was too sharp.

His breath caught. "Bella—" His voice was still harsh, but not, she thought with anger. Only she never discovered what he would have said because a sweet, musical voice interrupted them.

"Captain! I have grown bored waiting for you to recognize me!"

Alban swung around impatiently, to discover Mrs. Gallini herself, smiling up at him with undisguised pleasure. His brow smoothed. "Eloisa!"

"And here was I imagining you came because of me!"

I was imagining the same thing, Bella thought numbly as he took the other woman's outstretched hand. Worse, their eyes betrayed unmistakable intimacy.

"Captain Alban rescued me from Sicily," Mrs. Gallini told Bella and everyone else within earshot. "It is really thanks to him that I am here in England."

"How on earth did your wife persuade him to come to such an event?" Mr. Conway had asked.

"A certain lady's name…"

But it wasn't Bella's name. It was Eloisa Gallini's.

Bella stepped back into the crowd and let it close around Alban and the singer. She'd never felt so bereft in her life.

"Inevitable, is it not, that our two larger than life guests know each other?"

Bella came to herself as her hostess spoke beside her.

"I suspect they have both had adventurous lives," Bella managed.

"Indeed. And it would be remarkable if a man like the captain had not had adventures."

Bella cast her a quick glance. She had the feeling Kate was talking here about the intimate variety.

"In his past," Kate said.

She was right, of course, but that this beautiful, twice-married woman should even begin to imagine her feelings was unbearable. "Either way, it is none of our business."

"Of course not," Kate agreed. "But Blackhaven will speculate in any case. Come, let us sit here out of the crowd."

Since she didn't know what else to do, Bella sat, her lemonade glass still clutched in her hand like a talisman.

"Do you know," Kate said unexpectedly, "I always rather admired you. When we were young and in our first London seasons."

Bella blinked at her. "You did? I never imagined you even saw me."

"Oh, I saw. And envied. You so clearly didn't care for any of the trivia so necessary to the world of fashion, and you seemed quite indifferent to all the gentleman hunting in the marriage mart."

"I was," Bella said with the ghost of a smile. "But then, the indifference was mutual."

"I doubt that. I think you intimidated them. Clever women do, you know. I just learned early on to feign empty-headedness. Although it's true I wasn't as clever as I thought or I'd never have made the marriage I did then. After marriage, a woman has more freedom to be who she wishes to be. Because of that, I thought it didn't matter who I married. I should have shunned them all, like you. Until I met Tristram—Mr. Grant."

Bella swallowed. "You're being kind. I just don't know why."

"Oh, I'm not kind," Kate said. "Ask anyone. The captain is like you, all the more attractive because he doesn't care for appearance. And then there's the dash and the mystery. I imagine to have his attention is quite…exhilarating."

Bella had no idea what to say to that. She rubbed futilely at neck of her gown, as if that could stop the pain.

"He likes you," Kate said bluntly.

Bella shook her head. "Why are you saying this? To warn me? If so, it is quite unnecessary."

"Oh, I wouldn't presume," Kate said. "You were always much cleverer than I. I'm just rambling until you feel better."

In spite of everything, a smile sprang to Bella's lips. She gazed curiously at her hostess who really wasn't anything like she'd imagined. Like Mr. Tranter imagined.

"Do you know Mr. Tranter?" she asked impulsively.

Kate wrinkled her nose. "Until the Assembly Room ball, only by repute."

"He says he was once in love with a friend of yours."

"Between you and me, he once *eloped* with a friend of mine," Kate said dryly. "Her father caught them in the nick of time."

"Because of you?"

Kate blinked. "Lord, no, I had nothing to do with it. But I was glad for her. The man is an unscrupulous fortune hunter."

Although Bella's instinct was to trust in Kate's honesty, she had too many other things on her mind to dwell on which truth was closest to the mark: Kate's or Mr. Tranter's. People saw the same events so differently.

Kate stood. "Well, I shall reconvene our little concert for the last aria."

In the end, by popular request, Mrs. Gallini sang two more songs, both greeted with much deserved applause.

Bella, lost in her own thoughts, became aware that her aunts were both talking to her. Aunt Maria wanted her to stay seated because she looked too pale and tired. Aunt Sarah wanted her to take off her spectacles immediately and pay some attention to young Mr. Muir who seemed to like her.

Bella stared at her. "Mr. Muir? He's twenty years old! If as much."

"So what?" Sarah demanded. "I believe he has no fortune but his birth is good and he is connected by marriage to Lord Wickenden who is bound to do something handsome for him. It would not be an ill match."

Bella, suddenly short of breath, plucked at the neck of her gown as if it were choking her.

"Don't do that," Maria snapped. "It just makes you cough—and look deranged besides."

Bella sprang up. "Excuse me," she managed and bolted away from them. Her breath was coming in wheezes that she knew would dissipate in the silence of the vicar's hall. Or in the street beyond. She could just go home. The vicar's servant could convey her apologies. She didn't look to the right or left, for she didn't want to see Alban with Mrs. Gallini and she certainly didn't want to inspire a fit of coughing here.

With a faint smile affixed to her lips, she sped to the door with purpose and was soon on the other side. Closing it, she leaned against it for a moment and breathed. Then she hurried across the hall toward the room she'd seen the servant take hats and cloaks—and halted. A man already stood there, his hat in his hand.

"You're ill," he said, starting toward her.

"You're leaving," Bella blurted.

"It's a long ride to Whalen in the dark. Do you want to come?"

"Yes," Bella said. She smiled with difficulty. "But you know I won't."

He came to a halt before her, his intense eyes searching her face. At least she could breathe again.

With difficulty, he said, "I don't want to *hurt* you, Bella."

With a gasp, she flung away from him. "Why must everyone assume I'm so frail? I don't shatter with—" She broke off with a gasp as he seized her shoulder and spun her around into his arms. Before she could even think, let alone speak, he swooped and crushed her mouth under his.

Bent backward from the waist, she clung to his coat from instinct, not fear. He gentled the forceful kiss almost immediately, but it had been enough to give her a taste of his true passion and God help her, she wanted more. Not that he stopped kissing her, for he didn't, he merely scooped her up without releasing her mouth for an instant. She was aware of motion and a door kicked shut, and a lot of soft silk and fine wool against her arms and head.

They were in the vicar's cloakroom. And suddenly, she wanted to laugh because he was so careless of propriety and because there still seemed to be hope for her, whatever that meant.

His mouth loosened at last. "I can't give you a home," he ground out. "Nor even a legal status here or anywhere else. I have four ships and a set of men who'd murder your grandmother, or even their own, for fourpence."

She ignored that. "What is Mrs. Gallini to you?"

His eyes searched hers. She thought she'd surprised him. "I picked her up in Sicily, gave her passage to England. We were lovers on the voyage."

Jealousy twinged inside her. "And?"

"She was urgent and adventurous. Do you want more intimate details?"

She flushed. "No. I mean *now*. What is she to you now?"

His lips quirked. His eyes gleamed. In anyone else it would have been a smile, predatory or otherwise. "You are jealous," he said softly and kissed her mouth with such open sensuality that she almost didn't care about the answer.

He dragged his lips across her jaw to her throat. He held her by the hips, moving his own against her as he traced the neckline of her gown with soft kisses. She burned with sensation, thrilled to the male hardness pressing and stroking her.

"You're trying to distract me," she said breathlessly.

"How am I progressing?"

"Too well," she replied, incurably honest.

He straightened. "She is nothing to me. No one is. Except you, for some reason, and I can't have you."

Slowly, she lifted her hands from his shoulders and locked them around his neck. Her heart beat so hard she felt her whole body vibrate with it. She whispered, "Have you tried asking?"

"Don't," he whispered against her lips. "Don't."

"Don't what?"

"I wasn't talking to you." He sank his mouth into hers once more in a kiss so powerful that she moaned. He pushed his body hard against hers and she stumbled backward into the coats. "When I do ask," he muttered. "You'd better say yes."

Before she could haul herself upright, the door opened and closed and she was alone, staring at nothing. Slowly, she reached up and touched her lips, feeling them smile under her finger tips.

When I do ask…

They would find a way, because the biggest miracle had already happened. He cared for her.

Chapter Eight

BELLA WOKE EARLY the following morning. Originally, she'd planned to inquire about another cottage on the outskirts of Blackhaven. She still proposed to do so, although her enthusiasm seemed to have waned. All she could really think of was Alban and their passionate encounter in the cloakroom.

"When I do ask, you'd better say yes." Did he really mean to ask her to marry him? Was marriage even possible with a man like Alban? Shockingly, she wasn't sure she cared. She only cared that he might love her. And the very thought made her ridiculously happy.

She wore a fresh dress of fine muslin with printed rosebuds that made her feel almost pretty. It seemed a shame to cover it up with the old travelling cloak, but she needed to in order to have any chance of remaining incognito while she searched for her cottage.

Whisking herself quietly out of the suite before anyone else was abroad, she almost bumped into one of the hotel maids.

"For your ladyship," the girl said, holding out her hand with a curtsey and a sly smile. Between her fingers was a piece of paper, folded and refolded until it was thick and tiny.

Bella took it from her, her heart beating suddenly so loudly she was sure the maid must hear it. Fortunately, the girl hurried away, leaving her to the tortuous unfolding of the paper which she was sure had to be a missive from Alban. He must have returned from Whalen one way or another, or decided not to go. After all, there were the children at Roseley to think of. And her.

Although his writing was unknown to her, she saw at once that it was certainly terse enough to be typically Alban. She could almost hear him uttering the words.

Come to Blackhaven Cove at 8 of the clock.

He hadn't even troubled to sign it. Nor did it contain any of the soft endearments one might appreciate from a man making, essentially, an assignation. Laughter bubbled up inside her because it was so like him. In his eyes, it wasn't even a command. He expected her to understand the unwritten provisos, *if you wish, if you can*, and she did.

Hastily, she refolded the note and dropped it into her reticule as she hurried along the passage to the stairs, a different spring in her step, because she had a new and exciting purpose.

The town was quiet at this hour, with only a handful of townspeople and market sellers about their business. A few horses and carts made their way to deliveries along the back lanes to the high street and elsewhere, but there were no fashionable vehicles abroad. Ladies and gentleman of quality did not normally rise at this hour. At least not in Blackhaven.

Bella hurried through the streets toward the edges of town and the path down to Blackhaven Cove. She wondered if Alban would have brought the horses they'd ridden out to Roseley. She would enjoy a gallop along the beach.

But as she glimpsed the sea, she saw that the tide was in. There was not much sand to ride on. However, a rowing boat was pulled up on the beach and the solitary figure of a man stood with his back to her, gazing out to sea. From the angle of the path, the morning sun shone directly into her eyes, half-blinding her, even with her spectacles on, but she knew it was him and her heart drummed with fresh excitement.

He turned, walking toward her out of the sun, and her spontaneous smile froze on her lips. The disappointment was like a blow in the stomach. Not Alban. Mr. Tranter.

She recovered quickly, forcing the smile to stay on her lips. "Mr. Tranter. What brings you here so early in the morning?"

"The hope that you would come, of course."

Her eyes widened. "*You* sent the note?"

"Of course." He gave a faint smile. "I see I have disappointed. You were expecting another, which rather disappoints *me*."

She wasn't quite sure what he meant by that and didn't want to speculate. "Why did you want to see me?" she asked hastily. "And why all the secrecy?"

He regarded her thoughtfully, more than a hint of doubt in his expression. He sighed. "To be honest, I wished to ask for your help, but I can see now I was too impulsive, that it is neither fair nor kind."

In spite of herself, Bella was intrigued. "Well, you may always ask."

"Truly?" he said eagerly.

"Of course."

"It would commit you to nothing," he said anxiously.

"Exactly."

Mr. Tranter took a deep breath. "I wished to ask you to act as chaperone for a young lady."

Bella blinked. "I did not expect that," she confessed. "Which young lady?"

"Anne," he said reverently. "The lady I told you about? From whom I was parted by the lies of…supposed friends."

"Ah."

"It turns out she is not married at all. She held out for love of me and by chance discovered I was here in Blackhaven. She is being held more or less prisoner in her home just a few miles along the coast, but she managed to get word to me." He sighed. "In short, we are going to elope. Please don't be shocked, but you must see that for us, this is the only way."

"I can see that it *might* be," Bela said cautiously. "But sir, where do you intend to elope to? I cannot come with you to Gretna Green!"

"There is no need to go to Scotland. Anne is of age now, and I have a special license and an old friend who is a clergyman and will be happy to oblige me. I just wish to make Anne comfortable by having the presence of another respectable lady with her on the journey. It is not far. It will take but half an hour to row to Anne, and from there it is but an hour to my friend. After the wedding, we will all return to Blackhaven and there is nothing either Anne's father or Lady Crowmore's vengeance can do to hurt us."

Although the last sounded somewhat melodramatic to Bella, her romantic soul was touched by the lovers' story. If it was true. Kate had called Tranter a gazette fortune hunter.

She came to a decision. "I will come and meet your Anne at the least."

Tranter took her hand and squeezed it warmly. "You are wonderful," he said fervently. "Hurry, we have no time to lose. Let me help you into the boat."

Since the waves were showing an alarming tendency to lap around her feet, Bella was happy to oblige. Mr. Tranter had to get his feet wet as he pushed the boat into deep enough water to float before jumping in and seizing the oars.

Watching him row, Bella couldn't help remembering her first meeting with Alban, who'd worn no coat when he rowed her back to the harbor. And no clothes at all when he'd first entered her boat. Blushing as she recalled his golden body, muscles rippling in his back and arms, glimpses of his strong thighs and flat stomach with that tempting line of hair… *Go no farther!* she warned herself.

Mr. Tranter rowed strongly enough but with the faint awkwardness of someone to whom the exercise was rare. With Alban, the oars had seemed like extensions of his arms. Leaving the cove, Mr. Tranter hugged the coast, heading away from Blackhaven. She'd known this was going to happen and yet for some reason, she felt unable to relax as she usually did on the water. Trying to establish the normal sense of peace, she gazed all around her. Ahead, a small ship, perhaps a yacht, lay at anchor some distance out from the coast. Behind her, even farther out to sea, a larger ship sailed on in the same direction as their boat. It looked oddly familiar. She pushed her spectacles further up her nose, but the sea spray prevented her seeing clearly.

Mr. Tranter had fallen silent, presumably lost in thoughts of his lady love.

"I suppose your mother would have been a better chaperone," Bella observed. "Though I expect she couldn't have managed such a journey!"

Mr. Tranter permitted himself a small smile. "Sadly not."

He rowed on a little farther. Bella, still searching for her sense of peace, closed her eyes and waited for it to come. She even tried imagining Mr. Tranter were Alban, but it didn't work. His movements were too jerky.

She opened her eyes again, and found that they had left the coast some distance behind. They were heading, in fact, out to sea.

Bella sat up straight. "You need to row closer to the shore," she said urgently. "The tide is turning and the current is strong."

"I'm rather relying on that to give my arms a rest," Mr. Tranter retorted, his manner no longer quite so polite.

Bella, used to rudeness being directed at her, although not normally by strangers, blinked and looked around her for a reason. They seemed to be heading directly toward the yacht.

"I understood Anne was meeting us ashore," Bella said, puzzled. "Is she aboard the yacht?"

"Yes, with my tame clergyman," Mr. Tranter said mockingly. "Do you really believe everything anyone tells you?"

Bella frowned. "I don't understand. What is it I believe so gullibly and should not?"

"Everything," Mr. Tranter returned. "My poor foolish creature, there is no Anne. There is no clergyman."

"No elopement!"

"Oh, the elopement is true. Sort of. But you are my bride. Or will be when your family gets word of where you are."

She stared at him. "I'm afraid you need to explain yourself. You may indeed find me foolish, but I suppose I'm too used to conversing with gentlemen."

His eyes narrowed at the implied insult. "What, gentlemen like Captain Alban?" he mocked.

"Yes, like Captain Alban," she said firmly, "Who is, in fact, the greatest gentleman I know."

Mr. Tranter laughed. "Really?"

"Really!" she said furiously. "He, at least, would never think of abducting me!"

Mr. Tranter laughed harder. "What a wonderful mark you make! Who do you imagine came up with this idea in the first place? We're in this together, to divide the money we extort from your family. When they pay up, I'll marry you, and all you have will be mine."

Bella sprang to her feet and the boat rocked precariously. She didn't care. She was acting from appalled agitation.

"Sit down you little fool!" Tranter barked. "You'll have us both in the drink."

The drink. The sea, with Tranter's yacht straight ahead, where he meant to hold her hostage to her father's permission to marry. Not that she needed his permission, but Tranter needed him to disgorge the dowry set aside for her husband. And given that ruin was the alternative—in fact it was inevitable now, surely—her father would agree in total fury.

But further out was another ship, which might or might not help her, to which she might or might not be able to swim. If Tranter had told her the truth, if Alban had lied to her, she didn't really care whether she reached the other ship or not. She just knew she would go nowhere with Tranter.

"Why all the lies?" she wondered aloud. "Why the melodramatic story?"

"So I didn't have to wrestle you into the boat and deal with hysterics where half the town might hear you."

"I shall have hysterics now if you don't row me back ashore immediately." After all, everyone deserved one last chance.

"No, you won't," Tranter said dryly. "You'd overset the boat and drown. Be a good girl and sit down. And when we get aboard, I'll show you how kind I can be."

Slowly, Bella loosened the strings of her cloak and let it fall to her feet. Tranter's eyes lit up. "Good girl. You're really rather pretty, you know, once one actually looks. Take off the spectacles."

She glanced behind her, fixing the position of the other ship in her mind. It was almost parallel with the yacht now. Then, with regret, she dropped the spectacles on her cloak.

"Do you know," she murmured, "once one actually looks, you really are quite commonplace." And with that, she simply jumped out of the boat.

ALBAN STOOD ON the deck of *The Albatross*, gazing toward Blackhaven with something very like regret.

But he had several things he had to do before he could return there, not least deliver the French brandy which they'd taken possession of from a sister ship during the night. They were taking a chance, delivering it in broad daylight, but Alban had a personal appointment to keep.

"Captain," said Barnaby, his quietly-spoken lieutenant from further along the rail. He had the glass to his eye and was looking ahead but slightly further inland. "That yacht you wanted us to look out for? I think that's it."

Alban strode to join him, snatching his own glass from his pocket as he went. Even with the naked eye, the anchored yacht was quite clear, as was the small boat rowing toward it.

"He's moved it," Alban remarked, focusing the glass on the yacht until he could make out its ornately painted name. *Neptune*. "He must be up to something." There was someone on deck, a seaman in a woolen hat, gazing toward the rowing boat.

"Who?"

"Tranter," Alban said. "I made a few inquiries in Whalen. He borrowed a yacht from one of the young landowners there and is now offering to buy it for some vastly inflated sum. Which, of course, he won't pay."

"Keeps the owner quiet and the law off his back," Barnaby said with instant understanding. "And we care, why?"

"Because he expects to muscle in on our business without sharing his," Alban said.

Barnaby regarded him doubtfully. "Do we care about a couple of small deliveries?"

"No. I don't like the man."

"You don't like anyone," Barnaby said dryly.

"You wound me," Alban remarked with blatant untruth.

Even from his very cursory survey, the yacht did not appear to be in the best condition for a long voyage. Alban turned the glass to the approaching small boat. Tranter was rowing himself and a woman.

For the first time, genuine unease prickled up and down Alban's spine. Without warning, the woman jumped up, rocking the boat quite alarmingly. Something in the way she staggered and righted herself hit him in the stomach, even before he caught a glimpse of the face beneath the bonnet. He knew that bonnet and that old cloak. She'd been wearing them the day he first met her and whenever she wished to be incognito.

"Change course," he ordered grimly. "Head directly for the yacht."

The treacherous bastard had moved faster than Alban had imagined, to snatch the girl while Alban was too far away to demand a share of the proceeds. Of course, Tranter's proposition had only been made because he knew he was rumbled and wished to get Alban's acquiescence, if not his cooperation. Tranter had never meant to share.

Even as he felt the tug of *The Albatross's* change of direction, Bella took off her bonnet and dropped it. Her cloak followed and suddenly Alban couldn't breathe. Tranter had stopped rowing to gaze at her with a smug mixture of mockery, triumph, and lust. Alban would ram *that* down his throat along with all the rest.

And then she jumped.

With quiet deliberation, she simply jumped into the water.

Oh, dear God… "Launch the boat!" Alban snarled, striding down the deck, all the while keeping his desperate gaze on Bella's position. But she didn't go under. She was *swimming*, swimming toward *The Albatross* with strong, swift strokes. After a few moments of stunned astonishment, Tranter began to row after her. By good fortune, he missed his first couple of strokes, no doubt through sheer agitation, which granted Bella an extra few seconds.

Alban's own longboat was soon lowered into the water with all the efficiency he exacted. The crew heaved the oars to his demanding rhythm, and they ploughed through the waves toward Bella's bobbing figure.

Alban had more oarsmen and a bigger, better boat, but although he moved faster toward Bella, Tranter was still closer. And as the swine realized who his rival rescuer was, his eyes widened and he frantically redoubled his efforts.

Worse, Bella was tiring. Although her arms still struck out, she was covering less ground. In fact, she was only marking time as Tranter leaned out of the boat and grabbed her by the neck of her gown.

Alban tore off his coat. "Keep your pistol trained on that bastard, and if I don't kill him, shoot him."

With that order, which he knew would be obeyed to the letter, he dived into the water, shooting forward with such momentum that it took him very few strokes to reach Tranter's boat. Tranter was desperately trying to haul Bella's dripping, struggling figure on board. She was sobbing with the effort, but showed no sign of giving up, even though Tranter was so clearly winning.

Alban didn't hesitate, merely took hold of the side of the boat in one hand and leapt upward, releasing his flying fist into Tranter's face. The man's head snapped back and he fell in the boat, letting go of Bella at last, so suddenly that she would have slipped under the water had Alban not seized her around the waist. He doubted she'd even seen Tranter fall.

She saw Alban, though, a look of astonishment frozen for an instant on her exhausted face. With a sob, she threw her arms around his neck. His throat constricted as he turned with her in one arm to strike out for the longboat.

However, Tranter was not yet ready to give up. Something—an oar?—thudded into Alban's shoulder with enough force to hurt. And Alban knew it would come again, harder, before he could get out of range. He didn't mind the pain, but he didn't want his shoulder paralyzed, however temporarily. He needed it.

Alban solved the problem swiftly, while the oar was already lashing down for its second strike. Simply, and forcefully, he tipped up Tranter's boat and kept swimming.

"Alban," Bella whispered in his ear.

In any circumstances, his name on her lips did something to him. In this fraught situation, he wanted to kiss her to oblivion. But there was no time.

"Alban!" Tranter screeched behind them amidst massive splashing. A quick glance showed him clinging on to the upturned boat. "Don't be like that, Alban! I was driving her to you! We can still work together... Alban!"

Alban ignored him. Eager hands were already reaching out for them from the longboat. Grasping onto the side, Alban heaved the exhausted Bella upward into their hold.

"Keep her warm, take her to the ship and tell Mr. Barnaby to look after her," he commanded breathlessly. He glowered at Cairney, his coxswain. "With *every* respect."

"Aye, Captain. Where are you going?"

Bella, who'd landed in a wet heap inside the boat, loomed up, staring at him over the side. She was soaked and bedraggled, seawater and even seaweed running from her loose hair down her face and neck. And she'd never been more beautiful.

"To collect your share?" she asked clearly.

She might have kicked him in the gut. Certainly, he couldn't seem to breathe or speak. And then he found his voice. "Yes. To collect my share."

He swung around and struck out toward Tranter. At least his men wouldn't let her jump again.

Tranter clearly couldn't swim. Clinging to the upside-down boat with one hand, he paddled furiously with the other, moving slowly in the direction of the anchored yacht. From the yacht itself, came no move to rescue him. The same laconic seaman stood on its deck, watching events with apparent interest but no desire to intervene.

Alban, who'd swum like a fish even in boyhood, caught up with Tranter easily.

"Look, I heard you were coming, thought we should move things forward as quickly as possible," Tranter babbled. "You hold her. I'll speak to the family—"

"Did you touch her?" Alban interrupted.

"God no. I spun her a tragic yarn to get her into the boat. Looking back, I should have kept it up until we were safely aboard the yacht, but there, it's worked out for the best. You can play the rescuing hero now and get a devoted wife along with half her fortune."

"Oh, I'll have *all* her fortune. And you—since you didn't hurt her—may have a quick death."

From desperate instinct, Tranter lashed out when Alban grabbed him. A fist connected painfully with his jaw just before he plunged the bastard under the water and held him.

Tranter's will to survive was strong. He struggled manfully, but Alban was implacable. The man deserved to die for what he had done and what he'd tried to do to Bella.

Bella. It was she who'd been abducted and frightened. Would *she* want Tranter to die? She was, after all, forgiving and soft natured. It was one of the things he loved about her.

Jesus, don't even think *love at a moment like this.* Then of what should he think? Of the plans he was trying to make? His hopes of rehabilitation and a legal return under his own name? His duty to care for his dead brother's children... None of which he could do from a jail cell, or while being hunted for murder.

With a groan of fury, Alban yanked Tranter out of the water and shook him, unspeakably relieved to hear his rasping, spewing gasps for air. Alban dragged the inert, wheezing man the rest of the way to the yacht.

"Here," he barked at the watching seaman. "Sail him and this tub to Whalen. The owner wants it back."

Chapter Nine

AMONG ALL HER jumbled emotions, Bella recognized shame, though she felt too cold and numb to divine the cause. Someone had draped a coat and a blanket around her. Almost mechanically, she clutched them closer. The coat seemed to smell of Alban…

To collect my share… "What is he doing?" she wondered helplessly. She hadn't meant to speak aloud. She hadn't expected an answer from Alban's men.

"Killing him, most like," one of them said laconically from the nearest oar.

Bella blinked, staring at him. "Killing Mr. Tranter? Oh dear, I don't think he should do that…"

"Seems to need killing to me," another sailor contributed. "Besides, no way for anyone to stop the captain when he's in that mood,"

"What mood?" Bella asked, twisting around from the seat she'd been given, to try and see Alban and Tranter.

"Captain don't have moods," growled the man who seemed to be supervising the others. Certainly, he was glaring at them while he moved to block Bella's view. "He makes decisions."

"'Course he does," grinned the first sailor.

"Ignore them, Miss," the sailor in charge advised. "We'll get you safe and warm on board and the captain'll look after you."

"On board?" Bella repeated in dismay. "Oh no, please, you must take me ashore at once!"

"Captain said aboard," was the apologetic yet curiously implacable answer. "It'll take too long to get ashore and people will stare at you being as wet as you are. Expect the captain'll take you back later."

Bella gazed down at the sea. It didn't look remotely inviting. In fact, she couldn't face going in again.

Alban had never hurt her. She'd always trusted him. And these men, the ones Alban had said would shoot their own grandmothers for fourpence… Surreptitiously, she glanced around them. It was true they had a somewhat wild appearance. Scars and missing teeth were quite common among them. But they were respectful enough. Once she was changed and warm, she could think again, and decide what was best.

"I'm Cairney," the sailor in charge said. "I'm the coxswain. Mr. Barnaby will look after you till the Captain comes."

"Who is Mr. Barnaby?" she asked.

"First mate. You'll like him. He's not so rough as us lot. Or the captain, come to that. Here, have a drink, Miss."

Bella took the flask he offered. "What is it?"

"Rum. You won't like it, but it's good for the shock."

Bella shrugged and took a sip. Although it burned, she didn't dislike it any more than brandy. "Thank you." She gave it back to Mr. Cairney, who took a healthy swig before replacing the stopper.

"Here we are miss. Can you climb up yourself, or will I carry you? You don't look as if you weigh more than a feather."

"Oh, I do," Bella said earnestly. "I can climb."

"Well, I'm right behind you if your foot slips off the rung."

She had to abandon the blanket to climb, but she managed to keep the coat by shoving her wet arms into its sleeves. She must have looked a pitiful figure as she stumbled aboard, shivering, miserable, and utterly confused.

Vaguely aware of Cairney murmuring to a better-dressed young man in a black coat, she supposed this must be Mr. Barnaby, and certainly he issued swift orders to Cairney and the men before he turned to her and bowed. "Madam. I'm Barnaby, first mate aboard *The Albatross*. Please follow me."

Bella more than half-expected to be conducted into the dark bowels of the ship, but on shaking legs that would barely obey her, there wasn't much she could do about leaving. Besides, these were Alban's men and seemed perfectly civil.

She followed Mr. Barnaby across the deck and down a flight of steep steps. Fortunately, there was a rail for her to cling to. At the bottom of the steps, Barnaby opened a door and ushered her into a bright cabin that felt instantly warm, no doubt due to the sun streaming in the row of sloping windows along one side. A round wooden table and four matching chairs with plush red upholstery sat in the middle of the room. Under one window was an open bureau.

Like some brainless insect drawn to the light, Bella moved forward to shiver in the warmth of a sunbeam, while Mr. Barnaby crossed the room to another door, which he threw wide.

"You'll find towels in here. I'll bring you some clothes that will do for you until your own dry. I'll leave them here in the main cabin. I'll call as I leave again. No one else will disturb you or enter without permission. This is the captain's cabin."

Of course it was.

"Thank you," she muttered in a slightly shaky whisper.

"May I bring the ship's surgeon to you, Miss? He's also an excellent physician."

"No. No thank you," she managed. "I'll be fine once I warm up."

There were no guarantees of that. Her family's obsessive care for her health stemmed from a constant stream of debilitating childhood illnesses. And it was still true that while everyone else had a cold that made them snuffle their way through a day or two, when Bella caught it, as she inevitably did, she was forced to take to her bed with pains in her chest and a racking cough that could go on for weeks. Aunt Maria was always convinced she would die.

But I will not be ill this time. I will not...

As Mr. Barnaby left, she shut herself into the bedchamber and stripped off her clothes. Since she'd dressed herself this morning, her soggy gown was not properly fastened and came off quite easily. As she seized the large, fluffy towel from the rail by the wash bowl, she finally registered the large bed against the wall. She knew a longing to climb between the sheets and warm herself there, but somehow, she couldn't do it. Not Alban's bed. If only she hadn't been so cold, she'd have blushed at the very thought.

So, she averted her eyes from it and wrapped one towel around her body, tucking it in under her arms. The other she used to rub furiously against the skin of her arms and shoulders.

She heard a knock at the outer door of the main cabin. Someone came in and she froze.

"I've brought you some gowns," came Mr. Barnaby's voice. "Choose what you wish. I'm leaving now."

"Thank you!" Bella called, and this time she was glad to note her voice was stronger. Dropping the second towel around her shoulders, she went back into the main cabin to inspect the gowns. Some of them were silk and very finely embroidered. All of them seemed very bright and exotic for England.

Bella grimaced. "Mrs. Gallini's," she decided with disapproval and no evidence whatsoever. The singer had no reason, surely, to abandon her gowns on Alban's ship. Bella picked up a scarlet gown, more suited for evening wear, although not, perhaps for the unmarried daughter of a duke. She'd never worn such a color before. Half-smiling, she moved to bask in the sun. She'd almost stopped shaking now and no longer felt too exhausted to stand. Dropping the red gown onto the ledge under the window, she began to walk briskly around the spacious room, eventually breaking into a run. She remembered from childhood that this was the best way to warm up.

Unfortunately, she was no longer a child, and when the door opened without warning, she skidded to an embarrassed halt. The flapping towel on her shoulders flew off and she had to grab at the other loosening under her arms. Worst of all, Captain Alban stood in the doorway, gazing at her in some surprise.

He, too, was soaking wet. She could see his skin through his shirt. And his breeches didn't leave too much to the imagination either. She swallowed.

"What are you doing?" he asked mildly.

"Warming up. I didn't know you were back."

His gaze swept over her, lingering on her naked shoulders. "Don't let me disturb you." He waved one inviting hand. "Carry on."

By this time, it seemed she could flush quite easily again. "I'm quite warm now, thank you." Ducking down, she made a grab for the fallen towel, but he moved faster and less awkwardly and got there before her.

When she straightened abruptly, he was much too close and made no effort to give her the towel. Instead, he held it loosely by his side.

"Why so shy, Bella?" he asked huskily. "You've seen *me* naked after all."

She had. All golden skin and hard muscle and... She swallowed and lifted one hand. It wasn't the cold that made her tremble now. "Please."

He lifted the towel, but didn't give it to her. Instead, he stepped closer. Hastily she stumbled backward but he came after her, and this time, she held her ground with conscious bravery.

He passed the towel behind her and placed it around her shoulders. She couldn't breathe for the pounding of her heart, and yet it wasn't an unpleasant kind of breathlessness. Not remotely.

His hands slid to either end of the towel, and tugged, drawing her against his wet, hard body. And then one hand was under the towel on her naked shoulder, softly caressing.

"What are you doing?" she asked in panic.

"Seducing you," he said at once. "Ruining you for the purpose of blackmailing you into marriage."

"I would never marry a man who did such things."

"You might if I tied your petticoat to the mast."

Her eyes widened. "You wouldn't!"

His eyes seemed to laugh at her, at once hot and mocking. "Have to dry it somehow. Be honest, Bella. It wouldn't be such an ordeal, would it?"

"What wouldn't?" she asked, as bewildered by her reaction to his body against hers as by his words. His hand moved under the towel, smoothing the skin of her back, making her shiver.

He bent his head. "Seduction."

"Not like this," she blurted, as his hand roamed back over her shoulder to the pulse beating so violently at the base of her throat. The towel now hung off one shoulder.

"Like what?" he whispered, brushing his lips across hers.

She gasped. His fingers slid under the towel over her breasts. "In mistrust. And hurt and anger."

"It makes no difference." His warm breath stirred her lips. Beneath the towel, his hand slipped downward over her stomach. Heat surged through her. Every inch of her thrilled to his touch. "You still want me, as I want you. We both know I can have you here on the deck. Or I can take you to bed and do it there. Would you like to choose?"

"No," she got out.

"Liar." His mouth closed on hers in a blatantly sensual kiss, while his finger caressed her skin. There was no denying what it did to her, what she wanted from him. She didn't even mind that the towel wrapped around her was coming apart. She only wanted more of this.

And yet it was too deliberate. His desire was real enough—the evidence pressed excitingly against her abdomen—but for the first time, she sensed no spontaneity in his embrace. It was calculated…to seduce? To punish? Both, perhaps. She'd hurt him.

"To collect your share?"

"Yes. To collect my share."

Stupid, stupid. And unkind. He'd rescued her from Tranter and from almost certain drowning, and she'd repeated Tranter's untrustworthy accusations.

"I didn't mean it," she blurted under his mouth.

He raised his head, staring down at her from hot, clouded eyes. His breath was erratic. It seemed to Bella that he forced his eyes to clear. And then, very slowly, he tucked her towel back around her and drew the second around both shoulders.

Without a word, he walked away from her and into the bedchamber. An instant later, he emerged with what looked like shirt and breeches over his arm.

"Never doubt an untrustworthy man," he said wryly. "It maddens him and causes him to behave badly."

Bella stumbled with the roll of the ship, and made another discovery. "We're sailing!"

"Of course we are. I have appointments to keep." The door clicked shut behind him.

BELLA WORE THE red gown because it was the first that came to hand. Of course, it was too big for her but, fortunately, the estimable Mr. Barnaby had also brought a selection of shawls. She tied one around her waist to hold the skirt off the floor, and cast another round her shoulders to hide the dress's unfastened state. Then she hurried up on deck in search of Alban.

At once, she missed her spectacles, abandoned in Tranter's boat along with her cloak and bonnet. She wished she'd just stood up and called for help instead. Wasn't that the way ladies were meant to save themselves? Although of course, ladies shouldn't really get themselves into situations from which they needed to be rescued in the first place.

"Where is Captain Alban?" she asked the first sailor who crossed her path.

"Forward, Miss," the man said cheerfully, pointing across the deck, toward the front of the ship.

Bella stumbled in that direction, trying not to fall with the roll of the ship, or trip over coils of rope as she went.

He stood with his back to her, one hand on the rail. Beyond him she could see the figurehead of a bird, no doubt the albatross for which the ship was named.

She said, "I can't stay away all day. My aunts will worry."

He didn't turn. "It seems to me, they worry anyway, whether you're there or not. If you truly want independence, you must learn to care less for what they say and think."

"And more for what *you* say and think?" she retorted.

"Well, no, that would be an alternative dependence, would it not? What do *you* want, Bella?" He turned at last, the spray sparkling on his hair and face.

"I want to go back," she said firmly. And right up until the words were out, she thought they were true. Then they simply weren't. She wanted to stay here, with Alban, to make things right with him again. To see him in his natural state among his men, to talk to him, know him. To feel his arms around her, kiss him, just *be* with him when no one could interrupt them. Her tongue cleaved to the roof of her mouth. It seemed impossible to take back the lie.

He turned back to the sea. "Unfortunately, I can't spare the longboat. I need it for my less than respectable appointments."

Hesitantly, she stepped forward until she stood beside him. Spray skimmed her face, cooling her burning cheeks. "Are you punishing me?" she asked with a sideways glance.

His lips twisted. "I had this idea that I was setting you free." He met her gaze suddenly. "If I'm wrong, we'll find a way to make it right when we return."

For no reason, tears sprang into her eyes and she whirled away from him.

"Bella." There was a stricken note in his voice. His hands caught her shoulders, gently turning her. "Bella, don't cry," he whispered. "I'm a fool but I'm not a brute. Not to you. I *will* make it right."

"I don't want it to be right!" Her voice broke. "I want to be with you."

With a sob, she buried her face in his chest and his arms came around her, holding her as tenderly as if she were the most precious porcelain. She felt his lips in her hair, softly kissing.

"I'd damned if I know why," he said ruefully.

She clutched the lapels of his coat. "Because I love you."

There was a moment of stunned silence. She wasn't surprised, but she couldn't, wouldn't, take back the words. His heart beat a strong, steady rhythm beneath her cheek. Then, he drew back, tipping up her face and frowning down at her.

"Why?" he asked.

She tried to blink away her tears which must already have stained her face and made her even plainer than usual. She sniffed. "I don't think I have a reason," she said frankly. "I know why I like you. I don't know what makes it love. Because even when it crossed my mind that you might really have conspired with Mr. Tranter, I still loved you. And though I wish you hadn't, I don't even seem to mind if you *killed* Mr. Tranter."

"I didn't," he said distractedly, searching her face. He shook his head. "You deserve a better man."

"I don't think one ever gets one's just desserts in this life," she said, and his breath caught on something very like a laugh. Smiling, she lifted her face to his and he kissed her, a soft, tender kiss that felt like a promise.

SHE ATE A midday meal in the captain's cabin, along with Alban and Mr. Barnaby, the ships surgeon Dr. Gowan, and a gruff older man called Nimmo who had a foreign-sounding accent.

The food was basic but warm and tasty, and she enjoyed a very good glass of wine with it. The lively conversation was surprisingly civilized and even learned. Whether self-taught or formally educated, these were well-read, knowledgeable men.

"Forgive me for asking," Dr. Gowan said to her once. "But are you short-sighted?"

"Very," she said ruefully. "And I'm afraid I've lost my spectacles. I don't think there's anywhere in Blackhaven I might purchase a replacement."

"I have some that might suit you. I collect them wherever I go."

"Thank you," she said in surprised delight.

When the meal was over, Barnaby and Nimmo returned to their

duties and Alban accompanied her to the doctor's quarters. Here, Dr. Gowan opened a trunk full of eyeglasses of every kind, each wrapped in lengths of cloth. Rummaging, he brought out several lengths and spread them open on his desk.

"Have a look," he invited. "I think these are the most suitable."

Alban leaned his shoulder against the door and watched. By means of trying on several pairs and gazing around her, using the clarity of Alban's face as a guide, she eventually found a gold-rimmed pair that seemed at least as good as the ones she'd lost.

"Thank you," she said warmly. "I'm afraid I have no money here to pay for them, but I shall send it via Captain—"

"There is no need," Dr. Gowan interrupted. "I can't bear to see people struggle needlessly."

"You're very kind."

At the door, Alban straightened. "With your permission, I'd like Dr. Gowan to examine you—to make sure there are no ill-effects from today's adventure, among other things."

"What other things?" Bella asked at once.

"Consumption," Alban said baldly.

Bella's eyes fell. She didn't want to think of illness and death. Not today when she'd just discovered love and had every reason to live. "What is the point? There is no cure."

"Have you been examined already for this disease?" Dr. Gowan asked.

"Yes, by Dr. Headley who said I am in the early stages of the disease, and by Dr. Dorrall who says it is not yet clear."

Alban said, "Gowan has unusual methods and unusual cures. It can do no harm, surely. I'm going ashore for an hour or two." And with that, he simply opened the door and left her.

Bella dragged her gaze from the closed door to Dr. Gowan. "Will you be in trouble with the captain if I say no?"

"No," he said humorously, "but you might be. In fact, either way, it is you who would have the trouble. Would it not be better to know?"

"Are you infallible, Dr. Gowan?"

"Of course not."

"Then what can you tell me that is more use than Dr. Headley's opinion or Dr. Dorrall's?"

"I don't know. Perhaps nothing, perhaps everything. At worst, I have no axe to grind, no money to make out of your health. I get paid whether you're ill or not."

Her eyes widened. "Do you mean those doctors lied to get more fees?"

Dr. Gowan spread his hands. "I have no idea. I don't know these gentlemen. But I do know it happens, particularly in fashionable society where the fees are substantial. Why don't we begin with a few general questions? And then you may you decide whether or not a physical examination would be a good idea."

She sank down onto the seat by the doctor's desk. "What kind of questions?"

Chapter Ten

Having overseen the delivery to the cove behind the Border Inn, Alban sent the boat back to *The Albatross* and walked up to the inn. Not for payment—that had been discreetly left under a marker stone as promised—but to keep his appointment with Mr. Johnstone.

He found him easily in the inn's quiet coffee parlor. Idly, Alban wondered if men like Johnstone were ever young, or if they never actually got old. For Johnstone, with his balding head, spectacles, and plain black, old-fashioned coat, looked exactly as he had twelve years ago. And would probably look the same in another twelve.

"Mr. Johnstone," he said, holding out his hand.

Johnstone's head snapped up from his newspaper, his eyes widening as they scanned Alban's person. "Good Lord." He jumped to his feet, taking the outstretched hand eagerly. "Mr. Lamont! It really is you! I'd never have recognized you, but now that I look, you're the living spit of your father."

"Don't say that," Alban said wryly, indicating that they should both sit. "How are you? How is Mrs. Johnstone? And the family?"

Mr. Johnstone beamed. "Well, I thank you, sir, very well indeed. They would send their greetings and very best wishes if I'd told them I was meeting you. But in truth, I was afraid it was a hoax and didn't mention you. My wife will be so happy."

"Hmm," Alban said, somewhat thrown by this effusion. "And what did you discover, sir? Is there a chance of pardon for me? The possibility of inheriting the Scottish estates?"

"You've already been pardoned," Johnstone said dryly. "According to Mr. Douglas, who handles your family's business in Scotland, Lord Roseley, your brother, petitioned the Scottish courts who dismissed the charges. Apparently, the Duke of Kelburn recanted and said he was mistaken in the identity of the poacher. Therefore, there was no crime and you did nothing wrong in freeing him."

Alban stared. "He recanted? When the devil did he do that?"

"Four years ago, when Nicholas asked for your pardon."

"But *I* was the poacher," Alban said. "Kelburn knew that from the beginning. I told him."

"Well, he didn't accuse you."

"He'd sacrifice Willie Kerr," Alban said bitterly. "But not the noble blood of a Lamont. Willie Kerr would have *died* for something he didn't even do."

"I know," Johnstone said. "Sadly, it is the way of the world."

"Not of mine," Alban said disgustedly.

Johnstone smiled. "But then, you were always a rebel, Mr. Lamont. Where have you been? What on earth have you been doing with yourself over those twelve years? No one could find you when you were pardoned, or when Lord Roseley, your brother, died."

"You don't want to know. Two questions, sir. Is there any reason why I shouldn't be the legal guardian of Nick's children, as Nick stipulated in his will?"

"None at all."

"And the Scottish estates are mine?"

"They are. You must send to Mr. Douglas."

Alban leapt to his feet, unable to be still. "In time," he agreed. "For the moment, this is what I wanted to hear." He paced to the window and back, longing suddenly to be back aboard *The Albatross* with Bella. Captain Alban was a hopeless match for her, but the Honorable Alban Lamont wasn't so bad…

His heart felt as if it was bursting. For she'd have taken him as Captain Alban. She loved him. He drew in his breath as if to drag back his escaping imagination, and swung around to face Johnstone once more.

"What do you know of this Radnor character that Marianne has married?"

"Nothing very much. He is beneath her in birth, was desperate for the aristocratic connection. And Lady Roseley is…not the kind of woman who manages well without a husband. Why—"

"Is he decent?" Alban interrupted.

"I've never heard anything against him. A few sharp business practices perhaps, but nothing illegal."

"I went to Roseley," Alban said abruptly. "The children were living there alone with a bunch of unknown servants, including one brute I wouldn't leave in charge of a dog. Neglected, barely fed. I know Marianne would never stand for that, but the thing is, servants would not dare behave so unless they were either sure they'd get away with it. Or were under express orders."

"But why would Mr. Radnor order such a thing? What would he gain?"

"If Leo died? Use of Roseley for Marianne's lifetime."

"On the contrary, *you* would inherit the lands and the title."

"But Radnor can't know that I'm alive. Nick didn't. You didn't. As far as anyone knows, Leo is the last of the Roseley Lamonts."

Johnstone stared at him in horror. "You really believe the children are in danger?"

"Less so now. At least the servants don't seem prepared to commit outright murder. I put the fear of God into them and wrote to Marianne. She should be at Roseley in a few days. And I'm keeping my eye on them."

BELLA SAT ALONE in the captain's cabin, on one of the dining chairs, her knees drawn up under her chin as she gazed out of the window at the rolling sea. Not for the first time today, she felt bemused. Because it seemed there was no longer any need to rush her life. According to Dr. Gowan, she was not about to die.

He was a strange doctor. He did not talk about humors and bloodletting, but had asked her a lot of questions about her life, her likes and dislikes, what she was doing when she felt ill, and when she felt well. He'd listened carefully to her pulse and her chest and examined her ears, her throat, and the underside of her eyelids.

Then he'd pulled up a chair and sat facing her, leaning forward to speak confidentially.

"I can find nothing wrong with you."

Bella blinked. "Nothing?"

"Nothing."

"But doctors have *never* found nothing wrong with me!"

"Well, you're not a particularly *robust* young woman, and I daresay you were a sickly child. I'm sure there were many times when there *was* something wrong. Now is not one of those times. But I hear no irregularity in your lungs or your heart that might cause concern. You don't have consumption."

"I don't?" She couldn't help sounding doubtful. After all, she'd spent the last two years growing used to the idea that she would not live to be old. "I do cough a lot," she said humbly. "My chest gets tight and I feel as if I can't breathe."

"So you said." Dr. Gowan regarded her thoughtfully. "And it happens only when you are acutely uncomfortable, when people are nagging you or when you are put in situations which you find intolerable. It seems to be your body's way of escaping those situations. The cough, the wheezy chest must all be very temporary reactions, for there's no trace of them, save for the faintest irritation I can see in your throat. In my opinion, you suffer from nothing more than unhappiness and a morbid shyness and sensitivity."

She frowned, mulling that over.

"Think about it," Dr. Gowan said. "You have not coughed once since being on board this ship. Despite being abducted and swimming some distance in a cold sea. In fact, if I am right, you have coughed less in the last week or so."

"I...I suppose I have." She thought about the Assembly ball, and the vicar's soiree.

"And I don't think," Dr. Gowan added delicately, "that you ever cough in the captain's presence."

She smiled. "He does seem to frighten it away…" She raised her eyes to the doctor's. "I'm happy with him so I don't cough."

"You may take from that what you wish," Dr. Gowan said hastily. "Though by the same token, you are clearly happy with me, too! Let us just say, you are more comfortable in certain company than other. Which is odd, perhaps since most well-born ladies would be having hysterics in this kind of company."

Bella laughed. "You wrong us, sir, and your own company!"

"Perhaps. Anyhow, my advice to you is simply to avoid the company and the situations that make you uncomfortable. And be happy."

It all made a strange kind of sense, though sitting here thinking about it afterward, she wasn't sure she liked the idea of being made ill by her own family. Still, it was true she was always worse around her father and eldest brother who constantly found fault in her and shouted about it. She thought of the suitors who'd courted her father's influence and merely tolerated her as a necessary means to that end. The elegant and fashionable who'd discounted if not despised her; the wits before whom she'd been tongue-tied and gauche. The dislike had been mutual in most cases. She'd been too shy to get to know strangers and had done nothing to make them want to know her. The result had been social misery, in stark contrast to the rest of her family's easy social success.

And then, barely a week ago, Alban had burst into her life in the most bizarre of circumstances…and it seemed as if the sun had come out. Love had come quickly to her in the end. For although it would have been easy to confuse easy companionship for love, she *knew* this feeling was more. For one thing, he wasn't always an easy or comfortable man.

She smiled. From the deck above, came a slew of shouted commands, and running footsteps as the men hastened to obey. The captain was back.

Her heart beat faster as she anticipated his presence. She felt the sudden surge of movement as the sails filled and the ship got under way. A few more shouts—she was sure she could recognize Alban's voice—and then hasty footsteps clattered down the steps by the cabin door.

She turned her head as Alban strode in and came to a sudden halt. He still wore the dark coat and light breeches that seemed to be his normal shipboard dress, but his clothes didn't matter. His presence filled the room, vital, commanding and yet curiously soothing. As if nothing was quite right without him.

He kicked the door shut behind him. "What is it? Are you well?"

"Apparently, yes."

He crossed the room to crouch down at her knees. "What did Gowan say?"

"That I am not consumptive. That lacking the spirit to tell my family to go to the devil, I cough at them instead."

A glint of amusement lit his eyes. "I doubt he said quite that."

"You don't seem surprised."

"I'm not. I'm no doctor, but I could see how different you were in different situations. After our first meeting, when you charmed me utterly, I saw you from the coffee house with your aunts. You looked…crushed. And you always recovered immediately when you were taken out of stressful situations."

"I am a poor creature," she said ruefully.

He took her hands and kissed them, one after the other. "You're nothing of the sort. You're just too kind to dig in your heels and refuse people."

"My aunts love me in their own way. It's just…Aunt Maria's eldest daughter died most tragically and she's convinced I shall go the same way. And Sarah is so fed up with her spinster's lot that she is determined I shall not suffer similarly, even if she has to tie me to an octogenarian fortune hunter or to a youth barely breeched."

His hand tightened on hers. "Well, now you may tie yourself to me. If you wish."

It was nothing like any offer she had received before. In fact, it was so casually made it brought a smile to her lips. She didn't even know—or care—if it was marriage he proposed. She reached out and touched his hair, his rough cheek. "I wish."

He dipped his head, kissing her hands once more. "You are wonderful, you know. You've no idea who I am, that my birth is as respectable if not quite as high-ranking, as yours." He drew in his breath. "I am Lord Roseley's second son, Leo's rebellious uncle."

"Yes, I know," she admitted.

He blinked. "You know?"

"I saw Leo's letter addressed to you. Alban is not a common name."

"Why didn't you say something?"

She shrugged. "It was your secret and it made no real difference except to my understanding of you. But I think we should have people look into your case, for it does seem harsh treatment. If you'd like to go home, that is."

"I'd like the opportunity," he said honestly. "Although I can't imagine staying there forever. My feet are restless, Bella, by nature more than circumstance."

She searched his eyes, which didn't look hard at all, but heart-stoppingly warm. "Do you think…I could come with you? On occasions," she added hastily, in case he might find this too constricting.

"I would like that most of all," he said softly, leaning toward her. "But my wife must do whatever she wishes."

She smiled because he'd said wife, and he paused, his lips hovering over hers. "You did say yes, didn't you?"

"I think I said it a long time ago," she whispered and kissed him.

With a fair wind behind them, they made good time back to Blackhaven. Bella couldn't help being disappointed as she came to the end of her voyage, but at least she knew she would see Alban again soon, that she had a bright future of unexpected happiness to look forward to. She wouldn't even mind her aunts' scolding. Life was too wonderful.

Alban came with her in the small boat, as did Cairney, the coxswain who rowed for them. For purposes of discretion, since it was growing dark, Alban ordered the man to row into Blackhaven Cove rather than the harbor.

"I don't see that it's *much* more discreet," Bella observed from her bench in the middle of the boat.

Seated opposite her, in the front of the boat, Alban shrugged. "An evening stroll in the town seems less likely to cause gossip than landing in the harbor directly from my ship."

"Unless there are people in the cove," Cairney pointed out, pulling strongly on the oars behind her.

Alban shrugged. "They're unlikely to be the sort of people we need to worry about."

Bella considered. "I don't think I care either way."

Alban regarded her, his eyes gleaming in the fading light. "Some of my wickedness is clearly rubbing off on you."

"It isn't wickedness," she said at once. "Just a disinterest in other people's opinion of me. Or you."

His knee moved, brushing against hers. "I should have brought you ashore at once," he admitted.

"Yes," she agreed. She smiled. "But I'm glad you didn't."

As they drew into the shore at last, Alban jumped out into the shallow water and plucked her up out of the boat as if she'd weighed no more than a kitten. Her instinctive protest died on her lips, for it was unexpectedly sweet to be carried ashore in such strong, steady arms.

Her heart beat faster as he let her feet slip down onto the sand, but perhaps mindful of possible onlookers, he released her with no more than the twitch of one eyebrow, before turning back to the boat.

Having helped Cairney drag it up the sand to safety, he took an unlit lantern from the bottom of the boat and gave it to Cairney. "Go to the livery stables and see that the two horses I bespoke are ready. I'll meet you there."

"Aye, sir."

Cairney ran up the path ahead of them, and melted into the distance.

"Where are you going?" Bella asked.

"To Roseley."

She glanced at him uncertainly. "With Cairney?"

"Well, I don't want Jenkins assuming I'll always come alone. He might forget to be afraid."

Bella sighed with unease. "I wish their mother would come."

"It's their stepfather I'd like a word with," Alban said grimly.

It was, perhaps fortunately, a quiet time of the evening, between dinner and later entertainments, so there weren't many of the fashionable abroad in the town. Nevertheless, Bella was sure someone would see them, that word would, inevitably, get back to her aunts.

"What will you tell them?" Alban asked abruptly.

"That Mr. Tranter abducted me and I jumped in the sea and would have died if you hadn't rescued me and allowed your doctor to look after me."

Although he didn't reply, his quick, warm glance, told her he was proud of her.

Inside the hotel foyer, they shook hands politely, and if his thumb caressed her wrist, and she squeezed his fingers just a little too much, no one else would have been able to tell.

"I'll call on you tomorrow," he said.

"I look forward to it," she said breathlessly. It was oddly difficult to draw her hand away and leave him, but she did it. When she glanced back from the stairs, he still stood there, watching her, and somehow that gave her happiness and her strength enough of a boost to reach the top of the staircase and walk along the passage to the suite of rooms she shared with her aunts.

The door opened easily to her touch.

Jenson squealed and dropped a tray. "Oh, your ladyship!"

"Bella!" Aunt Maria exclaimed, hurrying toward her.

"Oh, my dear, where have you been?" Sarah demanded, closing in from the other side.

Bella remained rooted to the spot with horror, for in the middle of the room between her aunts, sat her father and Sir George Beaton, the man whose offer of marriage had placed her in such disgrace as to be banished to Blackhaven.

The Duke of Kelburn's face was thunderous.

Chapter Eleven

AT FIRST BELLA was too startled by the presence of not only her father but her rejected suitor, to notice the fussing of her aunts and the maid.

Until the Duke exploded, "Stand back in God's name and let me see my daughter!"

Bella all but jumped out of her skin. As one, her aunts leapt to either side of her, Aunt Sarah bumping heads with Jenson as the maid, too, bolted for cover. Reluctantly, with inevitable dread, Bella raised her eyes to her father's.

The Duke of Kelburn was a fierce looking man in his sixties, with a shock of white hair and white, bushy eyebrows over steely blue eyes. His nose was aristocratically long and thin, his lips thin and curving downward now with contempt.

"There's nothing wrong with her," he uttered in disgust. "Anyone less than an imbecile could see that right away. But my God, girl, I take leave to tell you you're a disgrace! As for your aunts...what possessed you to allow something like that abomination in her wardrobe?"

"What, the gown?" Maria said nervously, peering more closely at Bella's presence. "To be sure, it looked a little different the last time I saw it."

"It got wet in the sea," Bella admitted. "If you would just excuse me, I shall change—"

"Oh no," her father said grimly. "You needn't think you're off the hook so easily! What do you mean, *it got wet in the sea*? How did it get *into* the sea?"

"Um, I'm afraid I jumped," Bella confessed. "You see—"

"You jumped in the sea?" Aunt Maria repeated, horrified. "Where?"

"From a little boat. The gown did not like the salty water, but perhaps it will improve with rinsing. If I could just give it to Jenson…?"

"Stand still," barked the duke, causing her to leap several inches into the air once more while he raked her over with his furious eyes. "What will Sir George think to discover you like this? Out alone without your aunts or even a maid or an escort of any kind? To return home in a cloak I wouldn't give to my scullery maid and your gown ruined with sand and seawater!"

"I suppose that is exactly what he'll think," Bella murmured.

Her father's brows snapped together. He glared at her. "Are you trying to be amusing?"

"Oh, goodness, no," Bella said fervently. The familiar sense of panic was rising into her chest from her churning stomach and her short breaths sounded more like gasps. If only he wouldn't shout, it would be so much easier to think, to hang on to the astonishing, vitally important thing that had happened. Surely that would provide all the courage she needed.

"Then explain yourself!" the Duke roared.

"Let the child sit down," Aunt Maria said, guiding her to a chair. Which is when she realized her brother Sebastian was there, too, sitting beside her in full regimentals.

"Seb," she said in surprise.

He grinned and ruffled her hair as if she were a child rather than a grown woman a year older than he. "Greetings, funny-face."

"What are you doing here? I thought you were in Spain."

"Got bored with the war," Seb said carelessly. "Decided to come home. It's all finished anyway, bar the shouting."

"I'll deal with you later," their father uttered grimly. "I'm still waiting to hear why my daughter is running loose about the town like a hoyden—an ill-dressed hoyden at that!—jumping in the sea and rolling, by the look of her, in the sand!"

"Oh dear," Bella said. "Well…" She drew in her breath. "It began early this morning when I took a short walk, as I often do before everyone is awake. I had just left the room when one of the hotel maids gave me a note from—" She broke off, frowning at Seb with sudden anxiety, for he was her favorite brother in a careless kind of way. "You're not wounded, are you?"

"Devil a bit," Seb said cheerfully. "It's healed completely."

"Yes, but—"

"*Will* you stick to the point?" roared their father, making Bella start once again.

When she drew her next breath, it wheezed slightly, and she had to remind herself she was no longer afraid or ill, that she had a future with the man she suddenly loved more than life itself.

"My apologies, sir," she managed. "I received a note from Mr. Tranter."

The duke glared. "Tranter? Who the devil is Tranter and what is he doing sending you notes?"

"To own the truth, sir, I rather wondered that myself," Bella admitted.

"He's an admirer of Arabella's," Aunt Sarah said a trifle smugly.

Sir George sat up in his chair, as if paying attention for the first time since she'd entered the room. The duke turned his wrathful eye on Sarah who subsided into silence.

"The note asked me to meet him at Blackhaven Cove," Bella said hastily. "It's only fifteen minutes' walk so I went and spoke to him and he asked me to bear a lady company while he…er…eloped with her."

They all goggled at her. She had an inkling this truth might not be as believable to her family as she knew it to be.

"Digging yourself deeper," Seb warned below his breath.

"What a hum!" her father said contemptuously.

"You're entirely right, sir, it was a hum," Bella agreed. "But he was very plausible, and I suppose I must be gullible, for I got into the boat with him and he rowed along the coast for a little. It was such a beautiful morning that I almost fell asleep and when I opened my eyes, we were much farther out and heading toward his yacht."

"His yacht," the duke repeated.

Bella hoped the simmering anger in his steely eyes was aimed at Tranter and not at her. "Well, it transpires he probably stole it, though he claimed it was borrowed. Whatever, his aim was to ruin me so that you, sir, would agree to a marriage between us."

"What rot!" the duke exploded. "You are of age, girl!"

"Yes, but if you don't agree to continue my allowances and to the release of such fortune as I have, I would not be much use to him as a wife. At any rate, I did not want to be his wife at all, so I jumped into the sea."

Her father regarded her with somewhat ominous fascination. "You jumped in the sea," he repeated. "And swam ashore, perhaps?"

"Oh no, I think we were too far out by then. But Captain Alban's ship was passing nearby and the captain jumped in and rescued me. They took me aboard *The Albatross* and he and his doctor looked after me, and then, when I was warm and dry, they brought me back."

She thought it only fair to miss out the voyage up the coast and Alban's departure in the longboat with the men and several barrels of brandy.

"Captain Alban," His Grace repeated.

Bella lifted her chin. "Yes, sir."

The duke exploded. "My God, girl, when I want a fairytale, I'll read a damned book! What is the matter with you, you dim-witted, hen-brained imbecile? Did you actually believe any of us would fall for this farrago of nonsense? Or do you truly believe it yourself?" In disgust, he swung on his sisters. "I blame you for this, Maria! It's not spa waters she needs, it's a lunatic asylum!"

Aunt Maria bridled. "As it happens, Kelburn, we *are* acquainted with Captain Alban. I'm not saying it's an advantageous acquaintance, but it's a fact nonetheless."

Kelburn stared at her. "What, the damned smuggler fellow? At best he's a mere trader! At worst a damned pirate! Is that who upset

Smedley's dignity? Come, Beaton, let's leave this madhouse until the full moon goes in."

Bella held her breath until the door closed behind her father and Sir George, who seemed almost as dazed as Bella, and then released it in a rush.

"Oh dear," she said shakily.

"Well, it's your own fault," Sebastian said, apparently amused. "You might have come up with a more believable story. Being abducted by an amorous stranger and rescued by a smuggler just ain't you, Bella!"

"Mr. Tranter is *not* amorous. He's a fortune-hunter," Bella retorted. "And believable or not, the story has the simple merit of truth!"

"Well, *I* couldn't have made it up," Aunt Sarah said doubtfully. "Is Mr. Tranter really a fortune hunter and a villain?"

"If he's alive…but I don't *believe* the captain killed him."

Sebastian let out a crack of laughter. "Are you actually having fun here, Bella?"

Bella couldn't help her glance of pure mischief. "Do you know, I believe I am? But what in the world is His Grace doing here?"

"Smedley," Aunt Maria said grimly, dismissing her lord and master with one wave of the hand. "He ran into Kelburn at Audley's and of course spilled out a lot of nonsense about encroaching sailors turning your head."

"But he brought Sir George! Please don't tell me he's still trying to persuade me to marry Sir George."

Aunt Sarah slid her gaze away. "You could do worse, Bella. Especially now that Mr. Tranter has turned out so badly. And if you've truly been all day on Alban's ship, you'll be very lucky to get another proposal of any kind."

"I expect Beaton will bolt," Sebastian offered with careless kindness.

"Well you needn't say it with such satisfaction!" Aunt Sarah said indignantly. "Do you *want* your sister left on the shelf?"

"Yes, if the alternative's tying her to that crusty old windbag," Seb retorted. "You do know he bored his first two wives to death? They died in self-defense."

Bella couldn't help her choke of laughter, which caused Seb to grin at her as her aunts tutted in disapproval. Aunt Sarah shooed him from the room while Maria dragged Bella into her bedchamber to change, for they were to dine with His Grace and Sir George in the hotel dining room.

TO HER ANNOYANCE, Bella slept in the following morning. Totally, exhausted, she'd fallen into bed early, but the excitement of her day at sea had taken its toll and she didn't wake until Jenson brought her some hot chocolate and a bread roll at ten o'clock. Aunt Maria, terrified that she'd caught a chill during her adventure, dosed her with more of the vile-tasting tonic she'd given her the previous evening, and refused to let her out of bed until after lunch.

As a result, Bella spent a pleasant morning in bed with her books—both *Pride and Prejudice* and a more obscure hand-written Scottish history that had lots of tales of her pre-union ancestors, long before they were dukes.

Of His Grace her father there had been no sign. Nor any of Sir George or Lord Sebastian, although they were all staying at the hotel. The Duke had apparently commandeered the largest suite of rooms at the top of the house, and Sir George a more modest chamber close by. But the only word they received from any of them was a scrawled note from the Duke enclosing theatre tickets for this evening—seemingly Sebastian's idea.

"I don't know whether Sebastian's being here is a good thing or a bad," Aunt Maria commented. "I thought at first it might deflect His Grace from you, but Sebastian's latest start seems just to have made him angrier with everyone."

"Why, what has Seb done?" Bella asked with interest.

"He says he has resigned his commission. Or will resign it, one or the other! Because his commanding officers are fools."

Bella blinked. "Lord Wellington included?"

"No, I believe his lordship was exempted," Maria replied scathingly. "But the question is, if he really has given up his commission, what in the world is he going to do with himself? His Grace cannot abide idleness."

"I can't see him in the diplomatic service like Harry," Aunt Sarah contributed. "Or in politics like Kelburn and Monkton."

"Then it has to be the Church," Bella said, laughter bubbling up at the very thought of Seb giving sermons. *"Go forth from this place of worship and indulge in wine, women, and idleness. Play cards! Fight! The good Lord put us here to enjoy life!"*

"Bella!" exclaimed both her aunts, scandalized.

"Not the Church, then," Bella agreed.

Still, in spite of her jesting, she did worry about Sebastian, in-between bouts of longing for Alban to visit and remembering everything he'd said to her, every touch, every kiss.

After luncheon, she was reluctant to go out, in case she missed him. But in the end, she gave in and accompanied her aunts to the pump room. After all, she was as likely to see him in the town as elsewhere. In fact, remembering, she found herself peering at the coffee shop opposite as they left the hotel.

IN THE WAKE of several of his most villainous crew, Alban strolled from the harbor toward the tavern.

Since his men were restive stuck on board with very little to do, he'd released them in relays into Blackhaven, with the warning that if anyone got into trouble he'd leave them to rot in prison. He didn't want them to think he was growing soft, because he was pretty sure they understood the reason they were anchored here for so long.

Alban wasn't so sure *he* understood it. At times, he found himself terrified by the speed of this feeling for Bella, and the strength of his will to act on it, to have her as his own. For in truth, she was not the type of woman he was usually drawn to—sophisticated, independent females who understood that the game of love wasn't really love at all. In fact, it was strictly temporary.

Bella didn't understand that in the least. Or the inevitability of his letting her down. And yet she expected nothing of him, was only just beginning to understand her own attractions. And so, he set wheels in motion to clear his path to her, to a name and a home. And God help him, he liked the idea of her greeting him there on his return from sea. Almost as much as he liked the idea of her voyaging with him.

Occasionally, he wondered what the devil he would do with her when he was bored with her. But somehow, he could never imagine that. There might come a time when he didn't burn for her as he did now, but she would always be his friend, quirky, intelligent, understanding, with her own unique perception of the world. She would always be…fun.

He guessed her family's bullying disparagement and her own lack of confidence had prevented some people, some men in particular, from seeing the gem within. And he was only too aware of the dangers to his own cause of breaking down those barriers and encouraging her to shine. He'd seen the way Lord Tamar and several other men looked at her at the Grants' soiree. Even Tranter, he suspected, wasn't motivated entirely by money in his pursuit of her.

But the truth was, she'd dragged him from his blinkered, narrow view of life where he only looked after himself, his men, and his business. For the first time that he could remember in his adult life, he wanted to make someone happy. And he wanted it with a force that scared him. Even more astonishing, he'd begun to glimpse his own happiness, and not just in the odd moments he was with her.

He paused, one foot on the tavern step. He should sail with the evening tide and come back in six months or a year…

And find her married to someone else. Or, hurt by his neglect, retreated back into her shell of crushed misery.

She loved him for some reason. *Him*. And she wasn't the sort of woman who loved easily.

Alban spun on his heel, away from the tavern, narrowly missing a fisherman who cursed him instinctively and then relapsed into wary silence when he recognized him. Alban barely noticed. He strode away in the direction of the hotel. She might deserve better than him, but by God, it was him she was going to have.

From habit, he cast a quick glance around the busy hotel foyer, but recognizing no one among the wealthy and fashionable, or among the staff carrying bags and portmanteaux, he went straight to the reception desk and asked for Lady Arabella Niven.

"Her ladyship has stepped out, sir," the clerk returned.

He had no right to be either disappointed or irritated. Besides, there were a limited number of places he was likely to find her.

"Very well," he said to the clerk. "I'll call again later on." He swung away and found himself face to face with a haughty, white-haired man of perhaps late middle years.

"May I enquire, sir, as to your business with Lady Arabella?" this personage said coldly. Hovering behind him was a young man in military uniform.

"No," Alban said, "you may not."

The older gentleman blinked in surprise, as if unused to being denied. An unpleasant suspicion slid into Alban's mind. He looked more closely.

"It is a civil question!" the gentleman barked. "What is your name?"

"Alban. What is yours?"

The officer behind him folded his arms and grinned a trifle wolfishly. The old gentleman scowled. "Kelburn," he growled.

It had been twelve years since he'd laid eyes on this man. Twelve years during which his features had got lost in Alban's mind, in a welter of fury and hatred and contempt. And then in indifference. Quite clearly, the Duke of Kelburn still didn't recognize him.

Alban tipped his hat. "I thought so," he said, and he walked on.

"And that's the last we'll see of *him*," Kelburn said with satisfaction.

Alban's lips twisted. *You couldn't be more wrong.*

As BELLA EMERGED from her bedchamber into the sitting room, her father looked her up and down and grunted. Then he scowled. "What are those ridiculous things on your face? Get them off."

He was her father. Wordlessly, Bella took off her spectacles. Aunt Sarah, who now had an ally in this particular fight, held out her hand to receive them. Bella pretended not to see and tucked them away in her own reticule before raising her now somewhat blurry gaze to her father's face.

"You'll do," he said grudgingly. "Beaton will meet us in the foyer. Mercifully, he seems prepared to overlook yesterday's behavior. If nothing else proves his good nature and his regard for you, that does. Because I haven't forgiven or forgotten."

Bella opened her mouth to point out that whatever Sir George's regard she still did not and could not return it. But the duke turned away, striding toward the passage door.

"I'm a busy man," he pointed out. "I want this business concluded by midday tomorrow so that I can return to London."

"What business, sir?" Bella asked in dismay.

"Don't give me that innocent look," her father said disgustedly, standing aside for the ladies to precede him out of the open door. "You know exactly what I mean, and this time, you'll do the right thing and accept him."

"I can't," Bella said determinedly over her shoulder. "I accepted another offer yesterday."

To her surprise, her father laughed, a sound of cruelty and anger that wasn't necessarily aimed at her. "You can forget that. I've taken care of it."

The blood rushed from Bella's face so suddenly that she halted. The duke brushed past her, impatiently giving Aunt Maria his arm.

"What have you done?" It came out as little more than a whisper which her father had little hope of hearing.

Sebastian caught her elbow and dragged her forward. "Was it Alban?" he murmured in her ear.

Bella nodded mutely, staring at him.

"We met him in the foyer," Sebastian said under his breath. "Asking for you. His Grace sent him about his business."

Bella blinked, unable to quite imagine that.

Sebastian's lips twitched. "That is, when he heard you weren't in the hotel, he left. With His Grace's verbal boot up his rear. If he noticed. What's going on, Bella? You can't really marry such a fellow, you know, however much you might like him. You must know he's encroaching, fortune-hunting, and Lord knows what else."

"Must I?" Bella said harshly, and tugged free of her brother to walk downstairs alone.

This turned out to be a mistake, for once they reached the foyer, the duke barked at Sebastian to escort his aunt, leaving Sir George Beaton to offer Bella his arm. And in all civility, she could not refuse.

They walked out of the hotel in silence, since Bella was furious at such treatment of Alban. Even if His Grace had no idea who he actually was, that was no excuse for such rudeness. Or such high-handed dismissal of her rights and wishes.

But then, she had never given them any idea that she would stand up for herself. Until even her refusal of Sir George Beaton was not taken seriously. Instead, they seemed to imagine it was something her father could reverse with a little more bullying from him and a little more perseverance from Sir George. And no doubt, that's what His Grace had told the poor man, which made him almost as much a victim as she was.

"I am glad of this opportunity to speak to you, Lady Arabella," Sir George said at last, as they walked along the darkening High Street. "I want to say I am very sorry for your trouble."

"What trouble?" Bella asked, bewildered.

"Your trouble yesterday. With fortune hunters and the like."

Bella gave a slightly twisted smile. "My brush with fiction? Or the lunatic asylum?"

"I'm sure the Duke believed you as soon as he had time to think about it," Sir George said hastily.

Bella drew in her breath. "Sir George, I have to tell you that I—"

"Have you been to the theatre here before?" His Grace's voice boomed. "Is it any good?"

It wasn't something she could shout over the voices of her father and aunts, so she closed her mouth and bided her time.

Chapter Twelve

When they were shown to their box at the theatre, she could see her father's wiles at work at once. He arranged the seating, with Bella and Sir George at the front of the box, her aunts and Sebastian just behind, and himself at the back where he could snooze his way through the play. In this way she would be seen in Sir George's company, rumors of the engagement would no doubt start up again and Bella would presumably realize the futility of going against her father, the rest of her family, Sir George, and the world. He really thought she would be crushed into it because there wasn't any other option.

But even before Alban, that would never have happened. He'd never understood her any more than she understood him. Even as a child, she'd regarded him as little more than a stranger who occasionally breezed into her life, found fault—loudly—and left again. When he'd spent any time at home, she'd avoided him because he shouted too much. She understood now that the shouting didn't necessarily betoken anger, but still it caused a dread in her she could never shake off.

She took her place obediently and, without fuss, put on her spectacles. She hadn't yet attended the theatre in Blackhaven, so she gazed with interest at the blue and gold paint and the plush blue curtains and seating. Of course, compared with London theatres, this was a small one, the boxes fewer and less spacious. But she suspected the same rule would apply, that the audience would pay more attention to each other than to the play.

Certainly, there were more interested stares and glances cast at her box than she was entirely comfortable with, though this could have been due to the presence of the duke himself. A few people bowed to her from other boxes, including Kate Grant. Bella dutifully inclined her head in return. Since no one seemed to be cutting her, she assumed her adventures of yesterday were not yet the subject of gossip.

"You have friends here," Sir George observed.

"A few acquaintances," Bella allowed, sweeping her eyes over the audience pit below. The eccentric Lord Tamar sat there in a torn coat. For once, his attention did not appear to be on Bella but on someone approaching from the entrance below the Kelburn box.

Her heart lurched, for Captain Alban made his way through the mixed, milling crowd and appeared to exchange greetings with Lord Tamar. As always, he attracted attention of which he seemed either unaware or utterly uninterested. From the row in front a group of young townswomen gazed at him with awe. When he glanced in their direction, the boldest one smiled and batted her eyelashes. He didn't appear to notice that either, for he simply dropped into the seat beside the artist and gazed about him, acknowledging boisterous greetings with brisk nods.

Did he know she was here? Was that why he'd come? Had her father's intervention made any difference to him?

His gaze lifted to the rows of boxes. He inclined his head a few times, once to Kate, before his gaze moved on in her direction. Her breath caught.

"Who is that man?" Sir George asked.

Alban's gaze connected with hers. His eyebrow twitched and he inclined his head as though she were no more and no less than anyone else. And then the moment passed as Lord Tamar attracted his attention.

Bella swallowed. "Captain Alban," she replied. And Sir George leaned out of the box to see better.

It was stupid to feel hurt or slighted. Of course he would not single her out in this company.

It was a kind of torture to sit through the comedy that that formed the first part of the evening's performance. Bella, who normally liked to lose herself in the play, could not concentrate on it. She sat on the edge of her seat lest Sir George spoke about marriage. It would be so much better for his pride if Bella didn't have to refuse him again. Really, His Grace had put them all in an intolerable position. And then she longed for Alban's presence, the reassurance of his company. How could the same man churn her up and soothe her at the same time?

Fortunately, Sir George seemed to feel all the awkwardness of proposing in public and sat for the most part in silence. After the comedy came an interval, during which she dreaded being invited by Sir George to take a turn along the corridors before the tragedy.

Sebastian said abruptly, "Kate Crowmore! That's who she is! I've been trying to place her all evening."

"Kate Grant," Bella corrected. "She is married to the vicar of the local church."

Sebastian laughed. "Kate Crowmore, a vicar's wife? You're humming me."

"No, I assure you it's perfectly true."

Sebastian stood up. "Well, if you'll excuse me, I'll just pop along to her box and pay my respects."

"I'll come with you," Bella said at once.

"Arabella, we have guests of our own," Aunt Sarah reminded her, with a quick glance at Sir George and then at the duke, who'd nodded off.

"We won't be long," Bella said hastily, and seizing her brother's reluctant arm, all but fell out of the box with him.

"Bella, what the deuce?" he demanded. "Never tell me you're thick with Kate Crowmore for I won't believe you."

"Actually, I like her much better than I used to. And besides, you know perfectly well I'm avoiding Sir—"

"Well, I can't say I blame you for that," Sebastian allowed, "but in this particular case, you might just have to give in to the inevitable."

"Would *you*?" she retorted.

"Sir George and I really wouldn't suit."

"You know what I mean. Shouldn't it be inevitable that you stay in the army until you're at least a colonel, if not a general?"

Sebastian cast her a harassed glance. "You can win all the arguments, Bella, but you'll still end up Lady Beaton. Ah, here's Kate…"

"Lady Bella!" Kate greeted her. "Come in and let me introduce my good friends, Dr. and Mrs. Lampton. Lady Arabella Niven and…Good Lord, is that you, Seb? Captain Lord Sebastian Niven, I should say—unless you've been promoted again since last I heard?"

"Why no," Sebastian declaimed, hand on heart. "As soon as I heard you were free, I gave up my commission to come home and marry you and now I hear you've married another! Lady C, you've broken my heart all over again."

"I happen to know for a fact you don't have a heart," Kate retorted. "Come and sit down and tell us what you've been doing!"

Since Sebastian's dramatic greeting had somewhat overpowered her civilized introduction to the Lamptons, Bella stepped aside and made to close the curtain between the box and the passage. She didn't want any of her family to find her too easily if they came looking. One hand on the curtain, she cast a quick glance into the corridor, which was blessedly empty, apart from one man striding along it.

She doubted she even needed her spectacles to recognize Alban anymore. His straight carriage and quick, rolling walk, no doubt from too many years spent on board ship, were quite distinctive. From pure instinct, she stepped out into the passage and closed the curtain on the box. And then she ran to him.

He caught her in his arms at once, pressing his rough cheek hard to hers before he turned and found her mouth. With abandon, she flung both arms around his neck and kissed him back.

"Was my father appallingly rude to you?" she demanded when she could speak.

He shrugged. "No more than I to him. In a civilized way. I think he was warning me off. I hear you're going to marry someone else."

"I hear that, too, but I never listen to gossip. I'll tell him who you are and he might—" He cut her off with another kiss, strong and sensual.

"I don't care," he said against her lips.

A faint movement behind froze her.

Sebastian's voice drawled, "Not sure you should be doing that with my sister. Damned sure you shouldn't be doing it in a public place."

Unhurriedly, while Bella cringed, Alban raised his head and released her, although he drew her hand through his arm.

"Captain Alban," Bella murmured nervously. "My brother, Lord Sebastian Niven."

"I'm going to marry her," Alban said quietly. The words thrilled through her. She still couldn't believe her sudden good fortune.

Sebastian narrowed his eyes, casting a quick glance up the passage where several people were spilling out of a box. "Maybe that's something we should discuss in private."

"Maybe," Alban said steadily.

"Bella, you'd better go back in to Kate. If His Grace wakes up and finds you've bolted—"

"You won't quarrel, will you?" Bella asked, looking anxiously from Alban to her brother.

"No," Alban said, urging her back toward Kate's box. "I'll join you in a few moments."

FACED WITH THE military young gentleman who'd accompanied the Duke of Kelburn this morning, Alban was surprised to receive as much civility as he did. Intrigued, he followed Lord Sebastian into an empty box, and drew the curtain.

"I suppose I should knock your teeth out," his lordship observed.

"You could try," Alban allowed.

"I could. But for Bella's sake, I thought I'd begin with the peaceful approach."

"Which is?" Alban inquired, taking a seat in the middle of the room, far enough back for his voice not to penetrate the adjacent boxes too easily.

"To point out," Lord Sebastian said carefully, "that most of Bella's fortune is dependent on my father's releasing it. If you marry her, I can't say you won't get a penny, but you won't get much more than that."

Alban shrugged. "I don't care. At the risk of sounding vulgar, I have enough money for both of us."

"My father will cut her off," Sebastian insisted, as though Alban had not perfectly understood.

"I think that would be an excellent idea. The whole parcel of them makes her ill."

Lord Sebastian blinked. "They shout," he allowed. "Damn it, I shout myself. But they care."

Alban met his gaze. "Your aunts might but they understand nothing about her. Your father wants to push her into marriage against her will, with a man more than twice her—who possesses, moreover, eyes like a fish. Or so I am reliably informed. All this just for her father's own political ends. Or financial ones. I neither know nor care which. None of you seems to imagine she has any value without a husband."

Lord Sebastian clearly didn't like that. "Unlike you?" he retorted. "Or do you fancy yourself her champion?" He sneered. "A man of your …profession?"

"My profession is neither here nor there. And no, I'm not her champion. She doesn't need one. She's stronger than any of them gives her credit for. And she wants to marry me."

At some point during this last speech, Sebastian's expression changed. It might have been when Alban mentioned Bella's strength.

The young lord's lips actually curved into a faint, almost rueful smile. "Maybe she does, at that. And maybe you're just what she needs. But if you're not, if you hurt one hair of her head—or her heart—I'll find you and kill you."

Alban stood. "Finally. A Niven man worth talking to," he said, and walked out.

As expected, he discovered Bella with Mrs. Grant and a couple he didn't know. More surprising was the fact that Lord Sebastian followed him in without showing any signs of wishing to punch him. In fact, he seemed more concerned with flirting with the beautiful Mrs. Grant.

Since the curtain came up shortly afterward, Bella was easily persuaded to stay until the next interval. Alban sat beside her, although the opportunity for private discussion was not great.

Under her breath, Bella murmured, "My father brought Sir George to renew his offer for me."

"I'll call on your father tomorrow morning," Alban said abruptly. "But I'm going to fetch the children from Roseley first. Just in case we have to sail."

"Sail?" she said startled. "Sail where?"

He shrugged. "Wherever we can find someone to marry us. I won't have you facing the condemnation of the self-righteous and the unimaginative."

"Such things don't bother me," she said, with such carelessness that he knew it was the truth.

"They bother me."

She searched his eyes. "What did you say to Seb?"

"That I would marry you."

She flushed adorably. "What did Seb say?"

Alban shrugged. "I don't think the words matter. It sounded like a mixture of threat and approval. With threat looming larger in the mix."

"He's quite handy with his fists," Bella warned. "And with weapons."

"So am I," Alban said sardonically. "But so long as neither of us hurts you, I believe we are both safe."

It broke his heart that she seemed surprised either he her own brother would care for her that much.

At the next interval, Bella and Sebastian returned to their own box. Giving in to Bella's dislike of confrontation, Alban did not accompany them. Instead, he bade farewell to Mrs. Grant and her other guests in order to return to his seat in the pit beside the odd but entertaining Lord Tamar.

Mrs. Grant stood to give him her hand. "Thank you for coming to see me! Whatever your motive."

"Pure pleasure," Alban said at once.

"Mixed with care, I trust," Mrs. Grant returned steadily. "Lady Arabella has more friends than she realizes."

"I'm very glad to hear it," Alban said, and meant it.

For Bella, it was all going too well. She'd seen Alban and had managed to get through the evening without Sir George re-offering her marriage. And tomorrow, tomorrow the matter would be concluded once and for all. She didn't look forward to the confrontation that would inevitably entail, but she was prepared for it. To be with Alban. Her happiness seemed to form a little bubble around her, fostering the foolish belief that nothing now could go wrong.

The first unease to pierce her bubble was as they crossed the hotel foyer that night and a vaguely familiar man stopped and bowed to them, waiting patiently for them to precede him up the staircase. The man's presence was so unexpected that it took a moment for his identity to register with her. Thomas Waine, the duke's chaplain.

"What is he doing here?" she muttered to Sebastian. "Did he travel up with you?"

"Yes," Sebastian replied. "And why do you think?"

There was a brief pause, while they exchanged goodnights with Sir George and then everyone except the chaplain walked along the passage to the suite of rooms she shared with her aunts.

Bella seized her brother's arm and held him back as the others entered. "Seb, has His Grace brought a special license with him?"

Sebastian nodded. "He's pretty determined, Bella," he said ruefully. "I'm afraid you're going to have to make a stand for what you want. If you want Alban, you'll have to fight for him. For what it's worth, I don't believe the fellow means you any harm. In fact, I almost like him. But the safest bet is undeniably Beaton."

"He doesn't make me feel safe," she said in small voice.

"And Alban does?" he asked incredulously.

A smile she couldn't prevent flickered across her lips. "Yes. But it's more than that. Much more."

Sebastian raked his fingers through his hair. "I'll back you up, Bella, but you'll have to tell him."

"I will," she said, giving his arm a quick squeeze before she released him and walked into the sitting room, where her father and her aunts were all seated facing her. She had no time to read her aunts' expressions, for the duke's face was so thunderous she knew she was about to be verbally annihilated. At the very least.

She stopped in her tracks, pulling ineffectually at her gloves.

"Answer me this," her father began with deceptive calm. "Did you sneak off tonight to meet that Alban fellow who's been sniffing around you?"

Bella bridled at this description. "No," she said truthfully. "Although in fact, that was what happened. He too visited Mrs. Grant's box."

"And I suppose you took no account at all of Beaton's feelings?"

"None," Bella admitted. "Although I managed to prevent him proposing to me again."

"Ha!" the duke barked in triumph. "He doesn't need to propose again. I have already accepted him."

"Then I wish you both very happy," Bella blurted before she could bite her unruly tongue.

Appalled, she stared at her father who, however, seemed to have too many grievances against her to even take that one in. It was Seb who sniggered and her aunts who stared at her aghast.

"Happy?" he exploded. "How can any of us be happy when you have so clearly lost your mind? To say nothing of your duty! Without any concern for your name or your family, you are trying to drag us all into the mud. Well, I won't have it, d'you hear? Tomorrow at midday, you will marry Sir George Beaton, here in this room by special license. Waine will perform the marriage and after that, I wash my hands of you. You'll be Beaton's concern, not mine."

It didn't seem worth pointing out that she'd never truly been any concern of his at all. None of his children had been except in so far as they could be useful to him. His sons were all fine, strong men with bright futures, especially Monkton, the eldest, guaranteed to reflect well on their proud father. Likewise, her younger sisters had all made splendid matches, bringing land and influence to Kelburn's already overwhelming collection. Only Bella had failed in that respect. Or at least he thought she had.

"I can't marry Sir George Beaton," she said firmly. "I have promised my hand to another, who as—"

"A damned, nameless pirate!" her father exploded.

"He is neither," Bella said earnestly. "Papa, I'm very aware this is not the match you would ever have chosen for me. But please understand Captain Alban is a gentleman and, moreover, quite wealthy in his own right. You see, Alban isn't his real surname. It's his Christian name."

Finally, she'd caught his attention. And everyone else's. "Not his real surname?" the duke repeated. "Then what the deuce is?"

"Lamont," Bella answered. "He is the Honorable Alban Lamont, brother of the late Lord Roseley."

Her father's jaw went slack with something very like shock. Everyone stared at her with varying degrees of disbelief and consternation.

"You didn't recognize him," Bella guessed. "But he knew you."

"I didn't know he was still alive," the duke said. "They couldn't find him when his father died…" The old burning ferocity broke through the temporary distance in his eyes. "So, *he* was Alban all along. And this man just happened to find you out of all the women in Blackhaven, so irresistible that he must have you as his wife. Maybe. And you fell for it?"

The contempt in his voice cut her, but more than that, there was something she wasn't seeing, something that was so obvious to him she deserved to be reviled for her blindness.

"Fell for what? Captain Alban—Mr. Lamont—is an honorable man."

The duke laughed mirthlessly. "Honorable! I doubt he ever meant marriage, unless it was to diddle you out of your money and run! He believes I ruined him when he was a very young man, and I could see in his eyes even then that he'd never forgive me. And he never has. You stupid, gullible old maid, you are his means of revenge!"

Chapter Thirteen

Alban left Blackhaven at first light, and just over two hours later dismounted in front of the Roseley House stables. Since there was no sign of the stable lad, he looked after his own horse and found it water and hay before he strode into the kitchen.

No one was there. Not even the cook. The hair stood up on the back of his neck. Of course, it was still early. They could all have drunk too much ale last night and still be sleeping it off. Or they could all have had enough and walked out, whether to Radnor or to another employer. He'd imagined his frequent, unpredictable visits were keeping them on their toes. The kitchen had certainly been cleaner and the children fed and cared for.

But now, he wished he'd simply taken the children with him to Blackhaven. Will wouldn't have minded much, and Bella or Mrs. Grant would have been happy to hire a respectable woman to stay with them until Marianne arrived. Stupidly, he'd been stuck in the knowledge that he couldn't care for children. Even after he knew that he really was their legal guardian and would not be arrested for being who he was, he couldn't be rid of the notion that he was not the sort of person who should be around children, that Alban's nefarious reputation would somehow rub off on them.

Or had he simply wanted to be free to pursue Bella and his own business?

He should have done this days ago.

Uneasily, he pushed through the kitchen and upstairs into the main part of the house. Some instinct prevented him calling out for Jenkins and the others. Something was wrong here.

Fear for the children twisted through him as he walked silently across the hall and up the staircase, along the winding passage to the nursery. He still hadn't seen a soul. The house remained eerily quiet. Even when he paused outside the nursery, his ear pressed to the door, no childish voices reached him. No sounds of play within. Of course, Molly could have taken them out, though it was unlikely in the rain.

Slowly, he lifted the latch and went in. The schoolroom was tidy and empty. He walked across it to the children's bedchambers. His mouth was dry with an unnamable fear, far greater than any he'd known before a fight or when sailing into unknown dangers.

His right fist clenched and ready, he opened the door and walked into Leo's chamber, spinning to face anyone who might lurk behind the door. No one.

And there was no one in Leo's bed either. It had been neatly spread up. From a vague memory of his own childhood and playing hide and seek with Nick, he looked under Leo's bed and in his cupboard. There was nowhere else to hide.

Frowning, Alban strode from there into Florrie's room, which was equally empty and tidy. He left, crossing the schoolroom and barged into Molly's room with barely a knock. He'd insisted she sleep here close to the children, rather than with the other servants. But her room was empty and her bed made, too.

Alban had had enough.

"Leo!" he shouted, striding back across the schoolroom to the passage door. "Florrie! Where are you? Molly!"

Leaving the doors wide open, he all but ran into the corridor. "Jenkins!"

Something struck him hard in the chin and he stumbled back against the wall. From sheer instinct, he drove himself forward again, but many hands slammed him back against the wall. Jenkins's ugly, leering face loomed over him.

"Yes, sir," he mocked. "I'm right here."

Testing the strength of his captors, Alban strained forward, but apart from Jenkins and the two who held him, three other men, one of them with a pistol aimed directly at him, formed a half circle around him. He was trapped. For the moment.

"Where are the children?" he demanded.

"We were hoping you could tell us that," said quite another voice, modulated and cultured and yet curiously grating.

A gentleman brushed past the man with the pistol and came to stand beside Jenkins. Of medium height and build, he was well-dressed and fashionable, if a little over-addicted to pomade.

"However," this gentleman proceeded, "it would seem you too have mislaid the wretched cubs. Which brings me to the next question. Who the deuce are you and what do you mean by trespassing on my property and ordering my servants?"

Alban had already guessed it. "Mr. Radnor, I presume?"

"You still have the advantage. Jenkins here tells me you claim to be Captain Alban. Alban is an interesting name in this house."

"I'm glad you find it so. Perhaps you'd oblige your ruffians to unhand me?"

"Perhaps," Radnor said. "But then again, you haven't answered my question."

The man had cold, calculating eyes, and yet behind that calm was unease, even fear. And anger, a huge amount of suppressed anger. Alban had seen it before in sullen men.

"Do I really need to?" Alban asked. "I think you know exactly who I am."

"Then I should indeed send for the magistrate. Oh, wait, that's me."

"Where is Marianne?" Alban demanded.

"Mrs. Radnor is in London. Your insolent epistle reached me instead."

"Then you know my concerns for the safety of my niece and nephew. Apart from the girl, Molly, your servants are unfit."

"Then you shouldn't have dismissed the governess."

Alban frowned. "What governess?"

"The one my wife engaged before we left."

Jenkins leaned forward, grinning. "The one I scared off two days after they left."

Alban understood. "And you wish to blame me for her disappearance? Really, if I could remember how to laugh, I would. Dismissing a governess would hardly be the worst of the crimes of which I stand accused."

"It might well be now that the children have vanished also."

A fresh burst of fear for them exploded through him, lending him strength. He lunged, swinging his arms so suddenly that he took his two captors by surprise. They were thrown forward, crashing into either side of Jenkins who cursed furiously.

Alban swerved, lashing out with one foot to trip the nearest bully. Then he confused them by charging not for the door but directly for Radnor.

"Shoot him!" Radnor screamed.

The blast deafened him, threw him forward, and yet he fell a foot away from the desperately retreating Radnor. Only then did he feel the pain. He stared stupidly at the pool of blood forming on the floor.

"Well, at least your man shoots straight," he said before the blackness closed in.

BELLA WOKE WITH a headache. She hadn't slept much during the night, but had tossed and turned with her father's ugly words ringing in her ears. She didn't believe them, of course, but still, the insidious doubts seeped into her brain. She remembered the times Alban had warned her against himself, had drawn back from her, almost as if he was ashamed, as if honor drove him away. Before the urge for revenge grew too strong again?

Her family had taken everything from him. The duke had condemned a man to die, knowing he was innocent, and then allowed Alban, only eighteen years old, to be driven from his home with nothing, and hunted into exile. With no home, no family, he'd grown hard in order to survive, had built his trading business in the company of harsh, rough, and no doubt dishonest men. Coming back to Blackhaven, seeing old friends like Will Conway, to say nothing of the children at Roseley, could only have reminded him how far he'd fallen. Because of the Duke of Kelburn. Who wouldn't want revenge?

But Alban wouldn't take it out on an innocent woman. Whatever had happened to him, he retained a sense of personal justice. He protected her, defended her, even from her own family…

Only why had he not taken her ashore immediately after he'd rescued her from Tranter? Why had he allowed the possible accusations of ruin to arise? That they hadn't was surely not his fault, despite landing discreetly in the cove. Was he using the circumstances to force her father's consent?

Or did he never mean to marry me in the first place?

She didn't believe it. She trusted him. And yet once the idea had crept in, it wouldn't go away. It was always there, virulent and clawing at the back of her heart. Because somewhere she still couldn't quite believe that a man like Alban could truly love her for herself.

And yet he did. She knew he did. He was coming for her today, and she would marry him with or without her father's blessing.

In this vicious circle of doubt and faith, she finally fell into an exhausted sleep. Though with her head aching, she did not feel remotely rested when she woke again.

"You don't look well," Maria said worriedly. "We'll go first thing to the pump room. The waters should do something to revive you."

"For my wedding?" Bella said in disbelief. "I won't marry Sir George today or any other day."

"You will," Maria said, just a little ruefully. "We all do his bidding in the end." Her gaze sharpened. "And don't give me that look! Despite appearances, you might take to be contrary, I have never regretted marrying Smedley. Now, drink your hot chocolate so that we may go out."

It seemed almost ridiculous walking between her aunts, going to drink waters she didn't want in a place she had no desire to be, just to please her family in this small thing before she disobliged them in the bigger.

"Captain Alban's doctor examined me on the ship," she said abruptly. "He doesn't believe I have consumption at all."

"A ship's surgeon?" Aunt Sarah said contemptuously. "What does he know?"

"A good deal, I think. He is a qualified physician, too."

"And to what cause does he assign your cough?" Aunt Maria asked. "And your difficult breathing?"

As she opened her mouth to reply, Bella realized the impossibility of repeating the doctor's words. How could she tell her aunts they smothered her to the degree that it was they who made her ill? Especially in conjunction with Maria's husband, or with His Grace or Bella's eldest brother.

Aunt Maria sniffed. "I thought so. But I do believe the waters are helping, for you've coughed far less since we've been here."

Because I've been happy. Because of Alban.

She contemplated quite seriously leaving her aunts in the pump room and going off in search of Alban. It would save the confrontation with her father and Sir George, which was planned for noon. But then she thought she might miss Alban coming to the hotel, and in truth, she would feel much more comfortable marrying him with her father's acceptance, if not his blessing. By his own blinkered lights, he probably believed he was doing right by her.

And so, having drunk the waters until forced to relieve herself, she walked back to the hotel, her aunts on either side of her like guards. Unfortunately, she saw no sign of Alban. Perhaps he wasn't yet back from Roseley with the children. Perhaps their mother had finally come and he had stopped to explain matters to her.

Entering the hotel again, she felt a strange mixture of anxiety, excitement, and dread. By this afternoon it would be concluded. One way or another, she would be with Alban.

And if he's done all this for spite? whispered the nasty voice at the back of her mind.

Of course he hasn't, she answered herself indignantly. *He isn't remotely like that.*

You barely know him, returned the first voice with contempt. *You have no experience of men or love.*

Be quiet!

So lost was she in her futile if silent argument, that she didn't notice Sir George Beaton until it was too late to avoid him. She suspected he'd been lurking in the foyer, awaiting her return.

"Lady Arabella," he said at once. "Might I beg the favor of a few words in private?"

"Oh, well, I don't think that would be quite…you know…" Her babbling faded into silence as she pushed her glasses more firmly onto her nose, gazing in astonishment at the unexpected sight of young Lord Roseley and his sister at the reception desk.

With them was Molly, the one-time kitchen maid. She looked quite red in the face, presumably through dissatisfaction with the superior hotel clerk.

"Excuse me," Bella murmured, going at once toward the little group.

"Arabella?" said Maria. "Where are you going?"

Bella flapped one soothing hand and kept walking.

"Mrs. Arabella Nieve," Molly was repeating loudly. "Don't deny her, for I know she stays in this hotel. And you'd better tell her we're here or she'll make sure you're sorry!"

At that moment, Florrie glanced round and saw Bella. Her little face split into a dazzling smile. "There she is!" she cried and ran to her.

Laughing, Bella dropped to her knees to receive the little girl, closely followed by her brother, in an enthusiastic hug. "Goodness, what is all this?" she exclaimed. "What are you doing here?" She rose to her feet, walking with her arms still around the children to meet Molly.

"Thank the Lord you walked in, ma'am, for I can't make this stupid man understand anything. You did say to come to you—"

"Of course, you're quite right," Bella said hastily. "Has something happened?"

Molly lowered her voice. "Nothing really. It's just we overheard Jenkins saying Mr. Radnor would be back today, and the children seemed so upset by the news that I was afraid they'd give me the slip and run off. So, we left together—"

"It was still dark," Leo said, his eyes gleaming with the excitement of his escape. "And Molly harnessed the horse to the gig and drove us all the way here herself!"

"Well that was very clever of Molly," Bella said warmly. "But did you not see the captain? He was going to visit you this morning."

"No, but we followed the road," Molly said. "Expect the captain rides across country."

"I hope he knocks Radnor down," Leo said enthusiastically. "And Jenkins, too!"

Somewhat belatedly, Bella became aware of the curious stares of other passing hotel guests, not least of them, Sir George and her own aunts. She hurried the few paces to the desk and fixed the open-mouthed clerk with a stern eye.

"I shall need a room for these children and their nurse, preferably one close to mine. Is the adjacent room still vacant? That would be best."

"Certainly, your ladyship," the clerk said humbly.

Bella eyed the children. "And I think maybe hot water for a bath."

"Of course, your ladyship. I'll see to it."

Bella took the children by the hands once more to find Sir George in her path, frowning with incomprehension. "But Lady Arabella, who *are* these children?"

"I believe we'd *all* like to know that!" Aunt Sarah muttered, while several other guests hovered nearby and pretended they weren't listening.

The lie popped into her head fully formed and perfect. It brought a gurgle of shocked laughter with it, but she swallowed that down and spoke to Sir George quite calmly.

"Why, they are mine, of course."

His jaw dropped. Aunt Maria moaned. Sarah made a sound like a growl.

"But...but how?" Sir George spluttered.

"By a secret marriage, of course," Bella said blatantly, sweeping away toward the staircase. "To Captain Alban. Come along children."

IT WAS ONLY once the children were settled in the room next to her suite, with Molly bathing them, that she began to appreciate fully what she had done with her impulsive lie. Not only to Sir George, but her aunts, the hotel clerk, and the several guests who had heard her.

Leaving the children's room for her own, she didn't underestimate either her aunts' humiliation or her father's fury. And yet the laughter still bubbled away just below the surface. She would have put it down to hysteria had she not felt so calm.

Opening the door into the sitting room, she wasn't at all surprised to see the duke there, pacing. She braced herself for his explosion of rage.

However, the look he turned upon her wasn't angry at all. She actually discerned amusement gleaming in his eyes.

"Well played, Arabella," he said wryly. "But it won't wash, you know. I've no idea who these children are, but they ain't yours."

Bella sat on the sofa and spread her skirts. "Why would you think that?"

"Apart from anything else, because you are always chaperoned," he said impatiently. "You've never had the opportunity."

Bella laughed. "I'm always chaperoned *in London*," she corrected. "But you must concede I was never there very often. I've spent months at Kelburn every year. Alone."

"You were never alone!"

"I might as well have been. I roamed the estate from dawn until dusk. You've no idea who I met."

"Don't be disgusting," His Grace snapped, his amusement clearly over. "You were closeted with your books!"

"Some of the time," she agreed.

Mr. Waine, the chaplain, whom she hadn't previously noticed, coughed politely. "Your ladyship does remember religion's requirement of truth."

"And of marriage," she returned gravely.

Sebastian grinned and threw himself onto the sofa beside her. "Well done. We all fell for it. Now who the devil are those children?"

Bella gazed at him in silence.

"Bella, you're not married," he said uneasily. "I'd know."

"Would you?"

"Admit it and let's move forward," the duke said, holding out his hand to the chaplain. Mr. Waine handed over a piece of paper which His Grace waved in the air. "Special license," he said with satisfaction.

Bella watched him lay it on the table in front of her.

"It makes no difference," the duke said. "No one believes you. You will be married today to Sir George."

"It makes every difference," Bella said, meeting his gaze. "Noon, I believe you commanded?"

The duke's eyes widened. He glanced at Sebastian, who took out his fob watch. "Half past the hour," Sebastian admitted.

Bella smiled. "And where is Sir George?"

Her father spun on his heel. "Find him," he barked at Sebastian and stormed out of the room.

Bella stood, casually picking up the special license and tucking it into her reticule before walking into her room and closing the door with a snap.

CONSIDERING SHE HAD just ruined her reputation, Bella felt surprisingly calm. Somewhere, she couldn't believe that it had been her mild, obedient self making all those scandalous claims. As she paced her bedchamber, laughter would surge up from nowhere, though it never quite made it beyond her lips. Anxiety usually interfered.

She needed to tell Alban that the children were here, and she didn't know if he'd already set off for Roseley and discovered them missing. She suspected so, since he'd planned to bring them here himself before coming here to confront her father. She hadn't exactly softened the duke up. He was unlikely to look kindly upon anything Alban had to say.

Eloping to Scotland, to Gretna Green, crossed her mind. It wasn't so far from Blackhaven, and Alban said he had inherited land in Scotland.

But first, she needed to see Alban. Unease intensified into fear as she imagined him being waylaid at Roseley by that brute Jenkins and his toughs, who might well have rediscovered their courage if their master was indeed expected back today.

Alban had said he would come this morning.

Bella stopped pacing around the room and opened the door. Her aunts, who were sitting together on the sofa, clearly in close confabulation, jumped to their feet in alarm.

"Bella, you're not going to do anything silly, are you?" Aunt Maria blurted.

"I'm going next door to see the children."

"Who are not yours," Aunt Sarah said firmly, "whoever else they might belong to. I know why you said what you did, but it won't wash. Kelburn hates to lose. If it wasn't for that, I suspect he'd wash his hands of you."

Bella sighed. "I wouldn't blame him." Without fuss, she left the room and walked down the passage to the children's room.

Bathed and dressed in some clean clothes Molly had had had the forethought to bring with them, they were investigating their new surroundings with interest. Both ran to her as she entered.

"Oh, Mrs. Nieve, do you think we can go to the harbor?" Leo asked eagerly.

"And the beach," Florrie added. "Molly says you can build castles out of the sand!"

"Yes, of course we can, just as soon as we find the captain."

"We thought his name was Nieve like yours," Leo said, gazing up at her solemnly. "Only now it seems it isn't yours either."

Bella sat, drawing them both with her onto the bed. "That is quite true. I am so hemmed in by convention and respectability that sometimes I like to be incognito. My real name is Arabella Niven. My father is the Duke of Kelburn."

"And Captain Nieve," Leo pursued. "They called him Alban, which is our uncle's name."

"It is," Bella agreed. "And in fact, the captain *is* your uncle. When he first came to you, he thought he was still in disgrace. Which is why he has been using Alban as his surname. I think all that is about to change. He was coming to explain things to you this morning and to take you with him until your mother comes home."

"Really?" Leo said eagerly.

"I believe so."

"Also," Florrie said. "You said we were your children."

"Yes, that was a shocking untruth," Bella admitted. "And I am very sorry for it. I just had to find a reason for you to stay with me and to—er—well, I'll try and explain it all better later! Um…when you heard Jenkins talking about your stepfather returning, did he happen to say when exactly he expected him? This morning? This evening?"

Both the children frowned with concentration, looking at each other.

"I think early," Florrie said. "He wanted everything ready last night before we went to bed."

Bella's stomach twisted.

"You won't send us back to him?" Leo said anxiously.

"No, of course not." She rose to her feet. "Let me just find Captain Alban…I mean your uncle, and then we can go to the beach. Be good and stay with Molly for now."

Returning to her own room, she seized her cloak and reticule and sped past her aunts before they could see what she intended. Even so,

Sarah sprang to her feet, making a lunge to block the door, but Bella was faster.

"I shouldn't be long, so don't worry," she gasped, flying out of the door and closing it hastily behind her.

Chapter Fourteen

THE DUKE OF Kelburn finally discovered Sir George Beaton in his bedchamber, where his valet was packing a trunk.

The duke was not surprised. He sat on the nearest chair and regarded his old ally sardonically. "Fleeing the field, Beaton?"

"Do you blame me?" Beaton retorted, pacing from the bed. "I'm sorry for it, your grace, but your daughter is clearly deranged and that benefits no one."

"No, she isn't," Kelburn said disparagingly. "Although I can understand why you might think so. In fact, she's being surprisingly clearheaded and a lot smarter than I ever gave her credit for. You don't believe that farrago of nonsense about those children, do you?"

Beaton scowled. "I don't know what to believe."

"Look. My daughter has been deceived by this fellow Alban. Or Lamont or whatever he wishes to call himself. Not that I believe he has yet wronged her in any way that might matter to you. But this story about the children is simply her weapon to stop the marriage to you."

Beaton paused in his pacing to scowl. "A marriage of convenience is a civilized affair. A reluctant wife is more of a millstone."

"That's the thing, Beaton, she won't be reluctant. Arabella has always accepted how things are and made the best of them. Once she's married, she will be all the help to you that you require. And she will be loyal in all important matters."

"It doesn't matter if she won't make her vows," Beaton muttered.

"You must allow a father to know what's best for her. We had an agreement, my friend. I can still make sure you get a cabinet post and the dowry we discussed, but without the marriage, clearly, you get neither. I value your support, Beaton, but I cannot trust it if you renege at this point."

"I'm not the one who's reneging!" Beaton exclaimed, throwing himself into the chair opposite the duke. "*She* is!"

Kelburn flapped one dismissive hand. "You're being ridiculous. She's just a woman and she will do as she is made to. Especially if you talk to her, play the honorable, rejected suitor, prepared to stand aside because of the respect and regard you have for her, despite the humiliation she's heaped upon you, blah, blah, and so on. I guarantee she'll look on you differently. She'll blame *me* for the marriage and spend the rest of her life making it up to you for her bad behavior."

Beaton, clearly wavering once more as Kelburn had known he would, fought a final defensive action. "If you can get her to the altar."

"I don't need an altar," Kelburn snapped. "I just need both of you in the same room in front of my chaplain."

Beaton hesitated, pulling distractedly at his lower lip. "When?"

"Now," Kelburn said.

Beaton stared. "And the cabinet post will be a good one?"

"They very best available."

Beaton stood. "Very well, marry us."

The duke bore his prize back to his sisters' sitting room, collecting Mr. Waine on the way.

"Get her out here," he said shortly to his sisters, who looked in alarm at each other and then back to him.

"She isn't here," Aunt Maria said at last. "She went out. Jenson's gone looking for her."

Kelburn tugged his hair in fury. "Can't you make the wretched girl sit still? Do I have to do everything myself?"

BELLA, IN FACT, had left the hotel before she realized she did not know

Will Conway's exact address, only that he stayed somewhere on Harbor View. She hastened first to the harbor and saw that *The Albatross* was still anchored beyond the bay.

She turned to the same old man whose boat she'd borrowed on her first day in Blackhaven.

"Weather's coming down, m'lady. Not sure you should," he said, even before she'd asked him.

"I'm not sure I should either," she said ruefully. She wondered how long it would take her to row out to *The Albatross*. And even then, she might simply discover that he wasn't there, but at Will Conway's. "Tell me, did you see Captain Alban come ashore this morning?"

"No, ma'am, that I didn't."

Which meant, surely, that he'd come early, before the old man arrived.

"Some of his men rowed in, though," the old man offered. "Rough looking lot. Wouldn't care to be *their* shipmate."

"Were they going to meet the captain?" she asked eagerly. "Had he summoned them?"

"Couldn't understand what they were saying, could I? Most of them are foreign."

"Where could they have gone?" she murmured, gazing around as though expecting them to be lurking close by.

The old fisherman looked at her in clear disbelief.

"Where do sailors usually go when they come ashore?"

Home? But no, not these sailors, most of them had no home, and if they had, it wasn't in this country.

"The tavern!" she said in sudden understanding.

"They'd start there," the old man allowed.

She frowned. "But the captain himself wouldn't go there, would he?"

"Would he not?"

"Ah," Bella said. "Thank you. You've been most helpful."

Although she understood perfectly well that low taverns were no place for ladies of quality—or indeed respectable women of any kind—

she regarded this as an emergency. It was already after two of the clock, and he'd promised to come before noon. Her father hadn't scared him off. Last night at the theatre had proved that. And if he'd ridden to Roseley and discovered the children missing, would he not ride like the wind back to Blackhaven to see if they'd come to her? He would be here by now.

Unless something had happened to him. Her insides twisted with fear. Alban was not a man easily intimidated or bested. He could, she was sure, look after himself in most company. But the combination of the brutal Jenkins with the mysterious stepfather feared by the children, was a different matter entirely.

She hurried through the bustling little market and along the street to the tavern. Her hope was that she would find someone skulking outside whom she might persuade to go and look for Captain Alban or any of his crew. However, again, the luck was against her and for once no one skulked on the unsavory doorstep. Nor could she stand around here waiting for someone to appear. People would notice her and wonder. And why on earth did she care about that? She'd just blasted her own good name with tales of children and a secret marriage that no one would believe in.

Before she could lose courage, she ran up the steps and pushed her way inside.

At once, the thick air caught at her breath. Stale tobacco smoke mingled with new. The sour stench together with that of old ale and unwashed bodies assaulted her nostrils, and turned her stomach, making her gag. She could barely see a foot in front of her own face, let alone recognize those of the patrons. Worse, the sounds of talk and raucous laughter died away almost entirely, and she knew everyone must be staring at her. Her cheeks burned, but she held her head higher and began to walk further in, peering at the people around her.

"Bloody hell," a familiar voice said, and Cairney, the coxswain, loomed out of the fog.

An instant later, a hand pushed him down by the shoulder and Dr. Gowan strode toward her.

"Bless you, ma'am, what the deuce are you doing in a place like this? Let me take you outside."

She turned reluctantly as he drew her hand through his arm and dragged her toward the door. "Is he here?"

"No, thank God," the doctor said grimly. "I dread to think what he'd say." He pushed open the door and a wave of gloriously fresh sea air assailed her choked nostrils.

"Where is he?" Bella demanded. "I'm so afraid he's in trouble…"

"There, there." Awkwardly, the doctor patted her hand. "The captain can take care of himself better than anyone I've ever known."

"Yes, but if he were ambushed?" Bella persisted.

"He's never ambushed," Dr. Gowan said flatly. "He's too careful. And he reacts too quickly."

She came to a halt a few yards away from the tavern and turned to face him. "Where is he, Doctor?"

The doctor shrugged. "He rowed ashore at dawn. Said he'd be back aboard by…" The doctor glanced at a gold fob watch in his waistcoat, and frowned. "By about now, dash it. We're all meant to be aboard, too, or be left behind. I'd better round up the men. The boat will be here for us any—"

"He isn't aboard," Bella exclaimed, catching his arm when he would have turned back to the tavern. "The old fisherman would have told me. Doctor, I think he's in danger, or worse, that he's been harmed in some way. Would the men come with me to rescue him?"

The doctor's jaw dropped. "You want to rescue Alban? It's we who'll need rescuing if we turn up somewhere we aren't meant to be. I've never known a man so secretive as the captain, and trust me, we all have things from our past to keep quiet!"

"No, you don't understand," Bella said urgently, and poured out the shortened story of children who were the captain's kin, of the brutish Jenkins and the mysterious stepfather who scared the children so much they'd run away to her at Blackhaven. "Alban meant to ride out there early this morning, collect the children, and return to Blackhaven before noon, when he was meant to call on me."

"He was?" the doctor said thoughtfully. Oddly, that seemed to be the part of the tale that finally convinced him of the captain's danger. "Where exactly has he gone?"

"To Roseley," Bella said urgently. "Cairney knows the way. So do I."

Dr. Gowan scowled. "Some of them men can't ride. Can we get a carriage there?"

"Yes, but I'm not sure how it will fare taking shortcuts off the road."

"Hire four horses for riding," the doctor instructed. "And some kind of vehicle, preferably one drawn by at least four horses. I'll meet you at the livery stables with the men."

KATE GRANT HAD just returned to the vicarage after visiting the sick of the parish, when Lady Maria Smedley and Lady Sarah Niven were announced by the awed maid. Kate, who was rarely put out, received them civilly and ordered tea.

"Is Lady Arabella not with you?" she asked. Unexpectedly, she'd found herself liking Arabella since she'd come to Blackhaven. She suspected each of them surprised the other and was glad of the budding friendship. But the older Niven ladies had always thoroughly disapproved of Kate and she was intrigued by their visit.

"Actually, no, that's why we're here," Lady Maria said bluntly. "We thought she might be with you."

"Sadly not. I have been out all afternoon and haven't seen her. My maid would have told me if she'd called."

The older women exchanged glances of dismay, tinging Kate's curiosity with unease.

"Is everything well with Lady Arabella?" she asked.

Lady Maria's mouth opened and then, under her sister's glare, closed again.

Kate's unease deepened. "Ladies, I am the vicar's wife. Even if I wished to, which I never have, I could not afford to gossip. If Lady Bella is in trouble, I would help."

Despite her sister's half-hearted gesture of silence, Lady Maria blurted, "We cannot find her. There was a quarrel and she left the hotel without a word. Her father wants her found immediately."

"Of course he does," Kate soothed, although every instinct told her there was more to this than a father's anxiety. "How long has she been gone?"

The sisters glanced at the clock on the mantelshelf. "About two hours," Lady Sarah said.

"Then I am sure there is no cause to worry," Kate said. She glanced from one to the other. "Er…is it possible Lady Arabella does not *wish* to be found?"

"More than possible," Lady Maria said grimly. "Our servants have discovered no sign of her in any of the public places in the town. Our last hope was that she was with you."

"Your last hope?" Kate repeated, startled. "Good God, ladies, what is it that you fear?"

"That she has gone…that she has been *abducted* by that encroaching Captain Alban who has filled her head with all sorts of nonsense. He wishes her ill."

Kate tried not to blink. "I would not have said so," she said cautiously. "On the contrary, I have observed him to show her a great deal of respect." She aimed for tact. "Am I right in thinking you are afraid because of a certain affection forming between them?"

They both nodded curtly.

"In short, that they have eloped?"

"We are beside ourselves," Lady Maria exclaimed, reaching for her handkerchief. "His Grace is enraged."

Of all the Duke of Kelburn's children, who would have thought it would be quiet, subdued Arabella who defied him? No wonder he was angry. Kate doubted he'd foreseen any such eventuality.

"I could send someone to his ship?" Kate offered. "And to Mr. Conway, with whom I believe the captain has been staying occasionally."

"Discreetly?" Lady Sarah said anxiously. "My brother is most anxious for discretion. My niece's reputation…"

"Of course," Kate said, rising to pull the bell. "I quite understand how the world works."

While the servants were dispatched, and a note carried round to Tristram in the church, the ladies drank tea in a civilized if somewhat nervous manner.

"Do you know, I think we should step around to the hotel," Kate said, "in case she should come home and no one think to tell you. Then we'll be overturning stones all over Blackhaven without any need."

The Niven ladies agreed, although clearly torn between their natural gratitude for her help and their agonized desire to keep the matter in the family only.

They were almost at the hotel when Tristram, on horseback, caught up with them. He leaned down from the saddle to Kate. "Something's is going on," he murmured. "A crowd of Alban's men were drinking in the tavern and all left together quite suddenly under an officer's orders. The tavern keeper thought Alban must be about to sail, but the men didn't return to the ship. They took the east road out of town."

Kate frowned as her husband dismounted, summoning a boy to hold the horse. They entered the hotel just behind the Niven ladies. "Why would a group of drunken sailors walk inland?" Kate wondered. "The brothel is on the south road."

"Lady wife," Grant said, hand on heart as though scandalized. "What can you possibly know of that?"

"Behave yourself, Vicar, the duke is waiting to pounce." Kate had spied the distinctive, white haired nobleman striding across the busy foyer with a servant at his heels. At one side of him scurried an attentive gentleman who might have been a secretary or a chaplain. A portly older gentleman walked at his other side.

"Well?" the duke barked at his sisters, before glancing around him somewhat belatedly for possible eavesdroppers. The reception clerk was busy with a fair, richly-dressed lady who looked vaguely familiar to Kate. An old gentleman was hobbling up the staircase with the aid of a stick. Two children and their nurse stood aside to let him pass. The duke's fierce eyes seemed to take them all in with contempt. And then they encountered Kate and Tristram.

"Nothing yet," Sarah said hastily in a very low voice. "This is Mr. and Mrs. Grant, who are kindly helping. Mr. Grant is the vicar of St. Andrew's Church in Blackhaven."

The duke scowled. "Is he, by God? I know your face, sir. And yours," he added to Kate.

"We met many times when I was Lady Crowmore," Kate reminded him.

"Ha." His Grace clearly remembered something about her. "This will be the country vicar."

"The one she threw herself away on," Tristram said blandly. "At your service, sir."

The duke was clearly about to dismiss them, with whatever degree of civility—or not—which he imagined they deserved, when Sarah spoke. "Mr. and Mrs. Grant know the town, Kelburn, and all its inhabitants, temporary and otherwise."

It was a slight exaggeration, but Kate suspected nothing less would have penetrated the duke's stubbornness. However, what the duke might have replied to the claim was never discovered, for one of the children on the stairs suddenly shouted, "Mama!" at the top of her voice.

Which for some reason acted like a sudden clap of thunder. The old gentleman on the stairs dropped his stick and the nurse spun to save him, while the child flew down the staircase. But the truly astonishing reaction was that of the smart lady at the reception desk, who suddenly turned, throwing out her arms in dramatic relief.

"Florrie! Oh, Florrie! There you are! What in the world are you doing here? Where is Leo?"

To Kate's continued amazement, the duke laughed and turned to the older of the gentlemen beside him. "And there you have it, Beaton. Of course they were not hers!"

The nurse, having restored the stick to the old gentleman, seized the little boy, who seemed to be rooted to the spot and all but dragged him downstairs with her. The young mother, clutching her daughter to her side, flew to meet them, snatching the boy from his nurse and glaring at her.

"Who are you?"

"Molly, ma'am," the girl whispered, clearly terrified. "The kitchen maid."

"Kitchen maid? What in God's name are you doing with my children?"

The duke strode forward. "I think we'd all like to know that," he said glacially. "Madam, you will excuse the informal introduction. I am Kelburn."

"Mrs. Radnor," the lady said, bewildered, taking in everyone, including Kate, who'd followed the duke to accost her.

"Mrs. Radnor, I believe we need to talk somewhere more private."

"I have no time, sir," Mrs. Radnor said firmly. "I had meant to stay here for the night, but now I see I must take my children home to Roseley at once."

The duke's eyes widened. "Roseley? You are Lady Roseley?"

"I was, sir. After my husband's death, I married Mr. Radnor."

The duke's gaze fell on the boy. "Then you are the new Lord Roseley. Well, well. It all begins to make sense."

"It does?" Kate said faintly.

"Madam, we shall accompany you," the duke said, as though bestowing a favor.

Several expressions chased each other across Mrs. Radnor's rather beautiful face, including astonishment, annoyance, and more than a hint of fear. "Your pardon, sir, but I cannot invite—"

"Madam," the duke said, low. "I have every reason to believe my daughter is being held in Roseley against her will."

Mrs. Radnor flushed. "Sir, you are insulting. Come, children."

Seizing her offspring by the hands, she took one step before the nurse—or kitchen maid, whoever she was—threw herself in front of her mistress.

"Madam, please don't take them back there," she pleaded. "They're frightened and it isn't safe for—"

"Stand aside. You'll wait here for the magistrate."

"M-m- magistrate?" the girl whispered in horror.

"You do not abduct my children with impunity," Mrs. Radnor said icily and sailed onward.

Interestingly, the boy, Leo pulled back. "I want Molly," he said fiercely. "And Lady Bella."

Of course, he was dragged onward and into the carriage Kate could see waiting outside.

"Have my carriage brought round immediately," the duke bellowed at the fascinated clerk.

"Right away, sir," the clerk said hurriedly.

"Do you know," Tristram said, apparently *à propos* nothing in particular, "what else is on the east road out of Blackhaven? The livery stables."

"So they are," Kate said thoughtfully. A gaggle of rough sailors hiring horses to take them…where? Answering Alban's call, wherever he was. And the Duke of Kelburn, for some reason, seemed to think that was Roseley. He was already on the way out of the door with his male companions while his sisters twittered about something in his ear.

"Oh, very well," the duke said testily, "but I've only room for one of you. And it will be a damned squeeze!"

"Sir," the distraught nurse tugged at Tristram's coat tails until he faced her in surprise.

"How might I help you?" he asked kindly.

"Sir, you're the vicar, aren't you? Please, you must help these children. I fear for them in that house."

"With their mother?" Kate said, astonished.

"No, ma'am. It's their stepfather they're afraid of. It's why we ran away in the first place because Mrs.—that is, Lady Arabella, told us to come if we needed anything. She can't take them there while Mr. Radnor and that Jenkins rule the roost. I don't know what they'll do behind her back without me to look out for them. And they're going to clap me in prison just for doing what the captain said and looking out for them."

"The captain?" Kate pounced. "Captain Alban?"

"So they say…"

"Do you know, Tristram, I believe I shall summon my carriage. Molly, you had best come with us and we'll do our best to keep you out of jail! Though you might have to sit up beside my coachman. Lady Sarah, might we offer you a seat in our carriage? I believe we all wish to travel in the same direction."

Chapter Fifteen

ALBAN WOKE TO throbbing pain in his shoulder and something wet and warm stroking the pain. He opened his eyes to see fading daylight at the high window of a bare-stone building full of straw. He could smell horses, hear the faint sounds of their snuffling and their shifting hooves.

He was in the stables at Roseley. And a dog was licking determinedly at the bloody wound in his shoulder. One of Radnor's men had shot him.

Alban sat up so suddenly his head reeled and the dog backed off in alarm. His left shoulder protested painfully, but he swore because there was no pistol in his pocket. Radnor or his men had taken it.

Hesitantly, but inexorably, the dog came closer once more. Alban fended him off with one hand, stroking the dog's ears while he investigated the wound. Thanks to the dog's ministrations, his shirt wasn't sticking to the wound, which looked clean.

"As I hope you are," he muttered to the dog. Taking his handkerchief from his pocket, he folded it into a pad, then shrugged out of his coat and ripped the sleeve off his shirt to bind the pad to the wound. Using his teeth, it wasn't too difficult, although he could have done with Dr. Gowan's expertise.

Judging by the messy straw, he'd lost a fair bit of blood, although not, he thought, dangerous amounts. Unless he'd bled somewhere else, too. He certainly felt dizzy as he dragged himself to his feet, past several stalls to the stable door which, inevitably, was locked.

Alban didn't doubt his ability to batter his way out of the door eventually. It was relatively flimsy and the hinges were partially rusted. If it came to it, he could probably rile one of the horses to kick it in for him. Although that would inevitably involve a lot of noise which would no doubt summon his captors and might damage himself and the horse more than the door. However, his brain was largely preoccupied for the moment with the question of why he was still alive.

Radnor needed him dead. And he was already shot. Why had they locked him up in here instead of killing him outright and burying him somewhere no one would ever find the body?

He frowned with the effort of remembrance. What had happened when he was shot?

He'd lain flat on his back, excruciating pain shooting through his shoulder, chest, and arm. The blood had whined and then roared in his ears and he couldn't move. He'd drifted in and out of awareness, listening to voices that hadn't made a lot of sense at the time, and then he'd been moving, bumping in the rough grip of two or three men complaining about his weight.

"Can't we just kill him?" one voice had said.

And then a voice he knew better, sniggering with vicious triumph. Jenkins. "No, the magistrates will do that for us. He'll be hanged for the brats' murders."

Of course. That was why he needed to get out, to make sure Leo and Florrie were safe. To take Bella away and marry her. And at some point, he really needed to kill Radnor. Even if it ruined his chances of inheriting the Scottish lands, it would be worth it. Bella would live with him on board and they could make their home anywhere they chose.

Marianne and the children would be better off without Radnor. Although God knew whom she would choose for her third husband if he wasn't there to keep his eye on things…

Stupid brain. Concentrate on the now.

Now was the dog's head under his hand, vibrating slightly as it growled deep in its throat. A warning growl. Was Radnor or one of his men coming? Jesus, had they found the children? Had they killed them already?

Either way, he could do nothing from in here. He had to risk attracting attention.

With a deep breath, he raised his boot high and kicked the door with all his might.

It gave a satisfying thunk and the wood creaked in protest. Unfortunately, he lost his balance and fell over onto his wounded shoulder which shrieked in agony. But Alban had learned never to give into pain in a crisis. He moved through it, staggered back to his feet and kicked the door again.

This time, he managed to stay upright, although he lurched like a drunk. Through his panting and the sounds of his own clumsiness, he heard a voice, *her* voice, speaking his name.

"Alban," it whispered. "Alban."

He'd lost more blood that he'd thought. He must have been lightheaded. Shaking his fuzzy head to clear it, he aimed his boot at the door once more, just as all hell broke loose in the yard beyond.

BELLA, DR. GOWAN, and two of the sailors who could ride, left the road and the carriage behind to bolt across the open country toward Roseley. As she rode, mostly in silence, Bella's mind drifted here and there, always coming back to Alban. Making sure that he was safe, recuing him from any trouble had become the most important thing in her life. Providing he was alive and well, she didn't care for anything else. Not even whether or not her father was right to accuse him of seeking revenge in her hurt and downfall. That wasn't the Alban she knew, and she *did* know him. She needed him to be safe. If he was, she could face anything, any pain.

"This way," she called, urging the horses through the woodland path that led to Roseley House. Dr. Gowan and the others followed her.

The doctor pulled alongside her as the path widened. "We shouldn't go charging in there. We need to find him first."

Since his words made sense, she slowed her mount. "We can tie the horses just at the edge of the wood and creep up to the house. There weren't many people around the last time we were here. Though there might be more now that Mr. Radnor is home."

"Exactly," the doctor said. Holding the horse with his knees, he appeared to be loading a wicked looking pistol.

"How long do you think it will take the others to get here?" Bella asked worriedly.

"Long enough for us to reconnoiter and, hopefully, be able to direct them if necessary. With luck, we'll find the captain before they even get here."

Although the light was fading, it was easy enough to find a place to tie the horses. Dr. Gowan directed the men to approach the house from either side while he and Bella approached the back. He seemed to forget very quickly that Bella was there, because as she walked beside him toward the back of the house, he glanced at her, blinking in apparent surprise.

"If I give the word, you must run back to the wood," he said urgently. "Stay there and wait for us. The captain will kill me if anything happens to you, and I can't say I blame him. I should have left you with the horses."

"I wouldn't have stayed," Bella said.

"No, I don't suppose you would." A smile flickered across his face. "You're good for the captain."

And she flushed with pleasure. More than anything she'd ever wished for in her life, she wanted to be good for the captain.

The house seemed as quiet as on her last visit, except that a few of the ground floor and first floor windows showed the glow of candle light.

"Money to burn," Dr. Gowan commented, since it was not yet truly dark enough to light candles. "But then, from all I hear, it isn't his money. What's in the outhouses?"

"I'm not sure." She veered toward the nearest one. "Stables, I think. A coach house."

Something thudded hard against the nearest door, making her jump out of her skin.

Someone was in there, trying to get out. "Alban," she whispered.

Without so much as a glance at the doctor, who couldn't have failed to hear the same crash she did, she ran. The door buckled outward again just as she arrived. Through the heavy breathing on the other side, she could hear the low growl of a dog.

She touched her hand to the door. "Alban," she said urgently. "Alban."

Nothing came back to her. She must have been wrong. Wishful thinking… Then who on earth was in there? Was it just the dog hurling itself at the door?

She pulled back one of the bolts.

"Miss," Dr. Gowan warned. He was aiming his pistol toward the house from which three men came running. "Halt! Stand still!" the doctor yelled, but it was too late.

Somebody's pistol went off, deafening her, and then the three men were upon them. Dr. Gowan went down under two of them, while a third grabbed at her arm. She stepped back, lashing out instinctively. By sheer luck, her fist connected with his chin and he stumbled, more from surprise than hurt.

"Why, you…" he muttered, lunging at her with considerably more power and purpose.

At the same time, the stable door finally crashed open and a dog leapt out snarling. Close on its heels was Alban, his eyes and hair wild, his torn shirt covered in blood. She let out an involuntary cry of distress, and his turbulent eyes flew to her. With a roar, he charged her captor and the two men catapulted past her and fell to the ground. She heard the smack of fist on bone twice and then Alban alone rose to his feet and turned to face her, breathing like a bellows.

Her heart twisted with the most intense joy and fear she had ever known. She couldn't speak. He was alive. Thank God, he was alive, but he was hurt and bleeding.

There was no time for talk. Other men rushed across from the house, including the large, hulking figure of Jenkins. Alban's two men came charging in from the sides, but it still left them outnumbered.

Alban let out a groan. "Dog," he said, grabbing the animal who'd preceded him out of the stables and pushing it against Bella's legs. "Guard!" And then he staggered forward, kicking one of the doctor's attackers off him and allowing Gowan to take care of the other.

But it was an uneven fight and one Bella saw they could not win. The dog at her feet seemed unsure why he was guarding her and growled at her. She barely noticed, merely dropped her hand to his head and he quietened.

Another gunshot rent the air, and Bella's fingers curled into the dog's fur. A gentleman strolled through the melee, his pistol pointing to the sky.

"Enough!" he commanded into the abrupt pause. "Surrender and I'll merely turn you over to the magistrate for trespass."

Julian Radnor, Bella thought. *The children's stepfather…*

"And if we don't?" one of Alban's men demanded.

The gentleman passed the spent pistol to the man beside him and took another from his pocket which he aimed straight at the tall figure of Alban. "Or I'll shoot you all, starting with him."

Instinct propelled Bella forward, the dog moving close beside her. Something rumbled in her ears, no doubt sheer terror, and it was getting louder. But it seemed Alban's men had the same idea as she did. Dr. Gowan, who was nearest, stepped deliberately in front of his captain.

"No, you'll start with me," he snarled, not in the least like the quiet, kindly doctor who'd examined her on *The Albatross*.

Radnor, who could have had no idea who the doctor was but must have heard his gentlemanly accents, wavered, then walked two paces aside to aim around the doctor. Another of Alban's men blocked him.

But Alban wasn't having that. He strode forward, torn and bloody and pushed between his protectors to face Radnor.

"What in the fiend's name—" began one of Radnor's men and then the growing rumble, which wasn't just in Bella's head after all, burst into the yard.

With a scream of horses, the hired coach swung dangerously around the side of the house, heading straight for the melee. Men hung off the roof and out of both doors, yelling and rattling sabers, brandishing fists and pistols. They must truly have been a terrifying sight to Radnor and his men, but Bella was so pleased to see them that she felt more pride than fear.

Before the horses even pulled up, men were leaping out of the doors and dropping off the roof, then rushing to face the enemy. Driving the horses, Cairney drew them to a snorting, whinnying halt, then leapt down to join the fray.

It wasn't much of a fight. Faced with such an alarming coach full of piratical sailors, armed to the teeth—had they really come ashore with all those weapons?—Radnor's men quickly discovered the better part of valor and surrendered.

Radnor himself took several, discreet paces backward. He was going to run and leave his men to face whatever Alban intended for them. Except, he stepped back onto Cairney's waiting toes.

Cairney seized his collar. "Going somewhere?" Cairney said into the sudden silence.

Alban, swaying slightly, said, "How the devil did you men get here?"

"Miss Bella brought us," Cairney said. "Just as well by the look of things."

Alban turned to where she still stood as though rooted to the spot, possibly because the dog was sitting on one of her feet.

"Oh dear." He began to walk toward her with deliberation, a hundred different expressions flitting through his turbulent eyes. "Now you really are in trouble."

Her throat went dry. Torn, wild, and bloody, he'd never looked so disreputable, or so downright dangerous. Everything in her strained toward him with a longing so powerful she couldn't speak.

It didn't matter. He came to a halt only inches from her and without pause, took her in his arms. One hand plucked off her spectacles and there, before everyone, he kissed her soundly.

He smelled of blood and sweat. His lips were hard, demanding, and sensual, shocking her. But she had never wanted anything as much as to be his, and this, surely, was his declaration. She let out a sob and flung up one arm around his neck to draw him closer, while the men's cheers echoed all around her.

"Now you're like me," he whispered against her lips. "Lost to all propriety."

Laughter gurgled up inside her, and with it came reality and anxiety. "At least I'm not bleeding. What happened?"

His whole body was trembling, as if he'd finally relaxed and given in to the pain. Wildly, she looked around for the doctor, but he was already there. So was Cairney.

Alban said, "Lock them all up in the house somewhere. Keep Radnor away from the others. And watch Jenkins, he's mean…"

"Aye, sir," Cairney said, and ran off.

Alban's gaze, full of a desperation she'd never seen before, came back to her. "We need to find the children."

"The children are safe in Blackhaven," she said in a rush. "Molly brought them to me."

His eyes closed and he swayed against her for an instant before he righted himself with the doctor's aid and began to walk toward the house. "I'm going with Gowan now."

"So am I," Bella said.

Alban frowned. "No."

"Yes," Bella said, and met his gaze. She held it, though it wasn't easy.

His frown twitched as though she had utterly baffled him. He seemed to have nothing more to say on the matter.

As it turned out, there wasn't much for Bella to do, except instruct the kitchen staff—who must have arrived with Radnor—to bring boiled water. She then passed Dr. Gowan the instruments, cloths, and bottles as he asked for them.

Alban lay still on the dining room table, impassive through all the doctor's surely agonizing ministrations. But his eyes followed Bella wherever she went, as though her face was a beacon in whatever hell of darkness he was going through.

"There," the doctor said, eventually standing back to admire the neatly tied bandage and the sling he'd made to support Alban's left arm. "The ball is out and the bone and muscle should heal nicely if you keep the arm still. Though your mess of a shirt is not the best setting for my work."

"Oh, I don't know," Alban said with unexpected strength. "The savage and bloody look has been known to obtain results." He made to sit and Bella immediately thrust out her hand to stop him. But Dr. Gowan merely took him by the elbow and eased him up until he sat on the table with his legs dangling over the side. Reaching out, he tapped one of the doctor's bottles.

"No," the doctor said. "I've numbed the wound as best I can. And I've already given you laudanum."

Alban tapped the bottle again. "I know. That's why I need help to stay awake. I need to sort this out before I can sleep."

"The morning will do," the doctor protested. "It's already dark."

Alban swept up the bottle, and the doctor snatched it back, grumbling as he uncorked it and measured out a dose which Alban knocked down his throat without a grimace.

He slid his feet onto the floor and stood for a moment as though testing his balance. "Good," he said. "Let's go and threaten Radnor."

Mr. Radnor was discovered in an ornate drawing room of fine proportions. He sat, apparently at his ease in the armchair beside the fireplace, while several of Alban's men lounged nearby, one picking his teeth with the point of a cutlass, another turning a pistol over and over on the table in front of him.

They all straightened as Bella, Alban, and the doctor walked in.

Alban looked around the décor. One eyebrow twitched, and it struck Bella that despite riding over here several times in the last week or so, he hadn't been in this room since his enforced exile twelve years ago. Wouldn't the rest of the house have drawn his curiosity if not nostalgic affection? No, for he hadn't meant to stay. He still didn't. This wasn't his home anymore.

"Do you like what we've done with the drawing room?" Radnor drawled. "Such an improvement from the drab, plain look I found when I first came here. Don't you agree?"

"No, it's vulgar," Alban replied without apparent interest. "My little niece and nephew are afraid of you."

"They are too timid," Radnor said with contempt.

"You ordered your man to beat them."

"They are insolent. They need discipline."

"For their timidity?" Alban inquired. "Or their insolence? Or just because they are my brother's children?"

Radnor flushed and made to rise.

"Sit!" Alban snapped.

Radnor fell back into his chair, an appalled, frightened expression on his face that he couldn't hide.

"Know this," Alban said softly. "Marianne may do as she likes with you, but you will never be in the company of her children again. I am their legal guardian and I am in control of their inheritance."

"You can't do that!" Radnor panted. "You are a wanted man! You should be hanged!"

"You should research your facts," Alban said carelessly. "Admittedly, so should I rather earlier than I did. But I am wanted for no crimes in England or in Scotland."

"You committed crimes here today!" Radnor all but screamed.

Alban glanced at his shoulder. "I'm the one who was shot. You're the one whose men are falling over themselves to accuse."

In the silence, Bella became aware of a rising confusion from the hallway.

"I don't care who you are!" a woman's frightened voice warbled. "Get out of my house!"

The door flew open and a lady all but fell inside, clutching two familiar children to her sides. Of course. This must be their mother, the elusive Marianne, once Lady Roseley, now Mrs. Radnor.

The lady stopped dead at the sight before her, but the children broke free of her with delight.

"Captain!" Leo yelled. "Lady Bella!"

Both children hurled themselves across the room at Alban and Bella. Smiling, Bella knelt down to catch Florrie, while Alban flung his arm lightly around Leo and ruffled his hair. The lady gave a little moan of horror, starting toward them, already beginning to call them back when her fearful gaze fixed on Alban, and she again came to a halt.

Her eyes widened. The blood drained from her face and her hand reached uselessly for something to steady her balance.

"Alban?" she whispered.

"I'm afraid so," he replied.

With a laugh that might have been a sob, she threw herself forward, much as the children had done. Alban had to release Leo to catch her in his good arm. His eyes closed briefly, and Bella's throat went suddenly dry.

Appalled, she recognized the emotion as jealousy.

"*You're* their captain? They never said," Mrs. Radnor cried incoherently. "They never said!"

"To be fair, they probably didn't know."

"*I* should have known!"

She drew back, sniffling, and beyond him, finally, her gaze found her husband rising to his feet, this time without Alban's objection.

Alban hardened his voice. "There are a few things we need to discuss."

"More than a few," Mrs. Radnor said grimly.

Leo slid away from Alban to Bella's other side. She grasped both the children's hands. "Mrs. Radnor, would you like to take the children upstairs to the nursery?"

Mrs. Radnor's frowned at her. "Who are you?"

"We seem to have forgotten the niceties of introductions," Alban observed. "Bella, my sister-in-law, Mrs. Radnor. Marianne, this is Lady Arabella Niven." A tinge of color entered his unusually pale cheeks. "My betrothed."

Warmth drowned Bella's foolish jealousy.

"You may trust her implicitly with the children," Alban added. "It was she who looked after them when they ran away from your husband."

It was Marianne's turn to flush. Mortified, she dropped a curtsey, which Bella returned.

"Forgive me," Marianne said. "Know you have my gratitude, and I hope we may talk later."

Bella inclined her head and led the children from the room. No one wanted them to hear or see what might happen next.

Chapter Sixteen

As the door closed behind Bella, Marianne said, "How does Roseley's disgraced and exiled rebel second son become engaged to an earl's daughter?"

"Duke's daughter," Alban corrected mildly. "Damned if I know. So, what do you want done with *him*?" He jerked his head toward Radnor.

Radnor sidestepped him and reached for Marianne's hand. "My dear, what are you doing here? I meant to have this all sorted out and your children brought to you—"

"Did you?" Marianne said indignantly, snatching her hand out of reach. "Then why did I have to hear of my children's distress from a letter intercepted by you and only sent on to me by a worried servant?"

"I did not want you worried," Radnor pleaded. "You were having such a delightful time in London."

"I read every word my children wrote to me," Marianne said in a low, quivering voice. "And I shall never forgive myself for leaving that man, Jenkins, in my house with them!"

Radnor spread his hands. "I am so sorry, my love. I was entirely misled in Jenkins. Be assured I shall dismiss him at once."

Marianne curled her lip. "You have been here since this morning and you have not already done so?"

"Be reasonable, dearest, I needed him to help me find the children," Radnor excused himself. "They left no word as to where they had gone."

"You would have sent that man to drag my children from safety?" Marianne pounced with even more indignation.

"My love, I said no such—"

Marianne narrowed her flashing eyes. "He told Miss Farnworth, the governess, that she was dismissed on your orders."

"He lied," Radnor said at once. "Of course he will lie to save his own skin."

"Unlike you," Alban drawled.

Radnor shot him a glance of venom. "My dear, let us talk away from this—"

"My bother-in-law is my children's guardian and protector," Marianne said at once. "He has every right to be part of this discussion."

"Yes, he does," Alban said impatiently. "So, let us cut to the chase. Marianne, what do you want done with your husband?"

"Done?" Radnor exclaimed in outrage. "*Done*, sir?"

"Like a rabbit," Dr. Gowan interpolated. "Or do you mean, in slang terms, done *in*?"

Radnor blanched.

Alban curled his lip. "Nothing would give me greater pleasure. Do you want him, Marianne? For I take leave to tell you, I won't have the children in the same house as him. If you wish him to remain, I'll arrange a separate establishment where you may visit them."

Marianne turned away abruptly. He could only imagine the way her world was falling around her ears. Johnstone was right. She was not the kind of woman who did well without a husband, but at the moment, she certainly could not stomach the one she had. He didn't know whether to feel pity or frustration for her poor marital choice.

"Shall I shoot him for you?" Alban asked. "No one need ever know."

"For God's sake!" Radnor exploded.

"No, for the children's sakes," Alban snarled. "You are an execrable man and you deserve to die."

"Don't," Marianne whispered. "I can't!"

"You don't have to," Alban assured her. "I'll do it and gladly."

"Alban stop it," she said, laughter quivering in her throat somewhere between tears and hysterics. "I can't live with your killing him, or my being responsible for it."

"Marianne," Radnor said softly, reaching out to her once more. "You won't regret this."

Again, she jerked back out of his reach, glaring at him. "Nor can I live with you in my house! I never want to see you again!"

"Marianne!"

She turned her back on him.

The door opened and Bella came back into the room. "Excuse me," she said politely. "I just wanted to tell you that the maid Molly has arrived. She seemed to think you'd dismissed her, but I thought that was probably a misunderstanding and left her with the children."

Alban stirred. "If you ask me, Molly saved their lives taking them to Blackhaven."

Marianne flushed. "Then of course she is not dismissed. Please ask her to carry on with her duties. I shall be up directly."

"Of course. Also…I'm sorry, this is your house, but Molly arrived with the vicar and his wife from Blackhaven, and also my Aunt Sarah, who seemed to think they might have to rescue me. Or Alban. I'm not very clear. I've shown them into the library across the hall for now."

"That's fine," Marianne said faintly. "We should have tea."

Bella's lips twitched and her gaze met Alban's for a breathless instant before she glanced away and turned to leave again.

"Bella," Alban said, instinctively reluctant to let her leave. He wouldn't have her treated as a servant in this house. "Please, stay."

When she glanced back at him, he could see at once that she wouldn't. He reached out his hand and her face cleared as she turned and walked across the room to his side. Amazingly, the strain went immediately out of him. How had she become so necessary to him so quickly? He, who'd needed no one since he was eighteen years old.

"Marianne is deciding her husband's fate," he explained, returning his gaze to his sister-in-law. "If you want him left alive, I would advise getting him out of the country."

"How? Where?" Marianne asked in despair. "Europe is at war!"

Alban shrugged. "One of my ships is about to sail from Whalen to Jamaica."

"Jamaica." Marianne brightened. "Could we make him an allowance on condition he stays there and never comes home?"

"Certainly," Alban replied, although without troubling to hide his distaste. But perhaps Marianne understood her husband better. One could only control with him with fear and money.

"But I'd never survive in Jamaica!" Radnor exclaimed.

Alban curled his lip. "Well, the alternatives are we hand you over to the magistrate, and you may survive as well as you can in prison. Or I kill you where you stand. You and your wife may fight that one out among yourselves, but I imagine I already know the result."

So did Radnor. "Jamaica," he repeated miserably.

"I think we should probably send Jenkins with him," Alban observed. "I'm reluctant to shoot the servant if I can't kill the master."

"Still the egalitarian," Marianne murmured, with a mixture of frustration and affectionate memory.

"Only up to a point. There's no democracy aboard my ships."

"I feel somewhat sorry for the Jamaicans," Bella said. "But at least there is no slavery now for them to exploit."

"Is that a vote for shooting them?" Alban asked.

"No," Bella said firmly. "And in any case, *this* situation is not democratic either."

"Then we'll send him to Jamaica. Cairney, take Mr. Radnor upstairs to pack a bag and then get him and Jenkins to Whalen. Take a couple of men with you when you go."

"Marianne!" Radnor exclaimed as he was marched ignominiously from the room. "Don't do this to me! I love you! Don't believe the lies of this *pirate*!"

Marianne turned her back, though she bit her lips in a helpless gesture he'd once found appealing. "But how will we get money to him?"

"We can make arrangements with my banker in Kingston," Alban said.

Marianne blinked. "*You* have a banker?" she blurted.

"Oh, I have several," he said wryly. "Shall we bring in Lady Sarah and the Grants and have tea?"

"By all means." Marianne glanced around uneasily. "And maybe you could confine your…men and their weapons to the kitchen?"

Alban jerked his head, and the men obediently followed him from the room.

As Alban and the men left the drawing room, Dr. Gowan paused to bow to Marianne and Bella and then he sauntered after them, closing the door behind him.

Marianne sank onto the nearest sofa. "What a most peculiar day," she said faintly.

"It must have been so very difficult for you," Bella sympathized. She sat on the edge of the sofa, feeling awkward. "And I'm sorry to have filled your house with sailors and frightened you. I'm afraid I asked them to come looking for Alban."

"*You* did?" She looked surprised, regarding Bella with rather more interest. "Have you known him for a long time?"

"No, not really."

"I've known him forever… It's so very strange to see him back here after all these years. I shall be so glad of him with Julian gone." She shuddered, no doubt overwhelmed by the betrayal and loss, and by what had so nearly happened to her children at the hands of one she should have been able to trust implicitly. She pinched the skin over the bridge of her nose. "Where will you live when you are married, Lady Arabella?" she managed. "Does your family have property in this part of the country?"

"I don't think so, no," Bella murmured. "In Scotland, mostly, and in Sussex."

Marianne's hand fell back into her lap. It struck Bella that she actually looked frightened, no doubt by a future that had just changed for her so dramatically.

"I believe," Marianne said in a voice that trembled slightly, "the Marshalls are looking for a new tenant at Haven House. It is rather closer to Blackhaven than Roseley, but it might answer."

"Thank you," Bella said hesitantly.

"I shall need him here, you understand…"

"Of course, I understand," Bella said kindly, although part of her couldn't help being irritated by the assumption of the other woman's claim on Alban. She had to remind herself that Marianne had had several shocks and must be feeling very low and isolated. Not to mention grief-stricken. She wondered if Marianne had loved her husband very much.

"You are such a good lady," Marianne murmured. "I am surprised…"

Exactly what she meant by that was lost in the entry of Aunt Sarah and the Grants into the room, and the exclamations and introductions which ensued.

"Arabella!" Aunt Sarah almost charged at her. "Captain Alban tells me you came to rescue him, not to elope! You foolish, ridiculous child! Are you hurt? He says not, but what do men know?"

"I'm fine," Bella assured her, enduring her aunt's thorough search of her face and body, presumably for traces of blood or broken limbs. "Quite unhurt."

Aunt Sarah sniffed and released her.

Although Bella's memories of Kate were hardly of a comfortable person, together with Grant she seemed curiously soothing, taking everything in her stride and making this very odd situation seem almost normal. Only Alban seemed restless, constantly pacing the room, never still.

When tea eventually arrived, Marianne sent for the children and gave orders for dinner to be served for her and her guests as soon as was possible.

"Oh, we couldn't intrude," Kate protested.

"But I insist," Marianne said at once. "You have all been so good, looking out for my children and me. And you cannot travel all the way back to Blackhaven in the dark. Of course you must stay the night…if you can bear a house with so few servants! We took most of them to London and I left in such a hurry they must be at least a day behind me in returning. But at least we have a cook…"

Bella cast a quick glance at Alban and found him still for once, watching her with quiet intensity from the window. For some reason, that look melted her bones. And then he dragged his gaze to the window instead.

"Oh dear," he said, with mingled frustration and amusement. "Brace yourself, Bella."

"Why?"

It didn't take long to discover. One of Alban's men who seemed to have constituted himself porter and butler, threw open the door to address Alban rather than the lady of the house. "There's an angry gent here with a gaggle of other toffs. Do you want me to let them in?"

"Oh dear," said Bella, who had no difficulty at all in recognizing her father and his entourage from this description.

Alban's lips twitched. But before he could speak, the duke simply pushed the sailor out of the way and barged in, Aunt Maria, Sir George Beaton, and Mr. Wain at his heels.

Marianne sprang to her feet in alarm. Her hand reached out as though to ask Alban to take care of this for her. And then, with a sudden frown, she seemed to recognize her newest visitors.

"Mr. Kelburn," she said severely, drifting toward him. "I believe I made it plain that I could not invite strangers—"

"Mr. Kelburn?" Bella's father boomed, stopping in his tracks to bow jerkily. "Madam, I have the honor to be the *Duke* of Kelburn. And *that* is my missing daughter!"

"I was never missing," Bella said mildly. "I merely wasn't with you. Papa, shall we—"

"Well, you're a damned fool!" the duke raged. "This time you have certainly ruined whatever was left of your reputation! Only a man who knows your wild starts as well as he knows your family would *dream* of marrying you now!"

Which was, presumably the purpose of Sir George Beaton's presence.

"Nonsense, Papa," Bella said calmly. "I am positively *surrounded* by family. *Both* my aunts are here to chaperone my visit to Mrs. Radnor. Although I am glad to see you, there was really no need for you to come at all."

Alban turned his head toward her. She wondered if it was in amusement, astonishment, or pride, but she couldn't look or she would break her father's gaze. The duke's face was darkening to a shade of puce she had never seen before. And yet, behind it, she was sure his eyes flashed with something like admiration. It almost seemed that all she had ever really needed to do to win him over was to stand up to him.

The duke turned his gaze, finally, on his hostess. "Mrs. Radnor. My apologies for descending upon you unannounced. But I know you understand a parent's anxiety."

"Of course," Marianne murmured, somewhat bewildered by this change of mood—which didn't last, of course, once his attention was caught by Alban's figure by the window.

"You, sir," he said with loathing, "have done your best to ruin my daughter. Never think I don't know why. I've even spoken to that Tranter fellow, who confirms everything."

"Mr. Tranter is a liar," Bella said hotly.

"And this fellow isn't?" snarled the duke. "Sir, I will speak to you later. First, I'd like a word with my daughter in private—with Mrs. Radnor's permission."

"Of course," their hostess said faintly.

Bella, anxious to get her father away from everyone else, led the way out of the drawing room and across the hall to the library where she'd earlier ushered the Grants and Aunt Maria.

The library was a much more pleasant place than the oppressive drawing room. It smelled of the books that lined the walls, old leather and slightly musty paper. She'd closed the curtains earlier, and the overall impression should have been one of comfort and coziness. However, as she turned in the middle of the room and watched everyone else file in—Aunt Maria, Aunt Sarah, her father, Sir George, and Mr. Waine—she didn't feel comfortable at all.

"This isn't exactly private," she observed to her father.

"It's private enough," the duke said grimly. "Close the door, Waine, and let's get this over with."

Bella's gaze flew to the closing door, through which she could just make out the figures of Alban and Marianne in the hall. Mrs. Radnor held his hand, reaching up to touch his cheek as he bent toward her.

Bella's heart seemed to stop beating. The snap of the door blocked out the unbearable sight, but she already understood everything. Marianne was his first love, who had only married his brother because Alban himself was banished. She was free, now, in reality if not in name.

Bella's fingers clutched convulsively at the neck of her gown, plucking it away from her skin, until someone dragged her hand away. She barely noticed, so lost was she in pain.

And she? What was Bella to Alban? An aberration? An amusement? A means to an end? The cruel revenge her father claimed?

No. I won't believe that of him. I can't.

With an effort, she forced her mind to function, to focus on her surroundings, on the voices buzzing irritatingly around the edges of her misery.

They were all looking at her. For some reason, her hand lay in Sir George Beaton's. She tried to draw it free, but his fingers curled, holding it, and she frowned.

Patiently, as though he'd spoken the words already, Mr. Waine said, "Repeat after me. I, Arabella…"

Her frown deepened, "I, Arabella," she said to please him.

"Take thee George Francis…"

With a jolt, she realized what oath the words were about to form, what she had been about to do without even noticing.

"But I don't," she blurted. "I already said so and I meant it."

"Oh, for the love of—" Her father cast his eyes to heaven. "Arabella, there is no other hope for you. Alban has ruined you in the eyes of the world. We are all very grateful for Sir George's trust and loyalty."

She regarded Sir George curiously. "Why is that?" she asked. "Why do you still want to marry me? What has my father promised you?"

Sir George flushed.

"Arabella, that is most unbecoming of you," Aunt Sarah snapped.

"Well, I'm sorry. I don't mean to imply my father would not keep his promise, because of course he would. He is a man of honor." Her gaze drifted to the duke. "Only I cannot see the honor in this."

"That is because you are naive and your head has been turned by that plausible rogue who is already stalking his sister-in-law instead. Bella, let us just be comfortable again."

Comfortable. She'd been so rarely comfortable, except in her own company at Kelburn, and even then, comfort had frequently degenerated into boredom. As a wife, as Lady Beaton, she would have her family's approval and she was fairly sure Sir George would not bother her much. She could live her own life as she chose, in a way that was not really open to her as an unmarried lady.

But…she would not have Alban.

Her throat closed up. Had she *ever* had Alban? Even without the complication of Marianne, *could* she ever have him, in any way that mattered?

She glanced at her aunts, at her father, whose face actually softened infinitesimally. "Bella," he murmured. "I've only ever wanted what is best for you. We all want that. Including Sir George."

She swallowed. "I know that." It wouldn't be so bad. Nothing mattered, after all, if she couldn't be with Alban. Her throat tightened.

"Proceed," the duke ordered Mr. Waine.

Mr. Waine drew in his breath once more and fixed Bella with a slightly nervous gaze. "I, Arabella take thee George Francis…"

"I…I can't," Bella said, abruptly, tugging her hand free at last.

Breathing was difficult. In just a few moments the paroxysm of coughing would begin. "I'm sorry, you must excuse—"

Her father leapt in front of her, furious once more. "I *must* do nothing of the sort," he fumed. "Proceed."

Arabella stared at him. "You can't!" she gasped, wheezing. "I won't say the words!"

"Yes, you will. You'll stay in this room until you do. Waine, get on with it."

Without warning, the door to the library flew open. Alban walked in, still wearing the torn and bloody shirt, looking every inch the pirate he was rumored to be as he strode directly toward her. Her heart tumbled over itself and she forgot to cough.

The duke turned, swearing beneath his breath. "Sir, you are not welcome at this family event."

"I rather think," Alban said, coming to a halt before Bella, "that it is the family event which is not wanted. May I escort your ladyship somewhere?"

"Anywhere," she said between white lips. Shame swamped her. Shame at her family's plotting, at her own ungallant part in it, and most of all, that he had witnessed it. And yet more than anything, she needed to be out of the room.

"You are promised here, Bella!" the duke warned as she laid her trembling hand on Alban's bloody sleeve. "You must be married now."

"I can't be," she managed. Her brain seemed to be working again. "You don't have a marriage license."

"Of course we do," the duke retorted, delving into his coat. "I had it from the archbishop myself."

"Then, where is it?" she asked mildly.

The duke held out one peremptory hand to Mr. Waine, who shook his head, muttering, "I do not have it, sir."

"We've heard quite enough," Alban snapped. "Even a special license requires the consent of both parties." And with that, he simply walked, forcing her father to stand aside rather than be barged.

As soon as he saw her in that room, Alban wished he'd put a stop to the nonsense before it had gone so far. It had been perverse pride, he supposed ruefully. He'd wanted to hear her refuse to marry Beaton, to convince himself he was doing the right thing. But when he opened the door, she looked so fragile, so ill, that his heart smote him.

Nothing could have stood in his way as he took her away from them. It didn't matter that he wasn't worthy of her. She needed him. On the other hand, bringing up the lack of license was a killer blow that pleased him.

"How did you know they had no license?" he murmured as he closed the door and led her toward the stairs.

"Because I have it in my reticule," she said, holding up the little bag that had dangled from her wrist for so long that it seemed to have become part of her.

His breath caught. "How very far-thinking of you," he said gravely, seizing a candle from the table at the foot of the stairs.

"I thought so at the time… Where are we going?" she asked.

"Where no one will look for you and you can stay out of trouble. Only you could be married through inattention."

She smiled faintly, although her lips were pale in the candlelight.

On the landing, he led her along the familiar left-hand passage, away from the nursery which was all she could have seen of the house before, and up the other flight of stairs to his old bedchamber.

He flung open the door and paused for the barest instant to let inevitable memory batter him. Nothing much seemed to have changed. It was a little airless through lack of use, but the room caught the sun for most of the day and it was not cold.

Releasing her, he went and lit the bedside lamp from the candle. He'd meant to let her sleep here in peace until the morning. But in the light of the lengths her family seem prepared to go to in order to marry her to someone else—and the discovery of the special license in her reticule—another idea was taking precedence.

"Wait here," he said abruptly. "I'm going to fetch G—"

"Do you still love Marianne?" she blurted.

He blinked at her. "I've never loved Marianne."

She cast him a skeptical glance, and his lips twisted.

Walking toward her, he added, "I might have imagined I did when we were children, but I haven't thought about her in years. I didn't even know she'd married Nick until Will Conway told me. She was beautiful and all the youths in the neighborhood were in love with her. I supposed I liked to win. In fact, I should be grateful to my father for throwing me out, because she's so manipulative I might have found myself married to her before I was nineteen. Why should you imagine I'm in love with her?"

"Oh, something she said," Bella murmured, not looking at him.

He came to a halt in front of her and tilted her chin up with one finger, frowning down at her. "And something you saw?" he prompted, understanding in a frustrated kind of a way. "In the hall perhaps?"

A flush rose to her pale cheeks.

"Well if the door had remained open, you would have seen me give her a peck on the cheek," he said impatiently. "Quite a cold peck at that, for one has to be firm with Marianne. In the same instant, I sent her back to her unwanted guests in the drawing room and listened shamefully to what was going on in the library. What were you imagining? That I made love to her in the hallway?"

Bella pushed her fingers under her glasses and rubbed at her eyes. "Oh, nothing," she mumbled.

This wasn't just irritating for him, it was hurting her.

"Bella, do you love me?" he asked abruptly.

She was so close he could feel the heat flooding through her. "You know I do," she whispered. "More than anything."

He caressed her chin between his finger and thumb. "And do you trust me?"

That was clearly a harder question, for her eyes widened. She even snatched off her glasses as if she could think better without seeing him. "Yes," she said at last. "Yes, I do trust you. I always have, even when I barely knew you."

"Then why would you think I would throw you over for Marianne or anyone else?" he demanded. "Why would I marry—" He broke off, frowning at her. "You trust me," he said, understanding. "It's yourself you don't trust."

She swallowed. "I'm sorry. I am not used to…this."

"You are short-sighted and a little clumsy," he admitted. She nodded, dropping her eyes and trying to break free of him. He wouldn't let her. "And you sometimes struggle to make conversation with shallow fools. Do you really imagine those things make you *less*? That they somehow make you a less attractive woman?"

She stopped struggling and stared at him.

"Do you think," he went on relentlessly, "that the fact that you prefer to write histories rather than ply your needle makes you a poor wife?"

"For some," she said shakily.

"For fools." He took her face between both hands, feeling his way, relying on instinct. "Bella, you are beautiful," he whispered. "With or without the wretched glasses. You are unique and enchanting and I would die for you. To marry you would be my honor, my privilege, one I'm a long way from deserving. I know that. And never think I'm the only one. Why do you imagine Beaton keeps following you around though you reject him at every turn? Even Tranter wasn't immune. In all the deals he tried to make with me, it was always he who got to marry you, never me. Until I scared away his few wits. And you do know Tamar wants to do a lot more than paint you? Nor is he alone. Why do you think I'm in such a hurry to marry you myself?"

"You weren't always," she reminded him wistfully. Her gaze dropped to his lips and heat surged through him. He stepped closer so that she could feel it, so that her delectable little body touched his at breast and hips.

"Because you upset my plodding, hedonistic life," he whispered. "You churned me up, filled me with notions that frankly scared me to death. And yet I couldn't leave them alone. I can't leave *you* alone."

He fell on her mouth, partly to prove his words, partly because he couldn't wait any longer. She was so soft and sweet, and her taste was all womanly temptation. Her mouth fell open beneath his and her tongue darted along his lips.

He groaned, knowing at last that this must happen now, before any vows or lines made it compulsory. It had to be with nothing to bind them except their own feelings, their own desires.

He released her, and barely able to walk, returned to the door and kicked it shut. When he turned back, her glasses lay on the floor at her feet where she'd dropped them, and her breasts rose and fell with her erratic breathing. She'd never been lovelier. Her eyes and lips glistened, from nervousness as well as need. But he would not wait. He dared not.

Quite deliberately, he advanced upon her.

Chapter Seventeen

Bella's mouth went dry. In the pale, flickering light, he looked rough and predatory and all she'd ever wanted. The closing of the bedchamber door had been somehow symbolic, and God help her, she welcomed that.

He halted in front of her, almost but not quite touching, Still, the heat of his body seemed to burn her like a furnace. Slowly, he reached up and pulled the ribbon from her hair, letting it fall in tangles about her face. His lip quirked as though in pleasure. His eyes darkened and glittered with something that thrilled through her to the pit of her stomach and lower.

His hand lifted once more. She thought he would draw the pins from her hair, but instead, he reached around her and began to unfasten her gown. She caught her breath and exhaled in a trembling stream.

It seemed that even one-handed he knew his way around women's clothing, for an instant later, the gown and under gown dropped around her feet in a puddle of fine muslin. Her shift quickly followed. A low moan escaped her lips as she stood naked before him, desperate to cover herself and yet afraid to move as his hot eyes devoured her from head to toe.

"Christ Almighty, you are lovely," he whispered. And then he touched her, drawing her in by the elbow until her naked body touched his carelessly clothed one. His good arm enfolded her, holding her against him as he bent his head and kissed her once more, a blatant, open-mouthed kiss that aroused and devastated.

"You're mine," he uttered against her lips. "Forever. Only mine."

She had no quarrel with that as she showed him by throwing both arms up around his neck. She tried to be careful of his poor shoulder, but beyond the inconvenience of the sling, he appeared to pay it no attention. The erection between his legs pressed hard against her stomach as he ravished her lips and throat, and then he lifted her right off the ground and strode with her to the bed.

"Tonight," he whispered. "And all nights."

She knew in her heart she would never have denied him, but the delicious melting weakness of her body, the surging heat of lust between her thighs as he kissed and caressed her naked breasts, took her by surprise. She didn't merely accept him, she *wanted* him with a fierce need she barely understood until his caressing hand found its way between her thighs.

She stretched luxuriously under him, loving his touch, like a cat. She even mewed as his hand left her to tear off what was left of his shirt and the rest of his clothes, hurling them to the floor. She stretched up her arms to him, her fingers already curling in need. He eased himself down onto her as she smoothed the skin of his naked back and shoulders with new wonder. The thrill of his weight between her legs was such that she couldn't help pushing her hips upward against him, and that was even sweeter.

But as if she'd been pushing him off, he eased off her on to his sound elbow, his hand leaving its sling to sweep up her thigh and inward. She cried out at his touch and writhed under the caress of his hand which was building some wild pleasure in her that she'd only known in dreams.

His heart thundered against hers, his breath labored as he kissed her mouth and her throat and breasts, flicking his tongue over her nipples, until ecstasy exploded between her legs, shooting outward to every part of her delirious body. His face weaved into her vision and he groaned as he took her mouth, as though riding the joyous wave with her.

She couldn't tell the moment he entered her body, for there was no pain, only some intensifying of the fading convulsions. Only then he began to rock within her and her eyes widened as she absorbed a pleasure that felt so different and yet so much part of all the rest.

His back rippled under her stroking hands, his dark, clouded face blissful and yet strained as it moved over hers. With his weight still on one elbow, he bent and kissed her, every inch of his body caressing.

"Oh my," she whispered against his lips. "Are we not meant to be married for this?"

His breath brushed her face, and then the most curious thing of all happened. His eyes lit and his lips curved, parting in the sunniest smile she had ever seen. For an instant, the world stood still as if in awe, and then joy tore her body apart and he fell on her, groaning, burying his lips in her hair, her neck.

The world came back to her, slowly, as he eased off her, turning her to one side with him so that he could stay deep inside her.

"*Now* I have ruined you," he said sleepily. "And will have to marry you myself. Unless you would rather Sir George?"

"Only if you have ruptured your wound and will be unable to do this again…"

He moved lethargically. "Oh, I will be able to this again many, many times. Although it would not be kind to you to do so immediately. Let me just lie here in you for a little longer and then…"

"What?" she asked. But his eyes were closed. She thought he might have smiled for the second time that night.

She lay wrapped in his arms, her limbs tangled with his, her whole body glowing while she gazed and gazed at the face she had once found harsh. Softened with love and sleep, it looked younger and more carefree.

"I love you," she whispered. She thought his arm tightened and he pushed against her, within her, but she couldn't be sure. The movement might have been hers.

IT WAS NOT quite light when she opened her eyes and gazed straight into Alban's. The memory of last night rushed into her mind, leaving her breathless.

"You're looking at me," she managed.

"I am. I'm wondering what you'll think of my plan."

"Tell me," she invited. Somewhere she couldn't quite believe she was lying naked in bed with Alban looming over her. "After you've reported on the state of your wound."

"It's fine," he said impatiently. "Gowan's a bit of a sorcerer when it comes to wounds. I barely feel it, though I'll probably need his ministrations again within an hour or two. Would you like to sail with me?"

"Yes."

His lips quirked and he bent to brush his lips against hers. "I haven't even mentioned where."

"I don't think you need to."

"I was going to suggest the west coast of Scotland, where we can investigate my inheritance and decide if we'd like to live there for part of the year or sell it and buy somewhere else."

"Grown-up plans," she observed. "Does this mean I may stop looking for cottages?"

"Unless you're desperate to live in a cramped shoebox." He hesitated, then, "You needn't consider money. I am a rich man by most people's standards."

"So, it doesn't matter if my father cuts me off?"

"Not in the slightest. On the whole, I'd rather it. I also thought it might be time to send Will Conway home with directions to look after Marianne."

"Doesn't he have his own estate to look after?"

"Yes, close-by. He's adored her since we were children. Perhaps this is his time."

She smiled, touching his cheek with shy tenderness. "I didn't realize you were so romantical."

"I'm not," he said with revulsion. "I'm practical. I need someone I can trust around the children when I'm not there. And talking of being practical… do you think Grant could be persuaded to marry us with someone else's special license?"

Her heart lurched. "I expect so. He could probably sort out the paperwork afterward, if necessary…"

"Would you like to do it before your family wakes up? Or afterward?"

"Before," she said with a shudder. And yet somewhere she would be sorry to have no one there of her own. "Kate and perhaps Dr. Gowan could be our witnesses."

"Then arise, Lady Bella, and give yourself to this rogue…before you give yourself to this rogue again."

She blushed, laughing, because she knew exactly what he meant. "I never thought of myself as wanton before," she said breathlessly, as he drew her very slowly out of the tangle of covers.

"I can make you a lot more wanton yet," he said huskily, his gaze stroking every inch of her.

"More?" she said in disbelief.

"Oh yes." With obvious effort he released her and walked around the bed to find his clothes. She couldn't take her gaze off his naked back and rear, and the muscles that rippled in his arms and legs as he bent and climbed into his breeches. Then he rummaged in the large chest by the opposite wall. "I wonder if I can still fit into anything I wore when I was eighteen? Look, I'll send someone up with water for you to wash in, while I go and see if I can find Grant…"

HAVING CLEANED HERSELF and her gown to the best of her ability, Bella descended the stairs to the sounds of commotion at the front door, which eventually burst open to reveal her brother Sebastian barging past one of Alban's men into the hall.

The sailor's fists clenched purposefully, but fortunately before he could use them, he noticed Bella hurrying down the last of the stairs toward them.

"Morning, Miss," he said cheerfully.

"Good morning," Bella returned.

"Miss?" Sebastian repeated, apparently outraged by this affront to her dignity. "Show some respect to La—"

"Seb, it's fine."

"You do know him then?" The sailor sounded disappointed, as though he'd been looking forward to another fight.

"Yes, he's my brother. But thank you for keeping watch." She turned to Sebastian once more. "Seb, what are you doing here?"

"Making sure all's well with you," he said peering at her. "And I see that it is."

"Why wouldn't it be?" she hedged, embarrassed suddenly in case the cause of her amazing new happiness was somehow written across her face.

"Well, Jenson and the other servants are in a terrible state. I came back to the hotel late last night and was immediately bombarded with tales of your abduction by pirates, and how His Grace had gone to rescue you, supported only by the aunts, old Beaton, and the wretched chaplain. And then, apparently, the real mother of those children you claimed as yours turned up breathing fire. No idea if the two are connected. At any rate, here I am, having ridden through the night—or what was left of it by the time I got enough sense out of anyone to discover where you were likely to be."

"Thank you, Seb," Bella said warmly, touched by this unexpected care.

"So, what the devil's been happening? *Have* you been rescued?"

A breath of laughter escaped her lips. "Yes, but not in the way you might imagine."

At faint sounds from above, she glanced up to see Alban running lightly down the stairs. Her stomach performed instant and intricate summersaults, bombarding her with memories of what he had done to her last night. Now, he wore a clean necktie and a black coat over plain breeches. Although they might have strained just a little over his broad frame, he still looked handsome in his harsh way, and almost respectable.

Behind him came Mr. and Mrs. Grant.

"Anyone I should have a word with?" Sebastian asked quietly.

She understood it was not verbal argument he had in mind.

"Oh no," she said at once. "The truth is, we came to rescue Captain Alban, and then the Grants and His Grace misunderstood completely and came after me."

Alban crossed the hall and Seb turned to meet him. They stood face to face.

"Niven," Alban said without expression.

"Alban. Or is it Lamont?"

"I suppose it had better be Lamont for today's purposes. Grant here has just agreed to marry us."

Bella's heart soared and she bestowed a spontaneous smile of gratitude upon the vicar.

"Dash it, Bella," Sebastian groaned. "His Grace will go berserk."

"As if he's never been angry with you."

"He's always angry with me," Seb said frankly. "The difference is, I don't care."

Bella met his gaze, warmed by his admittedly erratic protectiveness. Seb had always looked out for her, in his careless way.

"I don't care, either," Bella said. "Not in this. Besides, I have noticed His Grace rarely wastes his energy on things he cannot change. The best way forward is to present him with a *fait accompli*."

Seb scowled at Alban. "And you'll take care of her?"

"With my life."

Seb turned back to Bela, still frowning. "This is what's made you happy? This is what you want?"

She nodded wordlessly.

Seb's brow cleared and he grinned. "Where do we do it, then? Hurry before I sober up."

By the time the rest of Bella's family appeared, the "wedding breakfast" had reached a level of hilarity unknown to Alban without vast quantities of rum and dubious company. And yet amidst his pride in becoming Bella's husband, he was vastly enjoying himself, not only with her, but with her rakehell of a brother, the amiable vicar and his witty, beautiful wife, his brother's widow, and his small niece and nephew. Laughter and banter abounded.

Even Marianne, who'd been through so much in the last couple of days and who'd looked stricken when he'd told her Bella was now his wife, had come around. She had always been very much a creature of the present. And besides, he'd promised not to make any long voyages in the near future, and that while he was gone, Will Conway, who had always been devoted to her, would help in any way he could. This seemed to calm her panic and by the time they sat down to breakfast, she was infected by everyone else's high spirits and enjoying the company of her children.

Alban was glad to see that Leo seemed to have forgiven his mother her neglect, now that his stepfather was banished to the other side of the world. He and Florrie both thought it was a great tale that their captain had turned out to be their rebellious Uncle Alban, now restored to the bosom of his family. The wedding surprised them more, since they'd always assumed he was already married to Bella. However, they took this in their stride, too, and were delighted to be allowed to join the breakfast party.

The first coachful of Marianne's servants had arrived and it was a respectable butler who showed the Duke of Kelburn and his sisters into the sunny breakfast parlor. It irritated Alban that none of the servants from his childhood seemed to be at Roseley anymore. Marianne had allowed Radnor to dismiss most of them. The rest had left in high dudgeon. However, at least some of them recognized Alban, for he'd caught one or two of them gaping at him, and a footman had murmured, "Welcome home, sir," as he passed.

Lady Maria, who entered the room first, stopped so suddenly that Sarah walked into her and behind them both the duke cursed, not quite under his breath.

Marianne jumped to her feet as the gentlemen rose politely. "Your Grace, ladies, do come in," she said, with only a hint of nervousness. With a flick of her wrist she commanded the servants to set more places.

"Courage, my sweet," Alban murmured, closing his hand over Bella's where it gripped the table.

She smiled, twisting her hand to squeeze his fingers in return. "I'm not afraid," she said, almost in surprise. "Not now that you're here."

He thought his heart might burst.

"We usually have an informal breakfast at Roseley," Marianne was saying as the newcomers took their seats. "And this morning it seems we are celebrating."

"Oh?" the duke said without apparent interest. His scowl was reserved for Alban, while his sisters peered anxiously at Bella.

"Yes," Alban said. "I'm sorry if you don't like it, but I married your daughter this morning."

Silence enshrouded the room. Then the duke snorted. "It's another hum," he said, lifting his knife and fork as a plate was set in front of him. "You can't have."

"He did, he did!" Leo exclaimed.

"Lady Bella is our aunt now!" Florrie added.

"Oh Lord," Lady Maria moaned.

"Oh dear," Lady Sarah uttered.

"How?" the duke mocked. "You don't have a license."

"Actually, they did," Grant interpolated. "The marriage is true before God and the law." He smiled faintly, and yet, rather to Alban's impressed surprise, there was a hint of a steely warning in his voice as he added, "Let no man put asunder, and all that. Not that anyone here would."

The duke's eyes narrowed. "Jackanapes! I'll have you thrown—"

"Don't think you will," Sebastian murmured. "His father's the Earl of Boulton. It's a *fait accomplit*, sir. I was there myself. Be gracious."

The duke turned his ire on Alban instead. "So long as you know you'll get nothing from me. Not one penny."

Alban shrugged. "We neither want nor need your pennies. But since we are family now, if you find yourself short, I'll be happy to help."

The duke stared at him. Even Sebastian's grin had a distinct air of nervousness. Then His Grace gave a short bark of laughter. "You're not afraid of anyone, are you, boy?"

"No," Alban admitted. "I believe I owe that much to you and my father. So, you see, it wasn't all bad. I bear no grudges and have nothing for which to…er… take revenge."

"Lord Roseley's son," Lady Sarah said brightly. "It's not such a bad match, Kelburn."

"But will you settle, sir?" Lady Maria asked anxiously. "Bella does not keep well, you know, and you cannot drag her around the high seas! She needs—"

"Aunt Maria," Bella interrupted gently. "I have everything I need."

At this moment, the door opened again, and Dr. Gowan's head appeared around it. Finding Alban, the doctor nodded.

"Give a bottle to my father-in-law," Alban instructed. And the doctor duly entered, bearing a bottle of the finest French brandy. He bowed to Marianne and the table in general, and then walked up to the duke and set the bottle before him.

"What's this?" the duke demanded.

"A gift," Alban said mildly. "If you like it, there's a barrel waiting to be delivered to whichever residence you prefer."

His Grace stared. "I am a member of His Majesty's government. Are you trying to get round me with smuggled brandy?"

Alban raised his eyebrows. "Of course not. I'm always looking for new business."

The duke's lips twitched. "I might grow to like him yet, Bella, but don't count on it."

Bella's hand crept into Alban's. "Oh, I don't, sir."

Chapter Eighteen

TWO WEEKS LATER, Bella stood on the deck of *The Albatross*, at her husband's side. They were watching the glorious red and gold sunset as the ship sailed south from Scottish shores.

To some degree, Bella had grown used to the astonishing new happiness of life with Alban. She knew that it couldn't always be this wonderful. But moments like this, surrounded by the beauty of the rolling sea and the magnificent sky, his warm arm loosely at her waist and her head just resting against his good shoulder, would always be special.

"I like your mother's home," Bella said dreamily. "I think we'll be happy there. And here."

The house Alban had inherited in Scotland, though beautiful and old enough to capture Bella's imagination, was in need of repair. So, they'd set the work in motion, met some tenants, and looked around the land to see where it and the lives of their tenants could be improved. Alban was working on that, too. They would return in the autumn, all being well. Bella looked forward to that, but then, she was blissfully happy to be back on board *The Albatross*, too.

"We should buy a yacht," Alban said. "And let *The Albatross* earn its keep. The men get restive being stuck in one place too long."

"I know. And I suspect they all have their reasons for that."

"They do. I'm going to send it south to Spain and Africa. Do you want to stay in Blackhaven for a while?"

She glanced at him, determined not to be disappointed. "I like Blackhaven. Will you sail with *The Albatross*?"

He met her gaze. "Not this time. They can manage without me. I thought we could take a house in the town, or in the surrounding country."

She couldn't help her relief. She'd neither keep him nor insist on accompanying him against his will. She understood he would need his time alone, too. She was just glad that time wasn't yet.

She smiled. "A cottage?" she teased.

He swooped and kissed her. If it was meant to be punishment, it fell very wide of the mark. For though it was clearly meant to be quick and hard, she clung to his lips, softening the kiss until it turned into something much more sensual and tender.

"Would you like," he murmured against her lips, "to come down to the cabin with me?"

"For what purpose, Captain?" she asked with mock primness.

"Love," he breathed, and took her mouth again.

"Yes, please," she whispered, when she could speak, and his lips curved into a smile. They'd been doing that more often recently.

"Do you never tire of my constant demands on you?" he asked.

She shook her head. "No. I never will."

And she never did.

Mary Lancaster's Newsletter

If you enjoyed *The Wicked Rebel*, and would like to keep up with Mary's new releases and other book news, please sign up to Mary's mailing list to receive her occasional Newsletter.

http://eepurl.com/b4Xoif

Other Books by Mary Lancaster

VIENNA WALTZ (The Imperial Season, Book 1)
VIENNA WOODS (The Imperial Season, Book 2)
VIENNA DAWN (The Imperial Season, Book 3)
THE WICKED BARON (Blackhaven Brides, Book 1)
THE WICKED LADY (Blackhaven Brides, Book 2)
REBEL OF ROSS
A PRINCE TO BE FEARED: the love story of Vlad Dracula
AN ENDLESS EXILE
A WORLD TO WIN

About Mary Lancaster

Mary Lancaster's first love was historical fiction. Her other passions include coffee, chocolate, red wine and black and white films – simultaneously where possible. She hates housework.

As a direct consequence of the first love, she studied history at St. Andrews University. She now writes full time at her seaside home in Scotland, which she shares with her husband, three children and a small, crazy dog.

Connect with Mary on-line:

Email Mary:
Mary@MaryLancaster.com

Website:
www.MaryLancaster.com

Newsletter sign-up:
http://eepurl.com/b4Xoif

Facebook Author Page:
facebook.com/MaryLancasterNovelist

Facebook Timeline:
facebook.com/mary.lancaster.1656

Printed in Great Britain
by Amazon